The Mechanic's Curse

And Other Stories

Clive L Gilson

For the Rokers – Karen, Charlie & Guylaine

CONTENTS

Wind Freaks

IN THIS WORLD, MADE dark prematurely by a childhood illness, distance is gauged by the tap of a brass ferule at the end of a white plastic stick. The measured spaces between objects in this house are only ever changed after a considerable period of thought and an endless redrawing of mental maps. Evolution is the key. The owner of the house prefers a familiar shade and shadow. There are regular visits by cleaners and friends and helpers, and they all know the drill of place and space. The owner of this house is a time served veteran of bruise and trip and painful assimilations, having lived with this particular singularity in the old family home in North Devon for nearly half a century.

That sense of singularity, of personal uniqueness, is another key. Solitude has become a positive boon. It is a choice, and within these bounds a regularity of step and orientation allows for a three-dimensional, feeling, breathing immersion in a version of the physical world unknown to the sighted. Clues abound. There are always cyphers available if you know how to look for them. Life is a never ending, interlocking set of puzzles solved in non-visual ways. In this place of safety the answers may end up being the same as they are anywhere else in the world but the workings out are quite different. On this night all feels well with creation and heaven will remain warm and cosy so long as everything and everyone remains just so.

The bathroom, for example, is laid out in the same way whenever anyone cleans. The bather maintains that order in the interim. Bottles of shampoo and conditioner always sit at the head end of the bath, to the left hand side on a tiled ledge, shampoo furthest from the wall. The weekly refresh of soap always sits in the dish underneath the mixer taps. Care is needed here. When not using the much more convenient shower in the en suite, the bather must wait for the stored heat in the metal tap to dissipate before feeling for Imperial Leather. The bather must make a constant judgement of distance using time and innate renderings of topography. A fully drawn bath, however, is one of life's little luxuries and always worth that effort.

The toothbrush will be in the wall-mounted holder to the right of the sink along with the toothpaste. There is a cupboard above the toilet with supplies, but here again the bather has to be careful. There is always the risk of bruising on door edges if they are left open and the brushing of teeth with ill-found Deep Heat is, hopefully, a once in a lifetime event. The bather still winces at the thought of that fire-gummed evening, especially given a supposed heightening of non-visual senses such as smell that should guard against such mishaps. The blame fell ultimately on one too many scotches in mixed company on a rare outing to the Wrecker's Retreat bar at Hartland Quay Hotel.

In the bedroom clothes are laid out on the Ottoman at the foot of the bed. Always black; black underwear, black socks, a black tee shirt, a black jumper and black denim. There is a large wooden linen press opposite the bed, Victorian apparently, and each item of clothing has a slide out tray. Knowing the order of things is enough. Clothes are sourced on a semi-industrial scale, meaning that socks, underwear, tee shirts et al are bought in the same style and in bulk from a suitably well-stocked sports retailer. The method is straightforward. Anything other than black could easily become a garish melange and the dresser does not wish to cause offence. The near-flung worlds through which this soul walks out need no more startling. Black is useful. Black hides stains. Black is always stylish. Black has a certain moody quality about it. Black is timeless. Black is… cool.

With the latest time-check on the radio in the kitchen the bather's heart rate drops noticeably. Wednesday night. Bath and bed. Clean, crisp sheets and a fresh, plumped duvet, under which a flushed, pink-skinned body will slide into blissful sleep. That radio is now silent, it's comforting sounds replaced by the equally satisfying gurgle and swirl of hot water flowing into the bath. The bather kneels down at the side of the bath, regularly measuring the depth of the water against the enamel sidewall with hand-spans. This is a world where, for the want of a better phrase, pots must be watched no matter how long the boil.

When the heat of the day's emotions and activities blend into and then dissolve in the rising, steamy warmth of the bathroom, it is in these contemplative moments that the bather tends to reminisce, and often drifts back into memories of sight. After so many years these memories are little more than impressionistic sweeps of a thick horsehair brush on an old, over-painted canvas. Fields and skies and the shades upon a wall, those huge landscapes that fill the mind of the child at such a young age, were never really, never carefully categorised or memorised. They are layers of grain and granularity that merge and bleed into one another. The blind years far outweigh the limited and unreliable experiences of childish sight.

Six years in the visual, of which the first three bear little on the memory, are too few to create a meaningful sense of loss. As a child the bather coped. As a teenager the bather railed and spat but eventually came to realise that the louder you shout at the world then the heavier the blows that rain back down upon your head. It was only when the rages subsided that the bather found the depth and the majesty that underlies the sublime nature of complexity in translation and sensory awareness. With that maturity came a new appreciation of beauty. Once again the singularity is expressed. In the same way that reading a book is far more personally satisfying in the imagination than watching a film, so it is with the bather's unsighted perception of the world at large. The bather considers that for the unsighted there is philosophical shift, an inherent theoretical difference to the metaphysics of blindness, and all of it is expressed simply and elegantly by the Morse code tappings of brass ferules on skirting boards, on paving stones and chair legs.

At one hand-span from the top the taps are closed off. This is the "Eureka" moment in every sense. One hand-span is more than sufficient to cope with the Archimedean displacement of water caused by the ever-increasing volume of the bather's spreading, middle-aged body. One hand-span also means that same body will be covered in hot, steamy water, and with that immersion comes the melting. Every ache and every care will dissipate and be washed away, leaving just an empty mind bobbing along as gentle ripples wander across the water's surface while the bather settles unthinking into this amniotic comfort zone.

The bather stands up, feeling a slight pinprick behind the knees as circulation starts to flow freely after this spell kneeling beside the bath. The art in undressing is in the placement of the discarded clothes. The bather cannot simply kick the layers off for fear of mould and festering. Once the black tee shirt is removed, the bather carefully places socks, underwear and jeans inside that tee shirt and places the bundle down by the closed door, ready for the carry out to the dirty linen basket at the far end of the upper landing. If in any doubt the door's jamming acts as a suitable reminder to do the day's laundry.

A fleecy, calf length dressing gown hangs ready and warm on a hook on the back of the bathroom door. None of the friends and carers and cleaners has had the heart to tell the bather that the dressing gown is fluorescent orange. As the bather stands up and shifts carefully to the left there is the sound of a knee bumping against the wooden frame that hides the inner workings of pipe and valve and drain beneath the enamel bath. The bather grimaces and sucks in a short breath, but the pain is fleeting and the draw of hot water is utterly compelling. Left leg first. A slight twist of the foot to make sure that weight is anchored and there will be no slipping. The hot water tingles against the skin, but pleasantly so.

Right leg. The bather bends forward and rests hands on the sides of the bath before gently starting to kneel, feeling every inch of skin thrill to the heat prickle of submersion. Once kneeling, and feeling the water lap against belly and buttocks, the bather lifts up slightly and slides legs straight towards the taps before settling back down. The enamel head end wall of the bath is cold above the water line as a back comes to rest. Amid rising tendrils of steam, knees bending upwards slightly, the bather slides down until just a head covered in damp, greying hair is visible above the still waters.

Inner heat rises, and with it a human core drifts into sweet meltdown as water laps across stomach and breast. A mind empties, becoming one with the moment in heat and foetal simplicity. Time is forgotten. The moment lingers on. A house creaks and groans, hunkering down in the winter winds that blow up from the Southwest in Atlantic squallings that drive the rain horizontally across the cliff-tops. The sounds of boards expanding where central heating pipes run, of sash window frames shifting uneasily as gusts buffet and crack against the old stone walls, these are the sounds of long loved comfort. Deep in the heat haze, drowning under waves of still rising steam, just before the water starts to turn towards the lukewarm, the bather luxuriates.

But the moment has a purpose. The drift is sublime and yet is still a controlled moment. Reaching up and to the left behind a head, the bather feels for bottles. There are two, and while neither is of the Deep Heat variety, it is still better to test. Taking each bottle in turn the bather pours a drop of liquid onto fingers and rubs. The first bottle is the conditioner. It is out of place, but the bather supposes that these things are inevitable wherever human beings may roam. The conditioner bottle is put back in its correct place against the left hand wall. The bather sinks down into the water, covering a sweat soaked brow. Rising again, shampoo is applied and vigorously rubbed into a scalp. The process is repeated, but this time, feeling lazily replete, the bather uses the shampoo to wash down under arms, pelvis, stomach and legs. Once rinsed off again the final dose of conditioner is applied to dripping wet hair and the meditation at the head end of the bath begins again as chemicals feed hair for a moment or two longer.

A break in thought. A frown. The flat-line brainwave-drift spikes sharply. There is a call, an indefinite signal, a disturbance. These moments of equilibrium pivot almost imperceptibly on a fulcrum that has shifted a millimetre off centre. The bather senses rather than feels the chill slide of outside air as a breeze pulses slowly through the building. An impossible thing. All doors and windows are braced and barred against winter storms. This chill wind is just a gust breaking through the vent at the top of the double-glazed bathroom window. The imagined voice in the hallway is one of those momentary phantasms, a playful childhood friend obscured by mists and clouds. The familiar shade of black that remains at most other times solidly uniform behind these dimmed eyes has suddenly started to oscillate, deepening and shifting in three-dimensional planes that drag a body in towards the furthermost, darkest pit. The bather sits slowly up, feeling water run down a chest and a back from shoulders and neck and hair. The air is cold against exposed skin. Unnaturally cold. A sound. A house in motion in the black shadows exposed to a mind now very sharply awake.

Speed of thought. Sitting upright now, the bather takes stock. A storm. The house is mid-Victorian. Whatever technology and modernity is brought to bear on the place, its fabric is old and the natural world has a habit of disregarding human endeavour. This is just a natural thing, a moment of solitude writ large in the imagination. The bather considers this. Bath-time meditations are an open invitation to the monsters of childhood. A memory takes shape; a dog long gone to the sodden earth in the fields at the back of the house, but a dog that the bather sometimes fancies to see in the misty corners of the world. Perhaps that floorboard step beyond the door is a manifestation of loss. A dog is missed at times like these. The bather remembers how a dog would lie in the open bathroom doorway, facing out, guarding the alpha. A smile. A silliness. A whimsy in winter darks.

A nagging doubt. It occurs to the bather to remember the conditioner bottle. Why was it in the wrong place? A simple human error? A cleaner or a friend being forgetful or distracted? The thought is dismissed but it is too late. There is a sense of dislocation. The beam and fulcrum shift a little further from the centre and the world tilts. The bather places both hands on the side of the bath and begins to rise up, water cascading from abdomen and buttocks, making unwelcome noise, signalling a location, making the mark easy to find, but the urgency of the moment outweighs the tell.

Halfway towards the standing, neither in nor out of the foetal sac, the bather stays the move. Conditioner starts to dry out on a forehead. Again there comes that chill breath on the neck of the world. Stronger this time. Colder. The bather works hard to reach a state of conviction. Blood pulses in veins. The previously stilled heartbeat now taps out the rhythms of rising panic. Unseeing eyes widen involuntarily. A catching of inner airs again, a willing of the world into familiar shapes. They are one and the same, the bather and the house, both growing old and creaking in their joints and broken skins.

The skin of the night, that shaded veneer from behind which a person might peer out at the darkling terrors, stretches taut. The hint of a footstep. That vague recognition of sweat and musk. An essence of the doorknob rattle and the bone breaker's waltz. The bather sinks back down into the tepid waters of the drowning pool. Geography has warped. Paths and passages are bent out of shape. The bather thinks too quickly to form the familiar shapes that usually illuminate this darkness, a darkness in which the bather should be the more familiar. The bather gasps once, then twice, verging on hyperventilation. Washing over a face, these ripples, these half-formed childhood night-darks, drive an imagination in overdrive and chalk white fingers wrap themselves around a doorframe.

The bather screams inwardly, a last spasm, and then subsides, calming and stilling the beating of a heart. There is nothing more to do. The bather cannot move. The wind freaks are cracking the upper landing walls. The door handle. The door handle rattle. The half-heard howl from the back fields. The bather takes one last deep draught of air and holds a breath, sliding down beneath the black waters. Conditioner scum floats on the surface of the bath water above the bather's head. A bathroom door opens and wedges on a pile of discarded clothes…

Miss Jones and the Refugee

(Loosely based on Andersen's In the Duck Yard)

AN OBSCURE BUT HISTORICALLY rich family of age old standing first came to live in one of London's green suburban idylls when those self-same suburbs were nothing but virgin fields and meadows recently subsumed into William the Conqueror's new realm. At that time the family name was long and impressive; D'Agouteville perhaps or Cholmondley-Warner or some such thing, but, as with all families, the generations followed one after another, proving more or less that sons and daughters inherit a mixed bag of genes and ancestral memory. Despite the vagaries of birth right and ability, the family remained true to its long heritage in one respect, at least, and that was to its ancestral home. Fortunes varied, were won and lost, and the family name changed through the ages, becoming a proper product of each model of social propriety, until, at the very end of a long line of ancestors, there was but one member of the family left living. She was known simply as Miss Jones.

During the long sweep of days that passed during which the family had faded into its current state of dilapidated grandeur, the great city had, conversely, spread its teeming streets far and wide. Miss Jones and her ancient familial home now stood in much reduced status in the middle of this quiet and genteel suburban sprawl. Around her home there had come the houses of merchants and bankers, followed by the lowlier dwellings of middle class managers and finally there came the estate houses of the common workers.

The family shut themselves away behind the barrier of polite poverty, pulling up the rope ladder of social interaction. Safe behind their crumbling castle walls, the family's ancient lust for life dissipated, and the vitality of these new lives completely passed them by. Miss Jones, as the last of her line, lived a quiet and shrouded life that was bounded by the tightness of good old-fashioned values and good old-fashioned friends. From time to time she watched the new world of alien features and fads strut and crow and found it all strangely attractive, but the rules of the game quite prevented her from embracing such energy and liveliness. It simply wasn't done. Self-control was an art that Miss Jones and her family had perfected through many long years of carefully managed breeding and etiquette.

Miss Jones had few vices and few interests that could be described as hobbies, but she was very keen on politics. Of course, it had to be the right sort of politics, the sort that was supported by bazaars, whist drives and charity lunches attended by her sitting member of parliament. Nevertheless, and in the privacy of her own salon, she was quite vocal in her support of the poor oppressed victims of foreign dictators and of those unfortunates in far off lands whose lives were devastated by fire, famine and flood. It was widely reported in the leafier lanes of suburban south London that after the local church's recent summer fete Miss Jones had sampled the sherry and become extremely eloquent on the subject.

"When you see them on television sitting around their fires and singing their traditional songs, well, it's so moving. They have so much dignity in their suffering. If it were only possible I'd take just such a person into my own protection. I would be a good mother to her. It's in my blood, you know. We Joneses have always been that way inclined. But they are so far away and there is so little one can really do to help".

Mistress Fate heard this desperate plea and within a week Miss Jones found herself facing a very new and challenging situation, for which she was entirely unprepared. Walking home from a visit to a friend's house one evening at about seven o'clock, Miss Jones was enjoying the last of the sun's tree-dappled warmth. The birds sang sweetly in the hedgerows and the last of the house martins were diving and darting across the sky as they fed themselves up for their long autumn flight south. A few wisps of cloud on the far horizon glimmered red and gold as they reflected the falling of day into the purple dusk of night. All was well with the world as Miss Jones turned the corner into her own street and was almost bowled over by a young man running at full pelt in the opposite direction.

Miss Jones spun around in an anti-clockwise direction when the young man's shoulder hit her left arm with all the force and momentum of a battering ram. She lost her balance and her grip on her handbag as she stumbled and tripped over her own feet, falling backwards into a beech hedge that bordered one of the suburban gardens. The young man managed two or three disjointed paces before he too crumpled and flaked, finally tripping over an uneven paving stone and falling chin first to the floor. As he fell he thrust out an arm to try and cushion his fall. The evening's background sounds of bird song and bees buzzing their way from flower head to flower head were cut in two by the sharp retort of bone breaking on hard cement.

Miss Jones heard the sound of footsteps following on behind the young man and as she pushed beech leaves out of her face she was able to make out three other young boys heading towards where she lay suspended in the hedge. With a physical urgency usually reserved for athletes and Special Forces troops, Miss Jones launched herself into a standing position, braced her legs upon the pavement and picked up her handbag in the most menacing way that she could manage. The young man with the broken wrist was of some ethnic stock, while the three other youths were Caucasians and Miss Jones was no fool. She recognised the situation for what it was and reacted instantaneously.

As soon as she realised what she was doing her legs turned to jelly, her heart skipped several beats, and she could feel herself glowing all over with beads of perspiration. All that had been so clear for that vital second was now clouded in the fog of doubt and confusion. She was not the stuff of legend nor of heroism, being the sort of person who worried that she was letting her whole class down when her shoes got dirty, and here she was facing down three members of an alien youth culture, whose sole intent was to inflict grievous bodily harm on another vulnerable individual. It occurred to her there and then that if they couldn't get to the crawling thing behind her, they would probably take just as much delight in wreaking havoc upon the body of one of the genteel classes. Her resolve momentarily wavered. Nevertheless, centuries of fine and proper blood were coursing through her adrenalin swollen arteries, and with her unwavering sense of indignation on behalf of underdogs everywhere, she steeled herself for the physical punishment that was about to pour forth upon her head.

She looked straight at the charging youths and yelled at the top of her voice, "You'll have to answer to me to first!"

The sound of running footsteps had already caused curtains to twitch in the front rooms of the houses of those who lived close enough to the road to have heard the disturbance. The sound of Miss Jones's defiant voice being raised in such an unlikely and, frankly, shocking way, heralded the full pulling aside of various nets and blinds. As soon as the good people of this suburban paradise realised that one of their own was in trouble with a posse of hell's skinheads, front doors opened and at least three elderly gentlemen were pushed and prodded out onto their doorsteps.

The three white boys, while hell bent on completing their terrible task, were not entirely insensitive to the weight of evidence that was being amassed against them. Their headlong charge towards Miss Jones and the stricken young man on the pavement behind her slackened off until they came to a skipping halt some ten yards away.

The gentlemen on doorsteps started shouting things like, "Bugger orf…We've called the police, you know…Go on, get out of it".

The boys shouted obscenities back, informing anyone who was listening that they knew where everyone lived and would be back later to get them. The stand-off lasted for nearly a minute before the sound of a siren in the distance saw the three of them break into a hectic run back the way they had come.

In no time at all, the entire street seemed to be filled with cars and uniformed officers, and an ambulance whisked the young man away to Accident and Emergency before Miss Jones had time to find out his name. She was, anyway, helping a very pleasant young policewoman with her enquiries and Miss Jones was on fine form as the policewoman took her statement. Truth be told she was probably a little tipsy having supped one too many medicinal Scotches from one of her neighbours' hip flasks when she said, "They're absolute scoundrels. Hanging is too good for them. That we permit such creatures to live and walk about on the planet! It wouldn't have happened in the old days, you know, oh no!"

Quite what would have happened in the old days Miss Jones couldn't actually say. She had a vague and hazy image in her head of one of her early ancestors running his opponents through with a large sword, and in her more candid moments she secretly approved of this approach. As it was she was quite content to end the day as she often did by toasting the world with another hint of single malt, safe in the comforting knowledge that the sun, like people, inevitably moves towards sunset.

Unfortunately for Miss Jones there was another sun of which she had taken no account whatsoever in her long and relatively restricted life, and at seven-thirty the next morning she was rudely awakened by a series of loud knocks at her front door. The adrenalin rush of the previous evening and the near quarter bottle of Scotch that she had drunk before bed had not mixed well and, when she opened the door to the reporter from the Sun & Mercury, Miss Jones was suffering from the unpalatable effects of her first hangover since her debutante years.

The next few moments were a horrible mixture of déjà vu and misunderstood questions, all of which left Miss Jones in a state of confused and bemused uncertainty. The photographer did at least have the dignity to let her change out of her dressing gown and slippers, but everything was still rushed, and she looked as if she'd just gone three full minutes with a welterweight boxer. The only saving grace was that the headlines painted a picture of a plucky citizen coming to the aid of a poor victim of racial abuse. Over the next few weeks both Miss Jones and the young victim appeared in the newspapers and on many of the news and current affairs programmes on the television and the radio. Their life stories were told and compared and much was made of the fact that two very different worlds had collided and, out of the chaos of the moment, had created a perfect picture of what the country should be striving for.

In Miss Jones's case her family background was investigated, and she was revealed to the world. All of the political parties identified with her recent struggle, praising her for her actions, and she was held up as a paragon of good old fashioned and traditional values by the true blues of the political firmament. Even those who thought her type was an anachronism in these modern times were forced to agree that she was very unassuming and brave. Cameras whirred and digital footage streamed across the closed world of conservative South London, so much so that nearly everyone in the neighbourhood wanted to invite Miss Jones to their parties, to their charity bashes and to their seasonal celebrations.

The young man, of course, received some publicity as well. His face appeared in print and on television screens and his own background was presented to the world, just as Miss Jones's had been. In his case, and although there was, obviously, just as much history to it, his family background was untraceable. He came from a remote region of a far-off nation that was locked into a vicious cycle of civil war and warlordism. As much was made of the tragedy in his homeland as was made of his broken wrist and the fact that no one could find the perpetrators of the attack.

Unlike the almost universal acceptance of Miss Jones in the media, however, some of the reporting that related to the young man tended towards the dark side. Some newspapers, tiring of the feel-good factor inherent in the immediate events of the day, started to ask questions about the presence of such people in the country. Numbers were discussed. Entry criteria were argued about and the cost of his treatment at the expense of the public purse became an issue for some of the more garrulous members of the establishment. When his story was set into the context of geography there were those who questioned whether any good could every come of a country that suffered from an apparently incurable case of Asperger's Syndrome. The final denouement was the revelation that the young man in question was waiting for his appeal for asylum to be heard by the government and he was not yet, by any right, a citizen of the country.

For Miss Jones, however, the social breeze, which she had until now only briefly caught the coat tails of, turned into a full-blown tornado. She was invited to parties and to dinners with friends and acquaintances, about whom she often knew only the bare bones. Nonetheless, she found herself positively enjoying the concentration of interest that surrounded her whenever the conversation turned to the state of the nation and to the whole immigration issue. She felt that she finally had something to offer to these discussions, basing her opinions on her direct experience with these poor unfortunate people. She was the queen of the chicken run with a bevy of hens and cocks clucking around her, hanging on her every insight and word.

In all of this, in the hurricane of press interest that engulfed the protagonists and in the quietly ebbing tide that followed as the story wound down onto the spools of microfiched newsprint, Miss Jones and the young man never actually met. In fact, under the strains of the moment and the inevitable riot of questions and counselling in the immediate aftermath of the alleged attack, they had never even spoken with one another. Their only real, physical contact had been when the young man barged into her by accident on a street corner. In the resulting confusion, with neighbours comforting Miss Jones and paramedics aiding the young man, they had no time in which to become acquainted. Their only indirect contact was when they exchanged thanks and some brief sound bites via a television link.

It should come as no surprise that Miss Jones's experience at the forefront of integration and social inclusion should provide her with the moral courage and the fortitude to deal with her next hot political potato. A year or so after the event on the street corner the government proposed the setting up an immigration processing centre in the borough where Miss Jones lived. Given her local fame as the woman who had a go, as the woman who stood up to racist yob culture, she was delighted to be asked onto the committee of the "Asylum Centre Campaign Group".

As she said on local radio one evening, "We should all do what we can to make this country socially and culturally cohesive, and no one knows that better than I do. But even after all of my experiences I have to say that we, the people of this borough, do not want this facility in our back yard".

The Beast Within

THROUGHOUT THE DARK DAYS of illness when he watched her life being sliced away in thin, almost transparent curls of prosciutto ham in the morbidly sweet-smelling delicatessen that served only the finest of cancerous dishes, Richard had never once doubted that he would cope. He thought of the slow unravelling of all that they had assumed and planned for in terms of food because she was, she had been, such a visionary in the kitchen, and ham in particular because of some long-ago account that he had read of island tribesman calling cannibalised victims of ritualistic ante-diluvian warfare Long-Pigs.

Richard cooked dishes for one now using a simple book of recipes probably designed for students. Her own library, a cornucopia of Rhodes, Oliver, Burton-Race, Fearnley-Whittingstall, Stein and David, sat on the bookshelves in his flat untouched, a small memorial to the days of splendour. More often than not now he grilled chicken breast, opened a bag of salad, and with a nod to past glories, made up his own salad dressing out of the last of her red wine vinegar and walnut oil.

When the time came to replenish the cupboards, he was sure that he would find something suitably pre-prepared in Waitrose.

After one such meal, with the wine cap unscrewed and never to be reintroduced to the bottle, Richard flicked through the digitally free channels on the television and came up blank once again. Nothing of interest. This did not surprise or annoy him. Richard told himself frequently that he enjoyed being phlegmatic. He had not been able to listen to the Archers since she died. Once it had been an evening ritual or, if they had been busy, a gentle Sunday laze in bed with tea and chocolate biscuits after early morning love-making. It is what it is, he thought, so there's no point in getting upset. By accepting the inevitable passage through the many stages of grief he was as certain as day follows night that he would surface again, would return to something akin to the skin that he had once inhabited.

With nothing on the box but the silence of his now solitary life, Richard got up from his armchair, walked across the open-plan living area of his small flat, picked up a packet of Silk cut from the kitchen worktop and withdrew one cigarette. He did not smoke in the ground floor flat, it being a rented space, a bolt hole that he could shutter against the world, so he opened the patio doors that lead out onto the communal gardens, leaned against the door frame and lit up. It is what it is.

The anti-smoking Nazi at his local Cotswold surgery, one Sister McGovern, had actually told him not to bother about giving up. He should go on holiday, get through the inevitable run of birthdays, anniversaries and Christmas, and then make the ultimate sacrifice with the New Year. He had, she'd said, enough on his plate. Richard inhaled deeply, stifling a rough, moist cough, and decided that he would not beat himself up too much about it. A drink and a smoke were fine and dandy things to indulge in given the unenviable circumstances of his life. He thought of them as strong but forgiving crutches upon which he could hobble towards normality. He mentally raised the rapidly cremating smoke together with his glass of something Tesco red to the evening sky in salutation to Fuhrer McGovern. They're not all bastards, he mumbled to a feral cat that was twitching its behind predatorily beneath his next-door neighbour's bird table.

A window slid shut in the flat above his, the owner, a florid, self-employed painter and decorator who made noisy love to his paramour every Saturday morning, evidently declining Richard's invitation to join him in his passive acceptance of the way of things. The first two fingers of Richards already raised and wine bejewelled hand strayed just a little higher than true stoicism demanded.

Richard had managed sexual congress once since she left him to fend for himself, a rather unsatisfactory affair, or shag as he'd referred to her in one of his rare drifts down to the pub with his son-in-law. The physical act was about what he'd expected. The primary assault had been over in a flash, a star-spangled whiz-bang that betrayed the months of unfulfilled marital passion during his wife's final, septic days. Richard smiled at the duality of the memories. He was clearly not as unfit as he'd thought prior to his hotel triste. The second and third waves of his sexual task force had gone in without meeting much resistance and established a strong bridgehead someway inland of the poor girl's own stamina. Physically he'd got his rock offs. It was sex, not lovemaking. What was unsatisfactory about it was the aftermath.

Beyond the sheer messiness of sharing intimate space with

another human body, all of which could be resolved by mopping up with man-size tissues, there was the inherently dirty feeling of betrayal. Ridiculous but true. His wife had been cold in her urn for months, and here he was, his ears ringing with the words of his counsellor about doing things for his own benefit now, still feeling as though he was committing treason. The thought of that night made him shudder on the doorstep. He could hear his wife cocking the firing pins for each member of the firing squad before which he sometimes dreamed that he stood. Emotional compensation; more wine and another fag.

What made it worse were the phone calls. In that moment of self-congratulatory euphoria, under the influence of the endorphin rush, he had exchanged phone numbers with the shag. Recently she had started to ring two or three times a day. Richard had added her by name to his contacts list, which meant that he could leave her to make plaintive noises on his voice mail. He instinctively deleted them after the first syllable.

In the old days, before that moment when he had looked into his future wife's eyes and known the absolute truth of his dependence on her, he had remained resolutely single. On more than one occasion he had been the bit on the side, the other man in the cuckold equation, and it had not bothered him one little bit. Now that he was single again, and even though the object of his momentary lust was reaching terminal velocity in the divorce courts, he could not square the circle of his crime. Her breathing in of air that should have been his wife's just made him angry.

It should, therefore, be easy, he thought, as he poured another glass of the dry red and pulled another cigarette from its snugly reassuring and mechanically sorted place in the packet, to answer the woman's calls and tell her that this thing between them was a one off, was done and dusted. The problem, which Richard acknowledged with a flick of his finger on the rough flint of the lighter, was that he had an addictive nature. When things got desperate he would take one of her calls, apologise and say that it was a hard time for him, and they would meet for another dose of something scabrous and itchy. Richard managed a low chuckle. Why, oh why, couldn't he take the great Billy Mac's advice and just get drunk and watch porn?

Questions about Richard's sexual reintegration with the wider world were, he felt, largely a distraction from the more important realisation that this thing, this disease, this inevitably bankrupting game of dice with the beast, was what is was. Acceptance was the key. Richard stepped out into the autumn evening, watching low, grey clouds scud across the treetops at the far end of the communal garden, and was about to make for a bench over by a massive Copper Beech, when he stopped, turned, and fetched from the flat the bottle and the packet of cigarettes. If he was going to muse, he thought, best to do it professionally.

The nights were closing in now, the leaves falling with the strengthening breeze that blew in the cold winds from the northern lands, a gift from the Snow Queen of yore. Despite showers earlier in the day that same leaf stripping breeze had dried out the bench seat, leaving streaks of dampness in the wood at the margins and around the rusting screw heads that held his weight as he sat down. It was not yet the full blown season for decay but already the manicured lawn was strewn with wet, black leaves.

Looking back at the block of flats he caught a glimpse of the florid painter caught in the glare of ceiling spotlights as he watched Richard in the garden, no doubt muttering about polluting neighbours and the irony of a survivor of one cancer ineluctably feeding the tumours of his own demise. The ruddy faced little man moved away from the window the instant that he saw Richard look back and wave a misty-blue hand.

After the initial shock of diagnosis, when he and she had sat in the consulting room of the breast surgeon, with the senior nurse on hand to translate medical tech-speak into plain English, when the tears had flowed between them like an automaton tableau depicting Victoria Falls, they had, he thought, even then, begun to move through space and time on different paths. His wife had borne the scars of mastectomy and lymph node investigations with bravery and a determination to overcome that awed him. The rolling months of chemo and radio, of Herceptin and consultation had bound their lives into a cycle of three-week blocks. Routes to and from hospital wore a groove in their souls, the shape of a tree being passed first in one direction and then another marking out a series of revolving, repeating steps. Nausea. Two days in bed with the curtains closed. Soundless days of untouched food trays and muffled footsteps on the stairs.

He should have sat with her for longer, but he found refuge in his study in between these bouts of impotent caring. Then, when the immediate global poisoning began to wear off she would surface and begin again the process of taking back her life, until the next blood test revealed neutropenia. Hospital walkways and the special care unit. The sound of the nurses voices became a soundtrack that played on a permanent loop during his last glass of comfort while she slept upstairs, worn away by the endless thunder of the chemotherapy cannonade.

She changed. Richard was forty-two when she was diagnosed.

Two years later, when the primary had been beaten, she looked fragile, like a Russian Babushka, although very much like a Ukrainian peasant woman, she still packed one hell of a punch. They tried to regain a sense of proportion, a semblance of normality, but despite every appearance of success, neither one of them could really make much headway against that constant fear.

In public they were an ideal couple, she always bright and bubbling, Richard quietly complementary, unflappable and devoted. Their first granddaughter came into the world and his wife made time to greet her by a sheer act of will. It was just a short moment, but it mattered.

Richard worked when the treatments allowed and loved her as best he found that he could. Behind closed doors he drank ever more and deeply, and somewhere along the line he stopped talking to her. Richard withdrew little by little behind the façade of the perfect foil to the recovering cancer heroine The truth that he only admitted to her in those final weeks when the friendship of all their years broke through the debilitation, was that he too was mortally afraid. He was terrified of losing her, and with her everything that defined who he thought he was.

The second diagnosis was incurable. Maybe a year, maybe two. She got nine months, by which time a second bout of chemo had been stopped because it was doing more damage than the multiple bloody tumours. Then, with no immune system to speak of, she really did become that little, frail old lady, wracked by pain and sepsis, until, with her family all around her, Richard had asked the doctors to stop the antibiotics. It had been pain relief for every single one of them.

For weeks after her killed her all that Richard could remember was her death face. When the morphine stilled her aching heart and burst his, when his tears fell on her cooling cheek and he spoke soft, sweet nothings to her ghost, she had sagged. The nurses did their best, but that face was simply not hers. The jaundice of enterochoccal sepsis and the deflation of pneumothorax coloured his memory of her. She was a foreign body, a simulacrum of what she should have been thirty years hence.

That had been the April shower that lasted all summer, but now, just recently, coinciding with the dulling of the year and the closing in of the nights, and perhaps with the woman in the hotel bedroom, he could remember laughter and life and fire in his wife's eyes. That was the fundamental problem that he grappled with as he sat on the bench in the communal garden outside his ground floor flat.

He poured another glass of wine and demolished it. He lit and smoked another cigarette. He emptied the last of the bottle and tried to savour it, knowing that, as usual these days, he had bought just the one. Richard was sublimely, drunkenly animated, talking rabidly to himself, the feral cat and the disapproving decorator in number thirty-four. His hands moved through the now low night air as he rehashed moments from these most recent of mourning days.

He found it difficult that the place where he lived, a quiet Cotswold market town, was always full of couples, weekending parents who had palmed the kids off onto Granny, or lovers sneaking off from a conference, usually middle-aged or older, and he always had to repress the urge to run up to them and ask them why it was they who could walk hand in hand towards a pension and a bus pass and not he and his darling girl.

Then again, he had noticed how often these weekending lovers found the time to spit and spat in between their lovemaking. He'd lost count of the times that he'd spotted that frosty look or overheard a tell-tale tone of voice, the sort that could lead to a recreation of the blitz or a glorious kindling of first-flush passion, and then he had to fight an urge to run up to them and tell them, implore them, to realise that it was all so fragile and that their time together should never, ever be wasted.

Most of the time Richard restrained these urges. He was in the habit of being unflappable, of being dependable, of being, well, Richard.

But he had one more thought, one more urge, one more moment of realisation. With the coming of memory there came the beast. In his most sanguine moments, when he maintained the façade of getting his shit together, he would remember her smile, would remember sketching her as she walked on a beach on Paros in the shade of a cliff with a small Greek Orthodox chapel at the summit, or he might suddenly feel her hand in his over the dinner table. He caught fragments of her conversation, stock phrases and expressions, her look of smirking, affectionate disapproval when he screwed up the do-it-yourself bodgery that was his household trademark. He smelled her skin in the aftermath of one of their rows, the one where she slept on the sofa and then crawled into bed on the Saturday morning with a mumbled apology because she couldn't remember what she had been so upset about.

With these memories came a primeval urge to howl, to bay at the moon, to call the pack to grief now that the alpha female had run down her last caribou. Richard downed the final swill of wine, and feeling his head spin under the raucous impulse he climbed up onto the bench, raised his hands to cup the lunar beauty of the now dark and clearing sky, and tilted his head back. The muscles in his chest tightened and from deep in his belly he gathered up years of frustration and loss, knuckling and kneading them into the shape of his anger and his own feral beauty before ejaculating one high, keening shock of wild sound into the damp night air in a body wracking orgasm of total and unadulterated grief. The hairs on Richards neck and arms and legs bristled. He felt his nails sharpen against the palms of his hand. The howling grew, flooding the air with pain. Richard bayed at the revealed moon as if all the worlds in the universe were barren and he, the last wolf yet living, could run no more.

A Life's Work

FROM A WINDOW HE can see Oak and Beech trees, green grass, striped in the cutting and rolling, and hedges running along a boundary from where small birds dart out to snatch scraps from a rustic bird table. He thinks they are finches, although he cannot be sure, never having spent much time with his head in bird watching books, but the beaks are short and strong and he remembers something about nuts and berries.

There is little that he can do now, except sit with memories and watch the world from his window. It's a sentimental process, this cared for waiting. The hospice is warm and the nurses are compassionate, and he thinks, were he younger and able to re-invent himself that he would marry one of them, the little rosy cheeked girl with the big chest, perhaps.

The drugs they give him tend to slow his thoughts down, but he thinks it a reasonable price to pay for a few more days without pain. The lump, it, that thing in his colon, demands that he expends his strength doing nothing. He thinks it funny that he is exhausted by waiting, by remembering.

He was a writer. He dealt in words, creating stories about other people's lives, their thrills and tragedies, the stuff of holidays and lazy poolside cocktails on Balearic islands, but he doesn't write things down anymore. Paper and pen are strangers. The thought of a keyboard fills him with dread. His fingers shake too much and what sentences would he, in his gammy handed haze, be able to construct now?

Life's business is complete; his work is done and now there is only waiting. He wonders, watching finches and sparrows busy at the business of living, whether he will be remembered or forgotten, whether the intelligence of the world, of mankind, will favour him by reading his books when he has gone.

It's not the waiting or the dying that's hard to do. The real nagging fear that binds him to what is left of his life is not knowing whether anyone will read his books or remember his name.

All for One

(Loosely based on the Grimm brother's The Traveling Musician)

THE 'DUNLIVIN REST HOME for the Chronically Ancient' had seen better days, nestling as it did between a SpeedyJob tyre and exhaust garage and a Shilling Shop distribution warehouse. Once upon a time the splendour of the home's architecture had been graced by green fields and sweet-smelling meadows, but now the house and its inhabitants' only claim to grandeur was the dusty tether that held their tired old souls to the swirling currents of modernity. Paint peeled from every windowsill, and the delicately pierced eaves dripped rust from the corroded iron guttering that hung to the fabric of the building for grim life, just like most of the inmates. The one simple, uncluttered vista enjoyed by residents was a patch of scrub land directly opposite the front door, a patch of land on which grew truly magnificent specimens of urban thistles. Pippin's field existed, such as it was, as a result of the wartime demolition of a row of terraced houses by a thousand-pound bomb. Such were people's retirement prospects in one of London's outer suburbs just a few short years ago.

Of the many residents crowded two and sometimes three to a room, most were in such a raw state of dilapidation that a high-backed plastic chair, a warm mug of something resembling tea and endless quiz shows on daytime television were the only stimulants they could manage. There were four residents in particular, however, for whom the prospect of one more day drinking thin soup and watching cheap soap operas was simply too much to bear. The accumulated spite and suffering caused by rough hands, tepid bed baths and endless days spent watching traffic through grey streaked windows forced their liver spotted hands to desperate action. One Tuesday morning, after another breakfast of stale toast and last year's raspberry conserve, Big Al Frasier nodded to one of his co-conspirators and whispered, "Pass the word on, Harry, we're go for Operation Sunlight straight after lunch".

Harry nodded back, adjusted the cuffs of his shirt so that they were set at regulation length under his smart blue blazer, and stood up very slowly so as not to dislodge any more of his vertebrae than were absolutely necessary.

Big Al watched Harry Cock, once a sergeant major in one of Scotland's finest regiments, parade out of the dining room, his head held as high and his back held as ramrod straight as his recalcitrant spine would allow. For all of his eighty years, his triple by-pass, his two replacement hips and his urgency in the bladder department, he was still a fine specimen of a man, just the sort you needed on a dark and dangerous mission. His fighting spirit was legendary in the home, where he constantly battled with the carers in a vain attempt to keep up some semblance of dignity in the most trying of circumstances. It certainly wasn't easy keeping your pecker up when you knew that your son had sent you to 'Dunlivin' because he wanted to extend the living room to make way for a home cinema, but old Harry wouldn't let the buggers grind him down. Anyway, all of that was soon to be a thing of the past if things went smoothly and their aged bodies held up. Big Al thought Harry was a brick, although he never said any such thing to the man's face, not now that he sometimes forgot the exact words he should use when he came over all emotional.

The third of the four conspirators, or Musketeers as Big Al preferred to call them, was Miss Peggy Grimalkin, or 'Wheels' for short. Peggy struck the fear of God into the soul, despite the fact that she had been chair bound for thirty years. She had obviously been a bit of a looker in her youth and, after lockdown at half-past eight, Big Al often wandered through the dreamy pastures of his own tender years and thought about what might have happened had he met her when they were both considerably more agile. It was best not to mention such things to her these days, however. Peg could give you one of those steely-eyed stares that made your knees tremble for all the wrong reasons, and she gave him the impression that she could impale a charging tigress at fifty paces with her size four knitting needles, regardless of undergrowth, wind direction or terminal medical conditions.

"Still", he thought, "she keeps herself clean, she's still got lovely hair and all her own teeth. She's bound to be an asset in a tight spot and we'll need some wheels if things get really sticky".

The only one of the four Musketeers who did not possess his own teeth was Dickie "Dog" Virtue. Dog, as he was affectionately known by the inmates, was a fixer, a King Rat sort of geezer, a man who instinctively knew how to play the game of survival. His procurement of a case of brandy and some Turkish Delight last Christmas had become the stuff of legend amongst those inmates whose memory had sufficient width to deal with real live events. What on earth the woman from the off-licence could have wanted with twenty litres of KY Jelly was anyone's guess, but the trade had made another season of miserable bad-will into a truly festive moment, a moment when they had all been able to remember what it was like to be five years old again. Dog was vital, Dog was one of the team, and even though he might sell his granny, God rest her soul, Big Al was sure that he could prevail upon him not to sell Peg unless it was absolutely necessary.

Big Al wiped up the last of the jam with his crust and popped it into his large, cavernous mouth, which was made all the more impressive by the hydraulic motions of his many chins. He had been a builder and a labourer all of his life and was still a bear of a man even at his advanced age. He was no longer six feet tall, having lost nearly a foot to general decay and a lifetime of hard physical exertion, but he felt happy in the knowledge that he more than made up for his reduced height by some impressive lateral expansion. His muscles were still toned and powerful, albeit shaped a little differently from his younger days, because you simply couldn't carry that much weight around without having an underlying physique capable of crushing small boulders between your knees. He preferred to think of his outer layers of fat as camouflage, as a shield against the austerity of the regime in which he found himself incarcerated. It felt, he sometimes thought, as if he were watching the world unfold through two tiny little portholes, but that world would soon end and a new world would be born. As soon as lunch was finished, as soon as they had all visited the bathroom and while the staff and the other poor inmates took their afternoon naps, the Four Musketeers would prize open the big sash window in Peg's ground floor bedroom and would make their break for freedom, armed with their carefully horded rations, a small but effective arsenal and assorted medical paraphernalia.

*

The rhubarb crumble was particularly impressive that lunchtime. It consisted of one part crumble, one part rhubarb and five thousand parts grey sludge and the sight of old Mrs. Bottomley's custard covered chin really had been the last straw. As soon as the staff room door slammed shut and the sound of contented snoring reached its usual two o'clock crescendo, the four escapees assembled in Peg's ground floor bedroom and made their final preparations.

Harry was as organised as ever, trailing a small, wheeled suitcase behind him that was covered in taped down lengths of flexible domestic waste piping, each one of which contained a stout, wooden shafted golfing iron. Dog, displaying his usual laissez-faire attitude to preparedness, wore his old tweed jacket, an unusually patterned pair of slacks and some water stained loafers. The only visible signs that he was prepared for the rigours of the road were a Swiss army knife hanging from his belt and a tube of denture fixative, which peeked out from his breast pocket. Peg had attached various wire shopping baskets to her wheelchair, which contained carrier bags full of clean underwear, balls of wool, her entire collection of knitting needles and enough boiled sweets to sink a battleship. Big Al had managed to squeeze himself into combat fatigues and a camouflage pattern baseball cap. He held a canvas kit bag over his shoulder, the combined effect making him look a retired butcher setting out for a survivalist weekend jaunt.

Big Al nodded to Harry, withdrew a mottled black crowbar from his kit bag and applied every ounce of his considerable weight to the task of inserting its flat end between the window and its frame. The team visibly tensed as the sound of splintering wood briefly obliterated the sound of snoring coming from further down the hallway, but no one stirred. One by one the aged, rusting nails that pinned the sash window permanently closed sheared and shattered. Harry and Big Al managed to push the sash window up as far as it would go. Harry then climbed through the opening as gingerly as he could and one by one the team passed out the bags, the wheelchair and finally Peg herself.

"Mind where you put your hands, Al Frasier", she hissed as he took hold of her just a little too familiarly for her liking.

Once outside, Harry closed the window, Dog checked that the coast was clear and the four of them set off down the street. Stage one of the plan had been a complete success and stage two required them to put as much distance between themselves and 'Dunlivin' as possible by teatime. Thick black clouds swept across the city skyline but thankfully the rain held off as the four musketeers hobbled and rolled towards the safety of the crowds in the nearest shopping centre, where they spent an hour attempting to blend in with the general population, before realising, as the shops began to roll down their shutters and the boulevards started to echo to the sound of Peg's squeaky wheel, that they would have to find somewhere safe to shelter for the night.

"Tell, you what", said Dog, "why don't we head down to the

Chavbury Estate? There's loads of empty flats down there…well, there always used to be. Don't suppose it's changed much recently".

"He's right", said Harry, "We'll need a roof over our heads tonight by the look of those clouds".

By the time that darkness had fallen and London's sodium orange suburban streets had taken on their ominous evening mantle, the gang of four had made it to the outskirts of the Chavbury. To be safe all they needed to do was negotiate the broken bottles and the carcasses of burnt out cars, fend off twelve-year-old muggers with their assortment of knitting implements and lofted sand wedges, and then break into a boarded up flat. Big Al could feel the tension and the heat in the mean city streets and he was starting to sweat profusely as he pushed Peg along in front of him. What they all needed right now was a nice cup of tea and a slice of fruitcake.

"I don't think I can go on much longer", Harry called out from behind a glassless bus shelter as he relieved the pressure in his bladder for the umpteenth time since their daring break out from Stalag Wrinkly. The fact that everyone could see exactly what he was doing was, from Harry's point of view, immaterial. Unlike the kids on the streets, Harry still believed in doing the right thing and as the bus shelter was the only half decent structure left standing on this particular street, it would have to do.

"Me neither", said Dog, "I need a sit down and a rest".

"And me", added Peg, as she finished another row of the scarf that she was knitting in case the weather turned nasty.

"What do you mean, 'and me'? You're always sitting down and

having a rest"

"Don't you go cussing me, Dog", Peg replied, giving him one of her looks and waving her knitting at his groin. Dog instinctively took a step backwards.

"Peg's right, boys", said Big Al, "we all need a rest. Anyone got any ideas?"

Harry finished watering the nettles behind the bus shelter and rejoined the group. "There's a place over there, just down from the shelter, where the door is open. We could try that".

"Zip, Harry", said Big Al, wheeling Peg away from Harry's partially exposed nether regions. "OK, you three stay here. I'll go and recce".

Big Al set off to reconnoitre the joint by the light of the street's one remaining lamp post, taking on a silhouette that looked like the backside of an African elephant being ridden by Mr. Potatohead. Dog, Peg and Harry formed a triangle, standing, or in Peg's case sitting, back to back, weapons at the ready, determined to protect their hard-won freedom and their supply of ginger nut biscuits against all comers.

It was pretty evident, even though Big Al had been away from the mean streets for some years now, that this was no ordinarily abandoned abode. The open door was made out of half inch steel plate, and judging by the array of padlocks hanging from various latches and catches, it was designed to prevent the delivery of more than just junk mail. Given the obvious levels of security employed to keep people out of the place, Big Al was a little surprised to find that there was no one on guard. Sloppy, he thought to himself as he peered inside the hallway. There was no carpet on the floor, the occupants clearly preferring to use carrier bags, cigarette butts and tinfoil as a floor covering. He could hear voices in the front room of the flat so he decided not to venture in, and instead inched his indelicate frame along the front wall of the building so that he could peer in through a window guarded by a sheet of metal security mesh.

In the front room he could see four young men, none of them older than twenty, lolling around on a flea-bitten sofa and smoking some very large looking cigarettes. On the floor by their feet there were bags of powders and pills and some neat piles of ready cash. Big Al understood. He had seen enough repeats of television cop shows to know that this was something called a drugs den and if he and his fellow musketeers were to stand any chance of converting the place into a bijou little residence for the independently retired, they would need a plan.

*

"Right, so you all know what to do", said Big Al as the four of them huddled together at the end of his pre-battle briefing. They all nodded solemnly and placing their hands in the middle of the huddle, one on top of the other, they exchanged flint eyed glances, took a deep breath and prepared to attack. They knew that this was the big one and that anything could happen in the next five minutes.

The Special Operations Pensioners crept up to the front door of the flat, where Big Al steadied his company of grey haired warriors, checked that each of them was armed and ready, and chopped the air with his hand, unleashing his elderly dogs of war on the poor, unsuspecting youths within. Harry went in first, seven iron at the ready, and made a beeline for the kitchen at the far end of the hall. He reached his objective safely, made a quick mental map of the room's layout, opened a large cupboard and found what he was looking for. The flat had an old, pre-industrial fuse box set low on the back wall of the cupboard and Harry's job was to kill the lights. Unfortunately, the plan had taken no account of old ironing boards, a defunct Hoover and piles of dirty washing, nor had it taken into account the fragility of Harry's back. He waved at his compatriots desperately, but Big Al just made chopping motions with his hand. With all the excitement and the adrenalin pumping through his veins Harry suddenly needed to pee very urgently, which is precisely where his old military training kicked into gear. You had to make do with whatever came to hand, and in this case Harry knew exactly what was needed. He unzipped and let fly, killing the lights and every other electrical appliance in the entire block with the torrential fizz and sparkle unleashed from his own personal water cannon.

As the flat flickered into darkness Peg wheeled herself into the living room, where the youths had been relaxing. She screeched like a banshee, running two of the youths over as they stumbled towards the hallway. She reversed back over them, stabbing them in their bottoms with her knitting needles just to make sure they got the message that you should never mess with a retired nit nurse.

Big Al followed her into the room and absorbed the other two charging youths as they crashed into his stomach. When they finally emerged from the folds of his military fatigues, desperately fighting for air, he picked both of the scrawny little runts up by the scruffs of their necks and deposited them on the pavement outside the flat. Just in case they felt like continuing the fight, both Dog and Harry were now positioned on either side of the doorway wielding frying pans in frenetic arcs above their heads while shouting and screaming at the tops of their voices.

Big Al retrieved the remaining two boys from underneath Peg's wheels, ejected them from the building and, once he was certain that the perimeter had been secured and that Harry and Dog were safely inside the flat, he slammed the huge metal door shut and leant his not inconsiderable weight against it. Harry lit some candles that had been lying on the living room floor and the four of them wedged the door shut with an old wooden plank. The battle-weary troop then panted and wheezed their way to the kitchen, lit the gas stove and settled down for a nice brew.

Outside on the pavement the four young men picked themselves up and fled towards the local multi-story car park to regroup. A new gang of vicious, drug crazed thugs had obviously taken their stash and their safe house away from them and they would have to get their revenge, but first they had various stab wounds and inflamed bruises to tend to. Meanwhile, in the kitchen Big Al took a puff on his inhaler, took a long gulp of his life restoring tea and grinned.

"Bloody hell, Peg, I thought you were going to steam roller the poor buggers", he said as he totted up the ready cash and the bags of gear from the living room.

"I wonder what these yellow ones do?" said Dog, digging a little mental furrow and sowing the seeds of a bright and blooming future for the four of them.

After a nice cup of tea, and having eaten a whole packet of ginger nut biscuits between the four of them, Harry checked that the front door was firmly wedged shut and that the rest of the flat was secure. Peg had already completed her ablutions and bagged the flat's only bedroom, so the men settled down on the sofa and tried to get some much-needed sleep. After the battle of Chavbury, the troops needed some rest and some liniment, and so, with the candles snuffed, Big Al, Harry and Dog let their eyelids drop and drifted off into the more than welcome land of dreams, a land where they were all twenty-five, raven haired and able to drink more than half a pint of beer before needing the toilet.

Outside, in the bleak, bottom numbing reality of the concrete jungle, the four young drug baronets finished patching up their wounds, smoked their last spliff and started to get really scratchy. They had a couple of notes and about five cigarettes left between them, having lost everything else that defined their world during their eviction from the flat about two hours earlier. They tooled themselves up with iron bars, a pocketknife and a length of metal chain, and were now ready to reclaim what was rightfully theirs. After some heated debate and a slap or two, the youngest and smallest of the four boys was despatched on a fact finding mission, and was told not to return until he had thoroughly investigated the situation and found out who and what they were up against.

Using his many years of experience in the breaking and entering of various types of house and small factory unit, the young drug runner prised open the kitchen window with a chisel and a length of coat hanger wire, climbed warily onto the kitchen work top, and set about the business of clandestine intelligence gathering. He noted the four washed mugs on the draining board, nearly fainting with the shock when he realised the place had been subjected to soapy water, but recovered his sense of cold, rational, Holmesian observation and started to make his stealthy intrusion into the heart of the enemy's camp.

Unfortunately for the young man, his powers of observation did not run to doorknobs and as he stole down the corridor towards the open living room door he completely failed to notice the knob of the bedroom door twisting slowly in the shadows behind him. Just as he was about to peer around the door frame to see what or who might be in the front room he became aware that the night air had suddenly taken on the consistency of treacle. He felt his chest muscles constrict and his stomach started to scream at him from inside that whatever else he might do in life, he most definitely should not turn around and look behind him. Of course, the young man had no choice in the matter, whatever self-preservatory advice his petrified gut might be giving him, and he turned to face the unknown demon lurking in the pitch black darkness of the corridor. He came face to face with two gleaming sparks of impish fury.

Peg, suffering from the combined effects of ginger nut dyspepsia and the thought that the bed would be full of fleas, had been quite unable to sleep. She had no doubt that the boys would be well away in the land of nod by now and so, with the coast clear, she could open the bedroom door and get some much-needed air. Just as she had been about to trundle down to the kitchen for a glass of water she heard the sound of wood under duress and guessing that something troublesome was afoot she had waited for the inevitable sound of footsteps in the hall.

The boy never had a chance. Before the scream could reach his larynx Peg's favourite carbon tipped, size seven knitting needle had slid home with deadly force somewhere between his thigh and his groin. The boy staggered backwards only to find his posterior fixed firmly in the vice like grip of Dog's false teeth.

The scream strangled in his throat, turning into a mewling whimper as he caught sight of the huge bulk of Big Al Frasier standing silhouetted in the living room doorway. He could feel something warm and sticky running down his left leg and faced with the combined wrath of the incredible hulk and his rabid guard dogs the boy dug deep and somewhere in the darker recesses of his motor neurone system he found the strength to leap over Peg, to hit the ground running and to dive headfirst through the plate glass kitchen window, preferring the possibility of death by a thousand cuts to the prospect of facing these hell hounds one moment longer.

As the last shard of glass hit the kitchen linoleum, Harry emerged from behind Big Al, holding a lighted candle and asked, "Anyone for a cup of tea?"

For the previous occupants of Flat 2a, Chavbury Villas the war was over. Faced with the terrifying ruthlessness of Big Al and his cunningly disguised Yardies, the local criminal fraternity decided that discretion would be infinitely preferable to the valour required to face down Wheelchair Peg, Dickie "Dog" Virtue and Harry "The Sergeant" Cock, and that is exactly how the legendary Frasier gang started out on the road to criminal infamy…

Where There's a Will

DANNY CRAIG LIVED FOR the future. His was a world of new technology, where television screens became ever bigger and where bandwidth expanded exponentially with the phases of the moon. When not at work patching network cables into routers and hubs for a local newspaper, Danny shared his home with his aged father and his demure, unassuming sister, Annie.

He shared his home but not his time, preferring, when not down at the pub watching Manchester City flatter to deceive in wide screen glory, to lock himself away in his room with his computers and his cable links to a very private world of digital opportunities. Danny found virtual reality far more rewarding than the unnecessary and irksome chores that comprised all manual forms of familial communication. Such things were, he told himself, outmoded. Unfortunately Danny and Annie were thrust unceremoniously into the analogue Dickensiana of real life when their father keeled over with a massive heart attack one Saturday evening while watching the family's favourite football team being trounced by Hereford United.

In the days that followed their father's untimely passing, brother and sister lived in a world of frayed tempers, compassionate overload and weary resignation. Death certificates were signed and lodged with the appropriate authorities, funeral arrangements planned and paid for, paperwork sorted and solicitors engaged to deal with the minutiae of closing down a life. Danny was sure that he could design a much more efficient way of dealing with the arcane world of paper and people, and regularly assailed his sister with critiques of off-line morbidity. If only they could deal with the stiff by clicking a button and filing its life away in some Interweb repository. When it came to the reading of their father's will, however, Danny found, in a rather brooding sort of way, that the world of flesh and bone took on a sudden fascination.

Danny stood outside the crematorium after a sparsely attended service making little attempt to disguise his impatience as he bade their one solitary guest goodbye. Annie, who's mortal soul was grounded in a much richer vein of sensitivity, couldn't help feeling that if this was all a life was worth come the final reckoning, then there was something infinitely sad about the infinite plan they were all a part of. Their mother had walked out on the three of them some ten years previously and a combination of family arguments and mortalities had reduced them to this paltry dynastic circumstance.

"Thought he'd never go", said Danny, turning to his sister as their father's ex-boss hurried back to his car and the comfort of paperwork. Rubbing his hands together as he blew on them Danny continued, "Ready for the grand unveiling? Shall we trot down to the solicitors?"

Annie sighed, stuck her hands in her coat pockets and followed her brother along Barlow Moor Road towards the offices of

Dawson, Dawson & Dawson, chosen by their father in happier times because he could always be sure of remembering the name of his solicitor when exceptional circumstances required the expertise of a legal beagle. The other advantage of the partners Dawson was that, unlike the new super-practices located at the heart of Manchester's business district, their fees reflected their clientele's ability to pay, which in the case of the now deceased Mr. Craig had never been very much.

Over a plateful of slightly stale tractor-wheel biscuits and weak tea in chipped china cups, Danny and Annie found out that there were no savings, no insurance policies and no investments. The only inheritance was the small, terraced house that they had grown up in and a few personal possessions. Much to Annie's horror, the elder Mr. Dawson spelled out the terms of the will in very short order.

"So, there you have it, I'm afraid", he concluded. "Miss Craig receives her mother's engagement ring and the… erm… Ming vase, while young Mr. Craig gets everything else, namely the house, which is paid for, and the furniture etcetera. I must say it seems a little one sided, but mine is not to reason…"

"Yeah, thanks", interrupted Danny, "I'll make sure Annie's looked after. Nice to have met you, Mr. Dawson."

Annie followed her brother out of the solicitor's office and back onto the street, where the weak light of a chill winter afternoon had given way to the dark pit of night like a coffin being lowered into the ground on a rain-soaked headland. Car headlights flashed in her eyes, momentarily dazzling her, as if a stray flash of lightning had reflected brilliantly on a brass handle just before the lid of the box disappeared from sight. Her tears, held back until now by the bleak austerity of the day, began to flow.

Danny didn't wait for her. He ploughed through the streets followed at some distance by his sister until, with the front door of their modest terraced home shut firmly on the outside world, Danny disappeared into his bedroom to play electronic games. Annie sat at the kitchen table and looked at her inheritance. She was the proud owner of some books, a few records, a wardrobe full of clothes and a bank account with approximately two hundred pounds in it, all of which was now enriched by one ancient diamond ring and a crudely painted blue and white vase. She spent the rest of the evening dabbing her eyes with used tissues and asking herself what other wonders life might have in store for her.

*

Despite his apparently uncaring treatment of her the previous day, Annie still firmly believed that her brother loved her and that he would, in time, learn to engage with the world in a more constructive way now that he was the effective head of the household. Breakfast that morning had been the usual hurried, monosyllabic affair, and when she returned home from work Annie was determined that she would sit her brother down and that they would have a thorough chat about the future.

"After all", she reminded herself on the bus that evening, "he did tell the solicitor he'd look after me".

Cold comfort awaited Annie as she stepped through the front door. Her brother had taken a couple of hours off work that afternoon and used the time to strip her bedroom, bundling her clothes, books and music into black bin liners. He had also packed her toiletries, cosmetics and personal knick-knacks into an old rucksack and together with the Chinese style vase all of Annie's worldly possessions were stacked in a small, untidy pile in the hallway. The poor young woman stood in the hallway in dumb silence as Danny explained the facts of her new life to her.

"Sorry about this, but it's mine now and I've got plans, none of which include you. You can't have order in a house full of women…"

"But it's not full of women, Danny, there's only me".

"Today, granted, but what about tomorrow? I'm a man of property now. There's bound to be something turns up. I've been chatting to a nice Russian girl on the Interweb and you never know. Anyway, as I was saying, you'll be leaving tonight. Can I have your key?"

"But where…where will I go, what will I do?" Annie whispered, feeling as though she were being sucked down into a whirlpool.

Her sad and lonely inner child wandered the dark corridors of a huge adult world, while at the same time she could feel the steam head pressure of outrage building in the magma chambers that brooded darkly in the spaces between her quiet outward persona and her molten core.

"Not my problem", answered Danny and he turned away, heading towards the kitchen where Annie could smell beans or spaghetti hoops cooking and toast burning.

She followed him into the kitchen. The table was laid for one person, with Danny's laptop already hooked up via means of temporary network and telephone cables in the place where she usually sat. The history of eruptions, being by its very nature violent, would have been proud to record the effects of Annie's full explosive force as it hit her brother's online world with maximum venom.

"Bastard! Bastard! Bastard!" she screamed over and over again as she emptied the pan of baked beans onto the keyboard and then turned her attention to the boy himself. By the time that she had whacked him with the frying pan six or seven times, kicked his shins repeatedly and doused him in an entire litre of Vimto, Danny's other worldly cool had been completely shattered.

As volcano Annie subsided into a state of uncongenial dormancy, she and her brother came to a bruised and battered arrangement whereby she could stay on in the family house for a few days until she could find somewhere else to live. Given her brother's obvious lack of filial concern for his sister and given Annie's disgust at his behaviour, there seemed little alternative but that she should vacate the premises.

Armed with her father's old address book, and after many disappointing telephone calls to old friends and distant relations, Annie eventually tracked down an ancient great-aunt who owned a crumbling Victorian villa that had been converted into bedsits. At first the telephone conversation with the old woman went very badly, with her great-aunt being extremely hostile to the memory of her nephew's long forgotten children, but, as Annie described her predicament and as the old woman remembered that it had always been the men in the Craig family who had been the cause of the greatest unhappiness, she eventually found it in her heart to offer the young woman one of her flats at a very competitive rent. Arrangements were made, the bed sitting room was cleaned and a week later Annie moved her bin liners and her rucksack into her new home. By now she had grown accustomed to the weight of her mother's old engagement ring on her finger and the Chinese style vase stood proudly in its new position on the fireplace mantelpiece.

The villa had seen better days, having matured over more than a century of irregular neglect into its current state of generally poor repair. Where once a stout Edwardian family had warmed themselves by the great living room fire and eaten roast meats on Sundays in the capacious dining room, there now existed within these walls a selection of small private worlds inhabited by transparent people who warmed themselves next to two-bar electric fires, who shared bathrooms and cooked tinned meals on single ring electric cookers.

Fortunately for Annie, she was still in such a state of shock that few if any of the shortcomings in her new home had yet registered in her consciousness. She was also blessed with the good fortune to have moved into one of the two ground floor bedsits, which boasted high ceilings, large sash windows and more than enough room to swing a cat. The two-bar was not effective in heating such a large space, but Annie's great-aunt assured her that the rooms were lovely and cool in the summer, which would be a blessing worth waiting for.

Over the course of her first week in residence Annie, who was naturally quiet even in happy times, impressed her great-aunt with her obvious inner sorrow, which the old dear thought only fitting for a woman of the Craig line, and the next Saturday afternoon Annie received her first invitation to call on her relative in her own apartment.

Annie knocked on the door to her great-aunt's apartment with some trepidation. In public the old girl bristled with an imperious air of confidence and hard-nosed, old-world defiance, but Annie was convinced that her private inner sanctum would be a shambling mess of decrepitude and cat infestations, full of strange smells and unfamiliar utility furniture that dated from the middle of the previous century. She steeled herself before entering the living room.

Annie was amazed to find herself in a most elegantly appointed salon, stuffed full of finely embroidered soft furnishings and antiques of obvious quality and refinement. In the middle of the room on an elegantly proportioned drop leaf table her great-aunt had set a Royal Worcester tea service, with one of those lacy three-tiered cake stands at the centre of the display. Drifting languidly from the speakers of a restrained but nonetheless modern stereo system Annie was sure that she could hear the dulcet tones of Leonard Cohen. Annie greeted her great-aunt softly and settled herself into the voluminous folds of one of the armchairs.

Great-aunt Edith poured the tea, keeping one eye on the cups and watching her great-niece with the other. As she handed Annie her drink, she went straight to the nub of matter. "So, you've experienced the true reality of life as a Craig at last, my girl. Not pleasant is it!"

"No", replied Annie quietly, "at least not recently. It wasn't too bad when Dad was alive. I mean, it wasn't exactly a life of luxury and he could be a bit moody at times, but I'm sure he did his best. After Mum left his heart wasn't really in it anymore, but he did what he could. As for Danny, I thought it was a phase, you know, something he'd grow out of".

"And here you are", said her great-aunt, "without a penny to your name, without anything that anyone would want to steal".

"It's true", said Annie sadly. "But then I've got nothing to fear either have I? I mean, who's going to bother with someone like me? All I've got is my mother's old ring and grandma's pot".

"You've got a heart, dear. What would you do if someone stole that or worse...if someone broke it?"

Annie sat in silence for a moment or two pondering the question of a broken heart. There had never been much in the way of demonstrable love in her father's house and she'd already cried enough over his death. As far as her brother was concerned she couldn't really remember the last time she'd really thought of him in affectionate terms. At best she felt a cold numbness in her heart, which she supposed was better than feeling nothing at all. Sitting here in this lovely room with a real fire in the grate and with Suzanne drifting out of the stereo's speakers, Annie felt that, even in her poverty-stricken state, life was still better lived than made into an excuse for not trying.

 Her great-aunt watched over her throughout the afternoon, revealing snippets of family history, and sketching pictures from her own life story, all of which seemed to consist of too many broken hearts and broken heads, until, with the football results due in and Leonard Cohen starting to become a little bit overbearing, she turned to her young relative and asked, "Do you want to stay for dinner? There's a DVD I want to watch and we could phone out for a curry".

By the end of the evening, which great-aunt Edith thoroughly enjoyed because of the company, two bottles of Lambrusco and because they watched quite possibly the best werewolf film ever made, the two women had become the best of friends. The old girl eventually retired, wobbling slightly as she went, and Annie returned to her own thinly proportioned bed on a promise to call round the next morning for coffee. She was to bring her mother's ring and the old blue and white vase.

*

In the days following Annie's departure from the family home and while she settled into her new bed sitting room, Danny Craig made changes. He no longer felt the need to confine his online activities to his bedroom and had spent many a happy evening hour running cables around the house and setting up a new wireless router. His main file server now sat in the living room, together with various and sundry stereo and television appliances. By virtue of the addition of a new hub, borrowed from his place of work, Danny could attach his laptop to his domestic network in any one of the bedrooms, in the kitchen and even in the downstairs lavatory. In the living room he installed a fifty-six-inch television monitor and was able to interact with online services in super-sized mode, which he found particularly useful when inspecting the assets and attributes of various potential brides from far flung lands such as the Czech Republic, the Ukraine and the Philippines.

Annie, knowing her brother from years of quiet observation, correctly suggested to her great-aunt that he would dedicate his newfound personal freedom and financial independence to the pursuit of private digital excess, and it was this that great-aunt Edith was thinking about as she lay in bed after a very pleasant Saturday in the company of her poor, disappointed relative.

Over coffee the next morning great-aunt Edith inspected first the ring and then the Chinese style pot. She consulted an antiques guidebook and after much humming and page thumbing, she turned to Annie and said, "Your father never was very bright, my dear. I don't think he meant to leave you in the shit, you know, I really don't. Unfortunately, he believed what he saw on television and I'm rather afraid that he watched a little too much of the Antiques Roadshow. The vase is quite nice, and certainly Victorian, but not worth more than a couple of hundred. It looks like Ming, but it doesn't taste like it, if you know what I mean. It's a reproduction. As for the ring, well, I remember the thing being passed down through various members of the family. It's even been pawned on occasion, our diamond engagement ring, but its only glass and nine carat gold. Your father thought, no doubt, that a Ming vase and a vintage diamond ring would be worth quite a lot and that you would appreciate them better than your soulless brother. As it stands, however, they're baubles and in no way do they compensate you for your father's sad loss".

Great-aunt Edith paused for a moment to let Annie take in what she was saying, pouring herself another cup of thick black coffee from the cafetiere. Annie simply stared into the steam that spiralled up from her own cup into the lazy Sunday morning air.

"The baubles may not have much monetary worth, my dear, but there's more than one way to skin a cat. Let me tell you a story".

Annie looked into her great-aunt's eyes and saw there a sparkle and an edge that quite disturbed her. She had always thought of centenarians as being small and spindly creatures with bent backs and osteoporosis, as dull animals with rheumy eyes and limited vocabulary, but her aunt's eyes shone with a strange mixture of passion, venom and audacity.

"I remember", began great-aunt Edith quietly, "when I first saw those baubles. Once upon a time I too had maiden aunts and one

Sunday, just around the time of the first Great War when I was seven or eight years old, my mother took me to visit her sisters in a house they shared near Macclesfield."

"I don't remember much about the rest of the day, but I do remember high tea. The four of us were sitting in the front parlour and I was especially looking forward to a slice of Aunt Cecilia's fruit cake. After tea was served my aunts opened a cupboard in their welsh dresser and fetched out a little green box and a blue and white vase, which they put on the table. My aunts and my mother seemed to drift off into a little world all of their own before, with a huge sigh, they put the items back into the dresser. Nothing more was said."

"On the way home I asked my mother about the vase and the ring, but she refused to say anything to me about them then or at any other time. It was only after the war, when I was about thirteen and my mother was sickening, that she told me about the precious things I had seen that afternoon."

Annie sensed that she was about to be initiated into a new world of family revelations and scandals. She sat up in her chair and gave her great-aunt the full weight of her attention.

"They were gifts, you see. Gifts from older, single gentlemen given to my aunts when they were teenage girls themselves. In those days, when the world was very different to this one, bachelor gentlemen of a certain class and attitude were often to be found in the company of young girls and boys. The camera was still a relatively new thing and artistic shots of fairies and such like were not uncommon. Of course, the constraints of time, place and social custom precluded, for the most part, any of the more common occurrences, and indeed very many great men undertook such friendships. I mean, where would Alice be without the Reverend Dodgson or Peter Pan without dear old Mister Barrie?"

"Unfortunately for my aunts, the gentlemen photographers in question were not of a literary bent, far from it, in fact, and paid the girls in cash or in kind for making artistic photographic plates in a room above a fishmonger's shop in Salford. Not one of the Craig family's better-known secrets. Your great, great aunts Cecilia and Florence were Boer War glamour models..."

Annie let out a small shriek made up in equal parts of horror and delight. In her mind's eye she could see gas lights flickering, shadows on red brocade curtains, and two nubile young ladies posing in shocking stocking tops for a row of whiskered bank managers and the outwardly respectable middle-aged scions of ancient clerical families.

"Oh, yes", continued great-aunt Edith, "yes, indeed! And if you think that's shocking ask yourself how another maiden aunt of this benighted family came to own and run a house like this and to have filled it over the years with antiques and curios from around the world. You see, my mother died soon after she told me about my aunts, and left to fend for myself and my brother, that's your grandfather, I took it into my head to enter into what, at thirteen years of age, I deemed to be the family profession..."

"My God", squeaked Annie, "You mean..."

"Mmmm" whispered great-aunt Edith, with a smile on her lips and a gleefully naughty sparkle in her eyes. "I did a few artistic poses for a local photographer, you know, under the counter shots, and then managed to hook up with a rather forward-thinking Archdeacon with a penchant for silk camiknickers and snakes."

"I remember thinking at the time how deliciously appropriate that was. Anyway, I kept mum about the whole thing for years, and as my darling cleric rose through the ranks of the established church, so my letters asking for financial assistance and moral guidance became ever more pressing, and that, my dear, was the pattern for my many years of success in trade."

Annie laughed out loud and long and then got up, plonked herself down on the arm of her great-aunt's chair and gave the old woman a huge, enveloping hug.

"You dear old rascal", she whispered as they rocked gently back and forth with the giggles and with the wide eyed sharing of new best friends. After a few minutes great-aunt Edith looked up, brushing Annie's fringe away from her eyes, and said, "Of course, it's all different now. The world has got a lot darker since we gave up the Empire".

Annie stayed with the old woman for the rest of the day, sharing with her a light lunch and a couple of large cognacs. As the two of them sat and chattered away about the old days, great-aunt Edith outlined her plan for getting even with brother Danny. Annie was impressed by her aunt's knowledge of things electronic, especially when shown the old girl's study, which was full of the latest techno-wizardry and broadband connectivity. She was even more impressed when she realised that her centenarian relative, having dispensed with a life of genteel blackmail in her early eighties, had subsequently taught herself not only the arts of silver surfing, but had also majored as a writer of hacking and viral software on a par with any young eastern European hotshot. Indeed, with the decline in rental income caused by the ever-increasing costs of insurance, red tape and health and safety initiatives, great-aunt Edith had financed some of the finer pieces in the apartment, including a real Ming chrysanthemum pot and a small Lowry, through her prowess at conducting phishing expeditions across the global email network in search of the details of other people's bank accounts. Digitally armed and dangerous, savvy and angry, the two women put their simple plan into effect; namely, he who lives by the Interweb shall die by the Interweb.

Great-aunt Edith showed Annie how to scan photographs and store them as images on the computer, using a collection of her very own black and white artistic poses from her early days in the glamour business, images which would now be considered at best cute but in most cases just as period pieces. Once the images were scanned the older woman copied down the details of Danny's email and web addresses from Annie's diary and set about the task of adapting one of her more subtle Trojan Horse viruses so that it would work specifically with Danny in mind.

Using Danny's known liking for foreign brides, the two women concocted an email purporting to describe a particularly ravishing resident of Gorky, embedded the virus in a picture of the girl and sent the email to Danny Craig. Sure enough, within an hour a message popped into great-aunt Edith's inbox telling her that Danny had opened the email, spent some minutes scrutinising the picture and that the virus was now safely and surreptitiously installed on his hard drive. All that remained for them to do was wait for a week while the nasty little bug trawled the Interweb in the low, dark hours of the night collecting images of the most bizarre, disturbing and perverted kind.

After a week of clandestine activity the Trojan Horse virus

despatched a summary of all the dreadful links, stories and pictures that it had found on its trawling expeditions in the howling hours and subsequently installed in a hidden area on Danny's hard drive. It then invoked a deletion routine, removed all trace of itself from the machine and let its digital DNA drift away on the ether that connects electronic superhighways to Acacia Avenues the world over.

That same Sunday morning, following an anonymous tip off, various large and burly members of the Manchester police force's vice squad battered down Danny's front door, dragged him out of bed and bruisingly bundled him into the back of a white van. The house was stripped of the appropriate electronic devices and following a brief forensic examination of hard drives, flash disks and sundry other items of magnetic storage, the Detective Superintendent in command of the vice squad charged the young man with a number of crimes related to the storage and distribution of banned materials. The haul was sufficient, he said with a satisfied grin, to ensure that Danny would be spending the better part of the next fifteen years on the "Nonce" wing at Strangeways.

Danny protested his innocence throughout questioning, throughout his trial and well into his first few days on G wing, but he soon found that it was best to keep a low profile. Given the nature of the evidence against him, no one believed his claims that he had been fitted up, and in the far from private world of lock-downs and slopping out, any mention of his sort of crime meant a bloody good beating.

Safe and sound on the outside and aided by the proceeds from Danny's own bank account, together with funds received from an unwitting, Canadian ice hockey player, Annie and her great-aunt employed the services of a very expensive legal practice in the heart of Manchester's business district. With the excellent advice of their own legal eagles easily overcoming the meagre resistance offered by the partners Dawson, they successfully overturned the terms of the will and shared the proceeds from the sale of the house, its chattels and the remaining technical gizmos that had not been confiscated by the Old Bill.

Annie settled into a life of sublime but quietly productive luxury with her great aunt, who, for her part had found an excellent reason to keep the home fires of her life burning brightly. She admitted to her great-niece that having crossed the Rubicon of a century of life she had started to get a little tired of things. Now, however, she couldn't possibly lay down the torch, not when she had so much to teach her rather naive young relative about living life to the full, the first lesson being how to behave and pose for glamour shots when in the company of rich, amateur photographers.

Glasshouse Tango

BROKEN GLASS UNDERFOOT. A heel twisting. A booted heel. Cuban. Grinding slowly, twisting, pressing down upon sharp but brittle fragments. He listens to the sounds of deliberate destruction. He hears his own breathing, soft and slow, beneath which he revels in the scratchy soundtrack of glass turning to powder. He looks up. Above his head he sees a splintered wooden roof truss, leached grey by sun and rain, made soft and spineless by ice and thaw and spore and worm. He smiles and walks slowly forward down the central of three aisles. The sound of denims, tight and boot-cut, brushing the skeletal remains of wooden glasshouse benches thrills him. He loves the solitude of the derelict. He adores the way that he and the sparrows and the rats and prowling cats can lay claim to a space once thriving with flora and green human thumbs, a place now effectively moribund. In the heart of the city, bounded by clogged arterial roads, constricted by the particulate cholesterol that forms diesel soaked platelets in veins, he can, despite a midriff heading south, still squeeze through relatively small gaps in chain link and board, losing himself in these abandoned places. There are always abandoned spaces if you know where and how to look for them. The city positively metastasises with them, an endless proliferation of corrupted cells wrinkling and decaying as neighbourhoods and districts fight through their endless cycles of dereliction and renewal. He has an Oyster card. He roams at will.

*

When he awoke earlier this Saturday morning he had felt instinctively that today would be a good day for trespassing. In spite of an intermittently wheezing cough, a remnant of thirty odd years on filter tips and cheroots, he felt generally and contentedly positive this morning. He decided that he would visit his new gem, his most recent shift along the twisting paths of West London's suburban DNA. Choosing the Piccadilly Line for a short hop towards the west he had taken the tube from Acton Town to Boston Manor, and skipping lightly across the main road opposite the station he had dropped down through streets full of solid, nineteen-thirties, bay-fronted, semi-detached houses towards the Manor Park boundary walls. At the back of the park, down where the scrubs still lay undeveloped behind the crumbling concrete block-work of an abandoned windscreen wiper factory, there lay the remains of an urban nursery. He had long ago scoured the factory bones, and felt no inclination to visit those rusting, rain and piss pooled halls today. His fascination lately focussed on the skeletal remains of these old glasshouses. His obsession consumed the time and dust caked bones of a memory, of a summer and autumn colour that, despite the fading years, was still brighter in his mind than any current shades of existence.

*

He breathes in deeply, drawing the aromas and chemical components of damp earth and late summer drowsiness deep within, and lifts his heel from the powdered glass underfoot. He looks around, counting the dirt crusted terracotta pots on a set of slatted wooden benches running along the left side of the glasshouse's rib-like wooden framework. Seven pots, all still upright and only lightly chipped, two of them full of dry, grey earth, trailing the brittle white stems of long dead plants, stems that crumble to the touch. Seven pots. The thick layer of compost and dust and debris on the workbench tops remains pristine in its dereliction. Nothing has been disturbed. It is over a week since his last visit and he worries that some other person might step through the shattered door frame and contaminate his memories with their own sepia tinged half-truths. He is relieved. All is safe and sound. There is no spoiling, not today, not yet. He is alone and the glasshouse is as yet an untouched crystal prism through which he splits the light of the world solely according to his own laws of physical abstraction.

Above him, hanging from rusty nails the raggedy remnants of shading blinds hang dirt streaked and grey, rotten through, and only truly held aloft by the strength of spider webs and seams of thickening, blackening grease and dust. There is stillness here, down behind the old factory, and he imagines that this local microclimate contributes directly to the blinds' frayed survival in a place where the seeming permanence of plate glass has already fallen and shattered. Perhaps, he thinks, the glass is more attractive to urban breakers, to the lymphocytic youths who infest diseased buildings when the infection of dereliction is still novel. There would, he supposes, be a purpose in throwing stones, that in the shattering of things these youths act as urban antibodies and serve to hasten concrete renewal. He can just about remember his own youth and can still take pleasure in imagining a crack and a tinkle, a smash and a delicate refraction. He instinctively understands though that in pulling down these blinds now the only gratification that anyone would receive would be a simple and grotesque smothering in dust and bird shit and spider eggs. It is precisely because of that outcome that he feels happy here, happy in the knowledge that the glass breakers have had their fill and moved on elsewhere. He is happy that as yet the moneyed princes of urban shade and shift have not turned their gaze his way. He is convinced that this is truly a forgotten place. It is his place. His place of memory.

He walks along the central aisle towards the middle of the glasshouse. He passes more pots, overturned and frost cracked despite their faded labels claiming Cretan origin, shattered in places, grinding away to red dust and mixing into the fading grey powders that were once glass roof panels. He steps over the crumpled remains of black plastic seed trays that litter the walkways and the spaces underneath the workbenches. A green gardening glove rots slowly, half turned inside out beneath the wooden racking. Glass and dirt and weeds bloom in the cracked concrete troughs and paths and accumulations of old topsoil, manure and John Innes composts. In a place where the original purpose is so clearly derelict, it amuses him that in this space where flowers once blossomed in neat rows and in managed orders there is now nothing left but black dust. As with his cats and rats and sparrows, the Mother God of planet Earth has a peculiar way of reclaiming formerly manicured spaces with such chaotic and vibrant maternal love.

He too has a reclaimed space, just along the aisle. It is right here in front of him. In the middle of the glasshouse he has moved the central row of benches and racking to either side, closing off the outer aisles, and he has placed a chair under the last remaining intact panels of glass in the roof. During a previous exploration of the site he found the chair buried under a tarpaulin in a hut at the far edge of the nursery compound, a slatted wooden foldaway chair with enough strength left in its metal frame to make it usable. On the back of the backrest are stamped the letters, "G.W.R." This is, he thinks, at least the third age that this chair has known, and it seems fitting that having given up the hurly of the station platform, this chair now rests with memories as he does. Around the chair he has swept the space clean using the last bristles on a worn out broom also found in the hut at the edge of the nursery compound.

He sits and arranges himself, hands folded in his lap, his legs formally neat, his back straight. He waits for the dust that he has raised to settle on the autumnal air within this skeleton glasshouse, feeling the slight shift in atmospheric temperature under these few remaining glass panes. He takes one last look around the place, and is comforted to see that the rusted pipes and valves of the industrially specified irrigation system seem as solidly fused and pitted as ever. He hears bird song. The ubiquitous Buddleia bushes that have sprouted in and come to dominate the walled yard are sweetly occupied. He tunes into the faint wash of flying insect wings, and allows his sense of place and time to drift beneath the sounds of fauna busy with living. He self-hypnotises, relaxing into his past lives, and he smiles softly with the drift.

The memories that come are random at first. He drinks water too fast at the kitchen sink while his mother warns him about hot boys and heart attacks in a vain attempt to slow down his childish enthusiasms. He smiles inwardly. Crazy woman. A boy whips a towel across his bare legs in the shower at school. Stevie Schneider, youngest child of an American service family living down the street when he was ten years old, takes a bath in a new-build house that they had broken into one summer afternoon. Police Constable Nichols on the doorstep talking to his father. Breaking images. Older now. Sally. Dinner somewhere and she complements him on the fact that the silk lining of his jacket matches his shirt. Ephemera. A shimmering prologue. But then the curtain lifts and a different woman enters his dream space to stand silently beneath a proscenium arch. He can feel her rather than see her. The lights are yet low. She is shadow. He never says her name out loud.

He slowly pulls out from his jacket pocket a piece of A4 paper, folded neatly into quarters. It is an inkjet black and white print of the only digital image that he has of her, an image snapped during a brief afternoon interlude in Oxford. In landscape shades of grey she rests on her front, on her elbows, on a hotel double bed, naked, pen in hand, filling in the harder clues in the day's Times Quick Cryptic. She is grinning at the camera lens, basking in the twin delights of a post-coital glow and the cracking of clues that he still cannot fathom. She is teaching him how to read these clues. He has spent these last year's practising every day in homage to her. He has an obsessive streak. He has not yet unfolded the quartered page. He knows the picture better than his own reflection. She never changes now, never ages, whereas on those mornings when he remembers to shave he sees an ever more distant relative of the person that he once was when he pretended to be an intelligent man.

The reveal has become an absolute ritual. He opens the page

along the short seam before the long. He smooths the picture out on his lap and opens his eyes the better to enter this glorious dreamtime with her. He smiles down at her, letting the memories flood forward into his visual cortex. Now she is standing there in front of a wooden dressing table mirror in that same hotel room with her hands on her hips. She wears a simple white blouse and jeans. Long henna-red hair flicks back and the look that she gives melts him even now, even here in the shattered glasshouse. Shared laughter. That slight twist of her left eye when she is utterly relaxed. And so the music starts. Birdsong morphs into the layered beauty of a Josquin du Pres Te Deum, with voices floating and melding in their devotion, voices that soar and cascade and lift the soul in pure and simple harmonic brilliance.

Almost as soon as those simple cherubic voices reach their crescendo so they start to fade away. The footlights of his mind's stage flare briefly before settling into a soft, yellow glow. There is a cough in the imaginary stalls behind him. The soundtrack cuts abruptly to the dark shadows of the one true dance. Emerging from the blurred and bleeding edges of the music, seeping into a definite shape and form, she is there with him once more, but this time she wears a calf-length red dress, tight across her hips and waist and bosom. He stands on the stage, arms held out as if taking her into the dance, and slowly he bends from the waist, twisting, shoulders drifting languidly through slow-motion demonstrations of the moves. His feet remain fixed. He is a bobbing mannequin, a robotic, mechanically slowed version of a human dancer. He starts to feel the power and the sensuality of the dance and so he starts to move, both in mind and in body. He moves purposefully across the stage, just as he drifts slowly towards the left-hand glasshouse benches. He crosses the boards with her under a spotlight, fusing with her, soul and bone and flesh.

He listens intently as the tango builds. A simple guitar and a drum, paced and sensual, repeating overlapping patterns. In the listening, in that shared understanding, they begin their silently exclusive conversation. He leads and she follows, but in the nature of the dance their fusing imbues each of them with elements of the other. Just as their bodies touch and slide, sending shivers and thrills through him, so their minds fix on the rhythms and the steps, merging into one space where his lead is accepted and then shifted through subtle degrees of harmony. He connects again with her across the years and the miles, and that connection is an embrace, an eternal constant in his mind, and through that embrace, within the sphere of music that surrounds them both, he feels as though he is born again in the dance. There is no past or future now. There is just the flow. He can be intimate again. He and she understand. They are one again. They are dazzlingly connected.

At that exact moment, diffused and incorporeal, that perfect connection shatters, as it must inevitably do. In the soundscape-blackened space behind his eyes he feels her shift and become separate. They slow, leaving the rhythm to flow on around them, and he pulls her into a close embrace, desperate to make these final seconds last forever. He smells her red, henna-laced hair. He lifts his right hand and runs it across her brow and down the left side of her face, letting her curls drift through his pale and slender fingers. She turns to look to at him with that slightly lopsided grin that she always showed him in the afterglow. He feels his pulse quicken as she moves a hand across his chest, lacing a finger behind a shirt button. His left hand moves down towards that dip where the small of her back melds into the rise of her buttocks. He presses his palm into her body. In the midst of the breaking apart they take their final steps in the dance together, slow stepping through the dissonant drift of a parting kiss.

His lips part. A tear falls. He is back in real-time. The tear falls onto his flushed cheek and runs down a hollow curve towards his upper lip. He has tasted these tears too many times. Already she fades. He no longer has the strength to hold her in the dream space, not like he used to. He is a shallow vessel now, a broken pot, a dry bed in which the flowers of his youth have faded into brittle, bleached whites just like these last remaining stems in the shattered glasshouse. As the music winds down he hears those words. Always those same words. They are the tear-words. He opens his eyes, holding himself in mid-embrace, alone in the middle of the abandoned glasshouse. His heel twists in frustration, grinding a potsherd to grim red dust, an instantly dried bloodstain on the crumbling concrete floor. He feels her ghostly fingers slip from his. Her face fades back into that indistinct haze of long fingered memory.

"I can't… can't see you any more…" he whispers, and once again the guilt rises, clawing at his viscera, the guilt that is and will forever be spliced with his love for her. He has learned not to think about their dreams of Buenos Aires, dreams of African drumbeats and brothels and long nights in the heat and haze of impossible Argentinian summers. It's all a cliché, of course, and he knows that. He also knows that he misses her every single day of his life. He knows that he was wrong in every way. He made a call and like so many before and since, it was plainly and simply wrong. That is the moment. That is always the moment when he knows, despite the bluster and the performance and the smoky shadow plays, that he is a broken thing.

The clichés burn brightly now. He lacks the strength to imagine with originality. He is a ghost of his former self, kept tethered to the physical world only by the drug delivered with her coming. He craves her presence. He flares brightly in her embrace. The withdrawal that hits him when the connection fades is almost unbearable. He is an empty man. His soul, like the glasshouse, is an abandoned space, dank, and dusty and covered in razor sharp shards of memory. He clings onto images of countless Miss Havisham's, images stolen from decades of films and television adaptations, as a shorthand way to describe his sense of self. He takes a slow walk back along the derelict path through the glasshouse and out through the broken fence, out and back towards the clatter and the bustle of the London Underground on a Saturday afternoon. He counts the steps as he walks, head down, hands thrust into his trouser pockets. He counts the steps just as he counts down the days, knowing that all things are numbered and that he is now the remainder, the lost fraction left over from an imperfectly balanced equation. The music has faded. His passion is spent. He is cold logic, an abstraction, a simple number, one among billions, no longer relevant as an individual, just an anonymous part of the sum, of the whole. He is a trespasser in place and time and memory.

He looks at his watch for the first time since he broke through the fence and entered the old nursery compound. It is nearly three in the afternoon. He wonders how time passes so quickly when all around him, when the days that he counts, seem to drag on and on and on. He remembers his morning optimism, his sense that the day would be a good day for trespassing. He shrugs and walks on. He supposes that when you anticipate the coming fix then all days feel good, and he allows himself a moment of respite. He is coming down. Things look bleak. He will stop at Adel's on the way back from Acton Town station and buy an overpriced bottle of Yellowtail. He will watch a film with a glass of red and drift away. He will work on something else tomorrow. He will appear whole again. And as he does the things that need to be done during the slow crawl of other people's days he will catch sight of faded white lace flitting along the edges of his unseen inner world.

There is always one last moment to overcome on these journeys into his past. He considers contacting her again. He knows where she is. It would be possible. But such a thing would require far more courage than he has ever possessed. As close as she might be, the distance between them is impossible to cross. He told her to go. He failed her. He was never brave enough to take that vital step forward. He was then, as he is now, fundamentally afraid.

Above him the clouds have thickened. Spots of rain begin to polka dot the pavement in front of him. One more heavy sigh from the Mother God. He uses up the last of his strength. He leaves his paramour to fade back into the glasshouse shadows just as he left her all those years ago, drifting and weightless, until his craving, until his desperate need of her memory, overcomes his cowardice. He reaches the station, stops and passes a hand through his thinning hairline. He needs that drink.

The Mechanic's Curse

Sunday September 19th, 2010.

Sir,

 (or Madam, although if you are the first to find this note at such a late hour and in this place, please do be careful)

My jacket you have already found, and in it this note, which is not my will, for there is nothing left to bestow, so let us call the document a testament or a caution if you would prefer. For my part, I certainly call it the latter.

Although the impulse to write this was born some time ago and some way from here, I've often visited this spot in recent days and the leap of faith required by me in leaving this note is no greater than that which you must make when reading it. I was first drawn to this particular spot one afternoon when walking west towards the end of all land. I noticed the signs on the bridge suggesting that those in need call the Samaritans. For your part I hope you never have recourse to such help. In my own case, I am some way beyond the price of a telephone call – in fact, in every way imaginable.

Please do not look over the edge. The Bideford bridge is high and makes for the strongest sensation of vertigo, and depending on when you find this note, there may still be what is left of my body in the narrows of the tidal drain. Do not worry. This body was broken long ago. All I do tonight is return to my constituent parts. And that is enough, I suppose. I have made my statement and backed it with the ultimate inaction – that is to simply let myself fall and to do nothing. I wish to do nothing about the inevitable consequence of such a choice. If only it were always that simple.

In short I have found peace at last. Could I have gone on in time and distance from here? No, I could not. Irrevocably, not. But such a bald statement, though true, leaves out the cause, and for that I must write down the circumstances of my life…so that you may understand the cautionary nature of my words and then, when the inevitable time comes for you, maybe you will resist temptation too.

At age eighteen I was like any one of you who reads this story at whatever point in the cycle of analysis and discovery that is bound to follow, be you the walker on the bridge, a member of the police, a paramedic, a coroner, a journalist, or even simply a reader of a local newspaper. My name is, or was, James, Jimmy to my friends back then. The rest of the details are in my wallet, also in the jacket hanging on the bridge, unless my primary discoverer has no heart.

Mine was a perfectly ordinary childhood. Born in thirty-six, sufficiently late between the wars to be able to fight in neither one of them, I watched most of the blitz, all of the inventive rationing, the later convoys heading south, and finally the black rimmed eyes of the widow through a child's direct but uncomprehending gaze. By forty-five I was nine years old, full of spitfires and heroes, no more so than when my father returned to our home from France. Although I always fancied him so, he was never a heroically injured pilot. He returned to me with both of his legs and his worst scar was from an accident with a welding torch. He was, as he often said down at the legion bar, just an ordinary Joe, a jobbing mechanic working on tanks, the Churchill if memory serves, but for me that was the year that my life began. I instantly adored anything mechanical from that point on in my life.

In all this I'm not saying that my mother and the collection of sundry aunts, and latterly Uncle Chuck, didn't do a wonderful job bringing me up in the hardest of times. Of course, they did. It's just that everything changed when my father got home from the war. I mean everything. My first taste of real hostilities wasn't the whizz of a doodlebug or the hospital train unloading casualties fresh from battle. The ugly truth about war came to me when my father took a strong dislike to my mother's collection of nylons and the new-fangled way that she did her hair. Bar one spell of leave between Africa and Italy, the old man had been away for four years nearly and I think mother had simply had enough of living her life in that seemingly permanent holding pattern between the hero's return and the black edged telegram. That's what he thought, too, so by forty-seven, by mutual agreement, I was living with the old man in Brentford.

My father got a job down at the old Trico factory on the Great West where they made windscreen wipers and similar accessories for what were still then essentially pre-war cars, and we two settled into mid-terraced obscurity. Being skilled with pretty much anything metal or mechanical, my father was soon in demand around the streets backing on to Griffin Park, fixing this and mending that, and as the post-war boom brought cars onto our streets, both he and I took to doing services and repairs to make a few extra bob, enough, in fact for the old man to come home proudly one evening in May fifty-two with a battered old Austin Seven. It took us four months, an entire summer as I recall, but we got the old girl ship shape, and by the time I was eighteen and working at Trico myself as an apprentice fitter, I was a chip off the old block. There was nothing better in life, for me anyway, than skin coated in grease right down to the whorls, bar maybe a rare Third Division South victory for the Bees. I was a practically shy lad, and nothing much has changed over the years. Cars and football were my entire raison d'être back then. It was a different time in a different century. We hadn't had the sixties and the rest of it to twist things round.

Fifty-four is a bad number. My unlucky number. It's the year that counts. For Napoleon it was eighteen twelve. I was eighteen in nineteen fifty-four and the old man was off drinking one Saturday lunch-time down at the legion with a couple lads from his old regiment. That spring we'd built a little garage in our back yard and I was sitting in the shade under its corrugated tin roof because it was one of those early summer days when the sky was blue and no one yet wore shorts and flip-flops. When I say garage, it was more a sort of lean to. We'd roofed over the old courtyard and knocked a double garage door in the rear wall so we could bring the odd car under shelter via the back passage. You couldn't do it now, not with cars the size they are and planning, but everything was smaller then, including the regulations.

As I remember I'd just done the brakes on the old Austin, had nipped inside to get a glass of water, and was then sitting on a pile of old tyres that we used to keep one of the doors from swinging shut. There was a knock on the door frame. I looked up and there he was, lounging against the door-frame like a young Clark Gable, and oh so dapper. Spats, I think, and a broad pin-stripe, with his jacket slung over his back, a well-proportioned man, with a smile that could cut chiffon in mid-air float. He was chewing American gum. He offered me a piece. He even had a slight Southern drawl, just a hint of Tara, to go with that pencil thin moustache and film star grin.

"So, you're the guy round here fixes things, right?" he asked

I was eighteen. It was nineteen fifty-four. I was reticent at the best of times. I just looked at him dumbly. He stood there leaning against the workshop door, just smiling at me, and then he shook his head.

"Sorry, kid. I guess I want your Pa."

He fished inside his jacket pocket and took out a crisp white card. No name. Just a telephone number. Kew, I believe.

"Get him to give me a call. You are on the phone, right?"

I summoned up the energy to nod just enough to confirm that we could phone him. We didn't have a phone, not then, nor a television, but we could always use the dog in the legion. Where a bit of extra cash was concerned the old man always drummed it into me that we say yes and worry about the actual job later.

"Okay. Get him to give me a call. Could have some work for him. Good work, if you know what I mean. An old Lagonda."

I should have asked him to leave then but I didn't. The thought of a real life Lagonda in pieces all around me was a small moment of contemplative heaven. He hung around, kicking at a couple of loose stones amid the cobbles. He let rip another smile, a huge fire-glow of a smile.

"Shy, huh? Me too, back along. Tell me one thing, kid, what do you dream of? What's your fantasy?"

I sat there, as mute as the sun was high. What did he want? I tried to think of something earth shattering. Brentford beating Arsenal in the FA Cup, maybe? No. He'd asked me what I really dreamed about. The stuff of my dreams was all around me; wrenches, a small lathe, screwdrivers, spanners, cylinder heads and grease guns. Machines were what I dreamed about, the sort that Dan Dare might fly, machines that could leap tall buildings, machines that would make the world of tomorrow.

Remember, this was the mid-fifties and we were just beginning to see the possibilities. This was a time of speculation. We hadn't quite got to Sputnik, but there were plenty of dreams; flying cars, nuclear power, rockets to the moon, the Mekon. My head was full of it. I never read anything remotely uplifting or literary, but I did read and re-read back copies of Practical Mechanic, The Auto and The Eagle, anything that showed you the improbable certainty of the future or how to fix the here and now. I surprised myself with how bright and bold I sounded when I answered him in one long torrent.

"I dream machines. I mean, that's what really happens. Before you knocked on the door and asked for my Dad, I was imagining what I called the Autocopter. Instead of a flying car with wings, which would be bloody useless round here, what if it could jump into the sky like a fly. I was reading about it, the army are doing that sort of thing, and what if we could do it here. Well, not here, there's not enough room, but Gunnersbury Park, perhaps, and everybody lands on the roof of where they work. You could…"

"Hey, kid, enough", cut in the gentleman at the door. "I get the picture. Okay. So, here's a thought. What would you pay for the ability to do just that, to be able to dream machines and then see them become real?

Quick as a flash I answered him from the bottom of my heart. "Anything!"

"You sure?" he asked, switching instantly to a stern and serious look, as if he had stepped into shadow. "Take a moment. You're absolutely sure?"

Right there, right then I knew exactly what I wanted. It was a perfect summer day, I was on my own, something I always found easy, surrounded by the world I knew, and it was so obvious. It was as though he were the child and I the hard-nosed grifter.

"Yes. Anything!" I said defiantly.

"Done deal, kid. That nuclear smile lit up his face again. "And tell you're Pa to call me. See you around some day. Be good."

With that he turned smartly on his heel and walked off towards the bottom of the back lane, heading for the main road, whistling Greensleeves as he swished the jacket hanging over his shoulder like a horse's tail.

Now, it would be wrong to let you think that there were any sudden great revelations, or epiphanic manifestations, nor was there any blinding flash of light and puff of smoke. When I say I wanted to dream machines, it is also true that I wanted to eat ice-cream, go to the Lyons Coffee House with Tom Miller from next door, sneak a pint outside the legion with the old man, and fix broken crank-shafts. I was like you and a million other kids just emerging into the world. I went to work. I ate, I drank, I slept and slowly but surely went from boy to man.

The funny thing was that when on the odd occasion I did sit and day-dream a machine or a new tool or some flight of mechanical fancy, then after that little moment of reverie I found that I could read a fully detailed cyanotype from within my head. I had an actual blueprint of the thing, whatever it was, stored away up top, complete with every aspect of the design such as geometry, dimensions, tolerances, materials and finishes.

The old man did eventually get around to calling the stranger on our doorstep but oddly the number wasn't listed. All told, that was that. I saw my mother once a week. I finished my apprenticeship, did my National Service for the fly-boys and then started out as a full-time employee at Trico. I dated a couple of girls for a while, both of them Tom's cast-offs, hung around in the background at the odd dance at the Hammersmith Palais, and really just did the normal stuff that everyone back then did. I dreamed the odd dream and filed the plans away, never thinking that there would be anything different in my world. I was always going to be my Father's son.

Then one afternoon at work everything started to change. We had a problem with a metal press, an old pre-war monster that should have been pensioned off with the ark, but British management had a blind spot when it came to investment back then and so we limped along with the damned thing for years, eking out ever thinning profits in the assumption that frugality is best. One afternoon, while the machine was in another one of its recalcitrant moods I sat idling away a couple of minutes thinking about how we could improve things, nothing spectacular, just a typical machine operator musing on how his job could be more efficient. Basically, my thought process went something like this; if we took the old girl apart and re-jigged her so that instead of one single repetitive operation on a large sheet we could punch out smaller lighter components and then fit them together later, we might be able to prolong her life while the egg-heads and the bean counters sort out the future. It meant a small re-design of the product, and given that spending money was anathema back then, I forgot about it.

A week later, while suffering another one of our down periods, the Production Manager and I had a bit of a set to. He objected to me being away with the faeries. I should be sweeping up the swarf or something similar. It all culminated with him asking me what I would bloody well do about it if I was so clever. I told him bluntly exactly what we should do. Thankfully one of our design bods was on the shop floor at the time and he overheard my ideas about the re-design. Instead of picking up my cards and heading down to the labour exchange I found myself ensconced with that same designer describing the detailed plans in my head. We got it right first time, and I got a change of career and damned good pay rise.

To cut a long story short, over the next two years I swapped overalls for a shirt and tie. While I never actually became a designer or a draughtsman, I did spend my days up in the offices coming up with tweaks and changes, some new designs and some pretty nifty solutions for the rapidly changing requirements of the good old British automotive industry. Bear in mind this was the period when we went from things like the essentially pre-war Jaguar XK 150 and hit the fast lane with the E-type. At first the old man, a foreman now, thought I'd sold out my class, but slowly, and not without the odd slanging match between me and him in the Legion, he and the boys on the shop floor came around. I seemed to make life easier for people, not just in terms of their workload, but when a company is successful and produces quality goods, then people's souls are fed.

It was sixty-three when our Managing Director called me into his office and there to greet me was the head of design at Imperial Engineering, then the single biggest and most successful British based engineering company operating in the wider world. Word spreads and like Johnny Haynes I was being transferred for a record fee and, frankly, a record wage. Harold Nottingham was the man's name, and he wanted an edge. Competition was starting to bite from Germany and Japan, and he paid well for the man who could dream machines.

So, was I happily married by then? The answer is no. As I said earlier, I'd dated, had the odd fumble, but a bit like Destiny, that Bond girl who reads the Tarot cards, I was so wrapped up in my work that I just never got around to the opposite sex. I had yet to have my 'Oh, James' moment. Leaving the old man and heading off down to the South Coast and the company laboratories was the biggest emotional event in my life up until that point. We shed a tear or two as I left him on the doorstep in West London, got into my re-assigned company Ford Prefect, and headed south. Did I have regrets? Some, but I was twenty-seven and still living at home, it was a bright April day, and it was time to spread my wings.

At the time I thought that the next thirteen years were the

happiest of my life. We started small, making improvements here and there across so many fields of the company's operational activities. Then they set me problems in new markets and with new solutions. The one contractual proviso I insisted on was that we never did defence.

They ran batteries of tests, plugging me into scanners and polygraphs and the like, but we never discovered the killer gene or the bump that made the difference. It was, we decided, a gift, like Leonardo's or Michelangelo's or, on occasions, Heath Robinson's. I had my own small team, my own design studio, and an apartment paid for by the company. I reached the age of forty without a real care in the world. I had little need of company, as devoted as I was to the day-dream, and even when the primeval urge did rise it was taken care of on expenses. Over one cup of tea I could save the organisation millions. Happy Days.

Happiness, of course, is a relative thing. I was rapidly approaching middle-age, but I was gifted, cosseted, and by now looking after my father, who had retired to the same South Coast area that I worked in. I felt settled and comfortable. My work was going well, and hardly ever a chore. I made a difference, both to the company and, I felt, to the world. I was a smug bastard, but then it was nineteen seventy-six. I wore bright colours, drove a rag-top and wanted for nothing, until, that is, Eva came on the scene. When she walked into our design studio, the new software specialist from America blew our tiny little minds. It was not that she was tall, leggy and blonde, although she was, nor was it that she held a double first from both Oxford and Harvard, although she did. It was her laugh, and the spark of life that she ushered into the by now dry and dusty world that

I inhabited. She was twenty-eight and a recent capture from Big Blue. I was in physical decline, readying myself for the inevitability of pipe and slippers, but in capturing my heart she restored the vital flow to me in so many ways, and that is how the nightmares began.

I suppose it's why I used the Bond analogy, although in my case it wasn't simply sex that changed my gift. While I'd had no compunction about eschewing love in favour of high-class satisfaction during my career with the company, Eva was something else, something foreign and exotic and untouchable. You got a full-on sea breeze in your face when she smiled at you. I lost my heart to her over the winter of seventy-seven, when the world around us was crashing down amid the discontent of post-war social failure. She stayed with me at my apartment, we drank good French Burgundies, snuggled under the new-fangled duvet when Channel storms lashed the windows, and I fell hopelessly in love. I don't remember her ever telling me that she loved me, not in so many words, but I didn't care. The rush of it all was utterly intoxicating. I could barely focus on the work at hand in our little studio because every time I sank into one of my reveries I saw Eva. The trick to dreaming machines is not having any distractions, and I was in deep, deep, trouble on that count.

But, of course, I was in lust and love and infatuated. She, it turns out, had done what she came to do. She had shagged the man with the weird machine-mind. She left us in the May of seventy-eight and no amount of begging on my part would convince her to stay, let alone be mine. She smiled that big American smile of hers and was gone. The sea breeze never blew for me again, no matter how long I stood on the sea wall. Eva leaving didn't help the machine imagining either, given that a broken heart fixates on the breaker. It took months to get the day job back in hand, but the night job, well, that was altogether easier.

As soon as it became clear that Eva was definitely going, I started to dream at night, something I had never experienced, not in the machine sense. I'd fallen of cliffs never to land, seen long dead aunts and travelled the world as a dread pirate, but never had I seen machines in my sleep. Dreaming machines had been a controlled, suggestive, conscious and programmed process until then. With the lights out my mind started to take me to places that I simply didn't want to see, a world of sliding Dali motifs and Bosch devilry. On the morning when I awoke from the first nightmare, the bedclothes drenched and bitten through, there was a new, steel, flat filing cabinet in my head. It remained without a name plate or any sort of reference system, but I knew what was in there. It was the inferno, the black pit, the desolation of millions. My nightmares brought forth Mars, the Destroyer of Worlds.

At first, I thought it a passing phase, a natural consequence of a failed first true love in late years, the absolute synthesis of heartbreak, and so I resolved to concentrate. Let the nightmares come, I thought, I can handle this, and during the day nothing else will matter. For a short while it worked well enough. The once sublime notion of closing my eyes for an hour during the day still worked after a fashion, but it became real work. I had to force the day-dream, and with it the results became less elegant and less refined. As the pressures of coping with my changed mental state started to fray the edges of my world view, I tried different strategies, like drinking until late to knock myself out, or when my liver complained and so did the company quack, I tried just not sleeping. I looked terrible and started to become more and more erratic around my colleagues.

In eighty-one my father died. The one safe haven in my life was sunk beneath the waves of madness. I became unknowable. The company hired shrinks and analysts, made or bought the latest medical diagnostics kit, basically did everything possible to protect its investment, but the truth of it was that I was frying on the inside. It got to the point where nothing worked. I popped pills and potions, tried yoga and meditation, but during the day I could dream neither nut nor bolt.

At night, however… oh, at night the flood gates opened. I dreamed of pilotless planes and of laser reflectors capable of incinerating cities. I dreamed of gas and severed limbs and burned skin. I spun on the vortex of man-made tornadoes and danced on the head of a pin withdrawn from splinter grenades. My mind was vengeance writ large, and that was when the company tried their one last, desperate stratagem.

They argued that if I let the nightmares out into the real world, then they might stop coming in dread night to torment me. By realising the designs I might release the pressure and restore myself to some sort of equilibrium. They promised safeguards, principally that they would reference the designs only for opportunities, techniques and technologies suitable for civil projects. By then I was so desperate to have someone end it all that I would have agreed to anything. I was the screaming vision seen by Munsch.

So, we cooperated. I worked with new colleagues and let open the gates of Hell, and for a while this new approach also seemed to offer some hope for a stable future. The endless throbbing in my temples, that explosive force held at bay by brittle bone and soft grey tissue, slowly dissipated. It never entirely left me, but it became manageable. I could live with it. The one side effect of giving free reign to the night darks was, however, that it became apparent pretty quickly that the day-dreams were shot. I was now a creature of the blackest night, but even then I thought that if we can turn this gift mutated into affliction to some good then all may not be lost.

What a perfidious man I was. For nearly ten years I shut myself away from all but the most trusted draughtsmen precisely because I did not want to see pictures or read news stories. I knew in my heart that my infernal machines of death would come into being. The company obeyed not the laws of the jungle, where the beast is simply what it is. The company was a global financial-industrial monster driven by the insatiable hunger of the market and by then I had become their principal source of profit. The inevitable, of course, happened. I saw a picture of a military drone in some war zone or other. I saw limbs and bomb blasts and the wreckage of a marketplace. I ran.

You would think that security was an issue, that I would be kept behind unbreakable glass, but that was never the case. Even in my most troubled times I was still allowed the freedom of an apartment on the coast, somewhere that I could retreat to on my own when the night freaks came calling.

I was an intelligent man. I knew that my place was bugged, and that they watched and listened. I was pretty certain that they followed me. I suspected that my clothes and my car were wired too, but it was no matter to me. My affliction came to my rescue. I dreamed counter-measures, had them made up, kept the prototypes and simply slipped out unnoticed late one night with a set of new clothes wrapped in water-tight plastic together with some cash. I stripped naked on the beach at Eastney, swam a little way out and then headed back to shore just a little way down the coast. I knew enough about cars to hot-wire a Vauxhall, put some miles between me and Portsmouth and then started walking. I have been walking slowly towards the end of land ever since.

I never dream during the day now. I never sleep at night. Mine is a continual waking, which, at seventy-four years of age, is finally taking its toll. Were I to close my eyes the nightmares would still come. I watch television through shop windows and see all of those things that you take for granted, but which I dreamed. The Never-Flat wheel. The liquid crystal imagination. The Fermat engine. The ion accelerator. The unlockable wrench. The bringer of death.

I have during these last years of wandering and beggary often considered the price asked of me by the man leaning against our old garage door. A soul? Heaven and Hell reduced to carbon ashes? The inventiveness of the torturer? Elevation to an Augustan God-head? No, I don't think it is any of these things. The price we pay for simply being human is that we so often forget that we always, always have a choice. By walking and keeping awake I've tried to stop the machines, but it is no good. I dozed for a while last night and dreamed of a field generator capable of cloaking a warship. It is, I think, time to stop.

Do I have any one last thought for you? Yes, I do. Think carefully before you answer any well-dressed man who springs up as if from nowhere offering you the world.

Farewell, friend.

But for the Moon

UNDER THE BROAD LIMBS of an oak, in a deep hollow that provided both shade and yet was open to the breeze that continually blew in from the sea, the old man lay down at midday, mopped his brow with a red, paisley handkerchief, and reached into his bag for the hard, round goats cheese and the hunk of heavy bread that he had picked up this morning when leaving his hut at first light. He fished out a small jug, the last of the rough, dry red wine and drank. He let a few drops fall from his mouth onto the kerchief and, rather than wiping away the dust on his face and lips, he just managed to smear it across his jaw and nose a little more vividly. It was a frugal meal but it would be enough to see him through to evening. It was a long walk down from the mountain to his one-time home on the coast, a place that he barely remembered other than for the fantastic whiteness of the walls and the deep blue cupola of their little church. He had a few pennies in his pocket, enough to sleep in a barn perhaps and buy a small piece of cooked meat and some potato. He crossed himself once before he ate the bread and cheese. God willing he would make the coast and home tomorrow.

He had chosen a simple life. It was, even after all these years, still strange to him that he chose life at all. When she died he neither embraced the opportunity nor did he slaughter himself in her memory so that he could be with her always. Everyone told him it was natural to be confused and that the pain would pass with time. He had three daughters, grown up and married when the fevers came and took his wife. He took no comfort then in the wonderful fact that the first of her grandchildren had called her Nana to her face before Charos stole her away from him.

"It is not as though you are alone, Michael", they had said. "You'll see. Give it a few months, let the grief come and be what it is, and you'll see. There will be new routines, new faces, it will all happen. You're relatively young, just fifty, you'll rut again."

He came to hate the laugh that always accompanied these lascivious suggestions. They meant well, he knew that, but how could they imagine that he could do all of these normal things without her. The priest offered a shoulder to lean on and a glass of raki. His neighbours spent weeks and then months cajoling him into living, inviting him to their homes, and sometimes, when the bitter tears really did fall, they even left him alone. In time, when he continued to hide behind the shutters, refusing to let the warmth of their smiles enter his heart, they stopped trying to help him all together, and he was secretly glad.

He had some savings, a little residue from a small property he and his wife owned and which he sold shortly after she travelled to the far banks of the river, so there was no need to work, at least not for a while. Maybe that was his mistake. Maybe he should have been more of a man, hiding his feelings and resuming the daily grind, putting on that happy face that she did so well even when the soul was blank.

He did not do that. He lived quietly, waiting for that moment each evening when the reds and gold of fiery day turned first to pink and orange, then to swirling purples and finally to the blackness of night. He waited and he watched and when the first stars sparkled into life, he greeted his wife and then got blind drunk. He was not brave enough a man to put a gun to his own head or to drive a knife into his own heart. He preferred the coward's way. Oblivion.

His daughters, of course, did their best. They invited him to Sunday lunches and on days out with the grandchildren. They popped their heads round the door for a quick visit and for a coffee. They held parties to which he was always asked, and he went along with it all at first. Oh yes, he attended their functions and their family gatherings but only so that he could stand there as if he were watching the world from inside a goldfish bowl. He found it hard to string a sentence together, not because he was slow, but because despite being considered an intelligent man, he simply could no longer be bothered.

Without his wife he was nothing. He continued to live without living. He gave up on business, spent hours writing hopeless paeans to her memory, and slowly the light in their eyes, these daughters of his with their busy lives and their boisterous men folk, ceased to burn for him. Yes, he had chosen a simple life. He watched as his daughters and their husbands bumped along with the endless cycles of living, working and with raising children. They found their way where he would not, and wilfully failing to understand that they too hurt as he did, he chose a simple life. He ran away from it all, throwing his hands up in the air and saying to anyone who might listen, "My wife is dead. What is the point of anything?"

He had been saying that self-same thing these last thirty years. From his old village he ran away with the last of his money to the city. He tried to lose himself among the crowds, tried to make himself become so small that no one would notice him ever again, so small that he might actually disappear. Always, always, when he waited for the stars, with a bottle of cheap hooch in his pocket, the moon would rise, and as he got drunk, he always thought he heard a familiar voice. He could never quite catch the full timbre and tone, and anyway some person or other would try to talk with him. People were like that in the city. They ignored you for long enough to make you think that you might disappear in a puff of smoke, and then one of them would turn around and say something. All that work, all that investment in anonymous fading would be utterly wasted. Always someone would come and walk across the void, filling it with humanity and possibility. No, the city was worse than his village.

Ten years after she died, nine years after he fled the village and soused himself in the gutters of the metropolis, he woke one morning and decided that the mountain overlooking his old home would be the best place for him. He would be closer to the stars, and to that damned incoherent moon, and he could sit without interruption, come winter snow or summer dust.

"Let the Bora blow itself out on my head", he said to himself, "and then we'll see what's what."

Money, of course, was almost non-existent now. He rented a shabby flat in the port slum and, when the coin for wine evaporated, he might work for a few nights as a pot-washer or something equally lonely. His worldly goods fetched a laughable sum, but who would need money on the mountain? He did need good boots, but that was all. He bought reasonably good boots, scrimping even then to make sure that he had a bottle or two for the journey. He walked under those stars, and always, when the moon rose, he thought he could hear a familiar voice, but it was so far off and so thin that he still could not make out the words. Maybe, he thought, he might find a shepherd's hut high up, somewhere where he could sit, wait for the stars and hear the moon a little more clearly. Yes, if he could just do that. It would be enough and now that he was sixty years old, he could wait for death. Surely the first snows would take him.

They did not. He became so good at sitting and watching and waiting that a local farmer who lived like a feudal lord in one of the bigger mountain villages employed him as a geriatric shepherd boy. It was enough to keep the wolf from the door, as indeed was he. It was a thing to wonder about. Why did he accept even that hand when all he wanted to do was die? Surely even he, wastrel and inconstant fool that he was, could sit on a mountain side and wait for the chill winds and sleets of winter to come and take him? He didn't have to do anything, he thought. He could simply sit, talk to the stars, drink, and maybe catch a word or two from that bloody moon. Surely he could just sit and fade out of the world as he had always wished?

It appeared not, for here he was twenty years later sitting under the oak. His legs ached from the walking, and his back was stiff. He shifted it against the rough bark of the oak tree, scratching a persistently annoying itch. Down here, down amongst the trees he could smell the wild thyme and smiled remembering her little herb garden all those years ago.

Was it really twenty years that he had sat on a mountain? Twenty years? He tried to measure the time, but he no longer had any reference points in the world below. Eighty seasons. Twenty shearings. What were they in the real world? He had not left the mountain side once in all that time. Twenty years of living on hard and rancid cheeses, the occasional slice of meat if the farmer took pity on him, thick, heavy bread, wild legumes and mushrooms, and, out of preference, jugs of the cheapest, roughest wines. He was more than eighty years old, ate appallingly, still communed with the stars and as a consequence he still drank too much, but nevertheless here he was. It would seem that Charos had, until now, never been interested in collecting his fee.

But then the moon…The old man knew now that he was but moments away from death. After a long life wasted he had just a few days, perhaps a few weeks left. He could feel it in his bones and in his waters, and now that it came down to dealing with the ferryman, the old man very much wanted to live. The moon had finally stopped shilly-shallying and only last night he had seen and heard her clearly. After all these years of mumbling and insouciance she had finally come to him. He looked up at that damned moon and saw that his wife sat there, in a little crater all of her own, looking exactly as she had done in the days before the fevers sunk her cheeks and turned her into an old crone before her time. She looked down on him, frowned and told him in no uncertain terms to stop being an arse. Her exact words. He laughed. For the first time in all these years he actually laughed. He laughed so much that now he had a sore throat and no voice. It was so like her.

It was as simple as that. He realised now why he could not die, not without climbing down from the mountain one last time. He must do that one thing he so signally failed to do before he ran away. He must put right the one thing that had been troubling him through all these years had he but seen it. It was not his wife's death that drove him to always seek a smaller place, always another bottle. The truth of the matter is that after he said farewell to the woman whom he loved with all his heart, he had simply been too scared to admit that he felt the same for all his family. He loved her so much and she died. He summed up his fear like this; if I love them too will the same happen to them? I could not bear it and so I will run away.

He sat under the tree for an hour, letting the noon sun burn and parch the earth. He slept for a short while, during which time he dreamed that he could see a chariot of flame bearing Charos towards him. He woke with a start, hauled himself up on his stout wooden stick, slung his bag back over his shoulder and patted the oak tree, thanking it for its tolerance of a foolish old man. His left leg complained with every step but he just laughed and told it not to be an arse. As he left the shade and headed down the mountain he said to himself, "That is why I cannot die. That is why I will live a little longer. I am going home to tell my daughters how much I love them."

A Question of Spin

(Loosely based on the Grimm brother's Rumpelstiltskin)

ONCE UPON A TIME there was a poor political lobbyist, which is in itself an uncommon thing. He spent many years at his trade but even after a lifetime of work the only true treasure that he possessed was his lovely raven-haired daughter, Emily.

Towards the twilight of the man's career a combination of luck and subject matter expertise finally gave him access to the country's top political hombre and in order to appear as a person of more significance than he really was he told the great politician that his daughter could spin the worst gobbledygook into solid gold prose.

"That's a talent worth having on the team", said the politician to the lobbyist. "If she's really as good at this presentational stuff as you say she is then bring her to my office tomorrow morning and I'll put her to the test".

The next morning the lobbyist and his daughter attended upon the head of state. After some polite preliminaries the young woman was taken into a room full of the most incomprehensible government policy papers, briefing documents and committee meeting minutes.

She was made to sit at a computer and one of the politician's more officious aides said, "Now, you're not to leave here until you've finished the lot. We want all of this bullshit turned into easily readable prose that gets our message across but also hides the skeletons in the closet. If you fail your father will never work in Westminster again". Then he closed the door and left her all on her own to finish the job.

So the poor lobbyist's beautiful daughter sat there and wondered exactly what she was meant to do. All she ever did at her father's office was make coffee and answer the phones. She wasn't even sure how to switch the computer on, let alone how to use a word processor. She had no idea how she was going to turn all of this officialese into plain and clear text.

No matter how hard she thought about it, she simply couldn't work out what to do and became terribly disconsolate and miserable. She tried to read one of the documents, but apart from recognising some of the more obvious words and phrases, she was completely stumped by all of the jargon and, realising that both she and her father would soon be the butt of jokes throughout the Westminster village, she started to cry like a baby.

Suddenly the door burst open and into the room stepped a small, bald man in a brown three-piece suit. He looked the girl up and down a couple of times and said, "Good morning, miss, why are you crying so bitterly?"

"Oh", answered Emily, "I have to rewrite all these official government papers so the common folk can read them but not really understand them. I haven't got a clue how to do it".

"It's just a question of spin", said the wee bald man with a chuckle. "Now, what will you give me if I translate all this stuff for you?"

"I'll give you my necklace", replied the girl. "It's real silver and diamonique".

The little man took the necklace immediately, sat himself down at the computer and looked at the first document. His fingers moved across the keyboard in a dazzling blur and in no time at all the printer was churning out a brilliantly concise, but simply worded version of events that answered all of the Prime Minister's needs. The little man continued working on the documents for the entire day until, with just five minutes left before the government official returned, he finished the last of them.

At five o'clock, and not a minute before or after, the official returned to the room in the company of the great politician. When they saw the pile of translated documents they were amazed. A few more minutes passed, during which the United Kingdom's glorious leader read some of the newly minted papers. He was so delighted with the results that he gave Emily a small peck on the cheek and one of his renowned, election winning smiles. Never one to look a gift horse in the mouth, he recognised a rather beautiful and useful filly when he saw one, and his thoughts turned to the Ministry of Defence, which was well known for the sheer head splitting boredom it induced in anyone stupid enough to read its papers. The lobbyist's daughter was told to report to the Chief Secretary at the Ministry of Defence the next morning.

At nine o'clock Emily was shown into an even bigger room than the one she had been in the day before. Around her were stacked nearly one hundred manuals, status reports, intelligence briefings and detailed planning exercises designed to cater for any military emergency. Once again the official in charge told her that she had just one working day to précis all of this stuff and turn it into something intelligible to the leader of the nation's government.

The young woman leafed through a manual describing the operation of the army's new standard assault rifle and began to sob. "What the hell is a slide bolt release widget?" she muttered, as her tears fell onto the brightly buffed parquet flooring.

There was a brief, peremptory knock on the door and with a flourish the small, bald man entered the room. This morning he was wearing a grey two-piece suit, betrayed in its modernity by the fact that the trousers were bell-bottomed flairs. The little man looked like he was drowning in the thing, the suit being at least two sizes too tall for him.

"So, young lady, what'll you give me if I spin this load of old tripe into something more coherent?"

"You can have my ring", replied the young woman. "It's real gold and has faux elvish writing on the inside".

The little man grinned at her, sat down at the computer and once again worked his magic, turning every one of the unintelligible documents into something resembling a primary school reading book.

"It's best to keep it simple if the Old Man is involved", he said as the final piece of paper emerged from the bowels of the printer.

Having collated and filed the last of the documents, the wee bald man slipped out of the door just in time to avoid the returning government official.

The great politician was so pleased with the results of the young woman's labour that he almost skipped around his office. In fact he was so delighted by it all that he demanded that she return the very next morning to work her way through an ocean of Treasury figures and policy documents. After all, he'd been in office for three years and he still didn't have a clue about the nature of the fiscal policy that his government was pursuing.

As requested, Emily presented herself at the gates of Her Majesty's Treasury the next morning. She was quickly ushered into the biggest office yet, where, emerging from the shadows, the Prime Minister took her hand and whispered, "Pull this one off, my love, and not only will your dear old Dad become my personal press secretary, but I'll bloody well marry you!"

Emily waited for the sound of footsteps on cold marble to recede. This time she didn't bother to open the documents or to read their contents, but instead she pulled half an onion out of her pocket and made herself cry, adding some loud gulps and sniffs just for good measure. As usual there was a rap on the door and in came the little man.

He'd obviously had difficulty with yesterday's oversize suit, so he'd made sure his clothes fitted him perfectly this morning. However, the combination of a loud plaid jacket, a striped shirt, tartan golfing trousers and white loafers somehow missed the sartorial target he'd been aiming for. He took his sunglasses off before he spoke.

"You know the drill, love"

"But I haven't got anything left to give you", said Emily, trying to look as sad and forlorn as she could. "My dad's just a poor lobbyist and you've already got all my dear departed Mum's jewellery".

"Then you'll have to promise me that when you're married to old jug ears you'll pass on a few snippets of information. You know the sort of thing; tips on cabinet reshuffles, early sight of government policy, juicy titbits about personality squabbles and all that jazz".

Emily decided that discretion was required in such matters, and once she was the first lady of the country then who knew what might happen. She promised the little man what he wanted and sat back to work on her nails while he converted every last scrap of paper in the room into a layman's guide to the country's tax and spend financial regime.

Within a year Emily and the great politician were married. Her father's new role as the Prime Minister's personal press secretary largely consisted of lunches with some of his old lobby friends and off the record briefings with favoured newspaper hacks, so all in all everyone was very happy. Emily didn't give another thought to the small, bald man until one day he suddenly appeared in her boudoir at Number Ten, Downing Street.

"Got anything for me, then?" he asked.

"And what if I say no", Emily replied brusquely.

"Then I tell him it was your Dad who inadvertently leaked the stuff about the pensions crisis to the press. Might mean an end to those lunches..."

The first lady suddenly realised how dangerous this little man might be and became extremely worried about where this might all lead. She promised him riches, a knighthood and a lucrative position as Chief Executive of a non-governmental organisation, but he was having none of it.

"No, I want gossip. Nice, fat, juicy gossip. That's what you promised me and that's what I'm going to have".

Emily began to cry and sob and wail so much that the little man decided to give her three days to come up with the goods just so that she would shut up. The last thing he needed was the secret service asking awkward questions about how he'd found his way into her bedroom, and, if he was being entirely honest with himself, he found Emily quite enchanting to be around. He felt sorry for her. Somewhere, buried deep beneath the outer layers of his hard-bitten, bottle-nosed hide, he still had a heart.

"Tell, you what", he said, "if you can guess what my job is in the next three days, I'll leave you alone forever more".

Emily spent the whole of the next night compiling a list of every possible job title that might exist in the world of newspapers, television and radio. When the little man arrived the next morning, she tried everything she could think of but it was all to no avail. He was not an editor, nor was he a hack, nor was he a plague of boils on the bottom of mankind.

The next night the first lady studied the shadow cabinet posts of all of the opposition parties in the country's parliament. When the little man came to her again she called him many things, including leader of the opposition, shadow trade secretary and old weasel features, but not one of these job titles were correct.

In desperation the first lady finally consulted one of her husband's aides and asked him to go onto the Internet and find out the names and job titles of every single spy in the world. It was a long job and the aide didn't return until early the next morning.

"I'm sorry, ma'am", he said, "but I haven't been able to find out the names or job titles of any spies. Apparently, they're all secret".

"Bugger", said Emily, pulling a large foolscap folder from under her mattress. She leafed wistfully through a couple of pages listing all of the extra marital affairs that her husband's cabinet ministers had been involved in since taking office. She supposed this would have to do.

"I did see one strange thing though, ma'am", continued the aide. "As I was walking through the civil service quadrangle this morning I saw a strangely dressed little man doing an odd sort of jig and singing a weird song. He was hopping up and down like a madman and crying:

I've got juicy gossip,

My diary's going to be full,

No more Mister Nice Guy

Now I've got all the bull!

"When he started singing I recognised him immediately.", continued the functionary. "Bullingdon Minor. We went to prep school together. Strange behaviour, I thought, for a man on the Arts Council. Then again, perhaps not. Those artistic coves are all a bit doolally."

Emily could taste the pure, unadulterated delights of victory.

"So what exactly does he do? For a job, I mean", She asked.

"Oh, erm, he's the council secretary, I think. Pushes paper around mostly, writes communiqués, that sort of thing."

Emily was over the moon when she heard that her tormentor was one her husband's more obscure minions, at least that was how she thought of all and any public servants. With the help of her husband's aide she checked the government lists and sure enough in the Arts and Heritage Yearbook there was a picture of the horrid and slimy toad.

The little man came to call later that morning and asked the first lady, "Well, what's my job, then?"

Emily thought for a moment or two and replied, "Are you a janitor?"

"No".

"Are you a nuclear physicist?"

"Ha, no! One more guess…"

"Well, then, you must be the Secretary to the Arts Council".

"You bastard", screamed the red faced little man. "Someone's sneaked on me, haven't they? How can I publish my diaries now?"

In his rage he stamped and stomped on the floor with so much force and spite that his left foot sank right through it and he fell through the rafters all the way up to his waist. Then, in an absolute fury of passion and anger, he seized his right foot with both of his hands and tore himself in two.

Emily called down for maid service and quietly slid her dossier on ministers caught in flagrante delicto back underneath her mattress. As she did so she made a mental note to slip out to the shops later that afternoon so that she could buy a nice new foolscap diary.

About Horses and Microwaves

SHE LIFTS THE PLASTIC film from a portion of chicken Madras, stirs it and puts the white plastic tray back into the microwave. She pushes the Start button and watches his dinner revolve through the meshed glass, knowing that the "ping" will make her jump. It always makes her jump.

He is watching Americans drive small white balls towards glory. She hates it because she thinks she might like golf, but getting paid more for four days work than most people earn in ten years seems wrong.

The kids are upstairs in their rooms, on the Internet, watching MTV or on the bloody phone again.

The window she looks through is framed in tough, durable plastic, better than the old wooden ones that always needed repainting. With their inserts and their twin panels of glass, she can barely hear the hum from the motorway beyond the trees at the back of the house. She hung new curtains after the windows were fitted, blue Gingham, but they need washing now that the grime and the sticky grease of the kitchen have had a year or so to settle.

She has the radio on, a talk show, listeners questioning a spiritualist about loved ones and stupid bastard tricks. She likes the voices, because they allow her to tunnel out of normality and break free from the sounds that surround her. She likes those commentators and their self-obsessed meanderings.

Empty plastic bags litter the kitchen table, along with half-finished homework and a packet of Shreddies from breakfast. No one uses the table anymore, preferring to grab drinks and squat in front of the latest early morning weather honeys. The microwave hums through another minute of agitated warming. It reminds her of flies on summer heat shimmies and the grass growing long at the fringes of the fields opposite her house.

The sun burnt her face this afternoon. House martins skimmed the hedges and the rooftops chasing insect food for their eave hanging youngsters. She stood there in the sun, alone, with a packet of old, soft carrots in one hand, feeding them to a horse that snorted at her for more.

'Just like home', she thought.

But feeling his skin, and his hard, waxy hair, running her hands up his face towards his ears, hearing cars behind her in the road, changed the pace of the day. It was the way he stamped his foreleg when he wanted another carrot. She feels the heat of the air from his nostrils, sees his height and his hauteur, even though he was just a nag in a field. It was a simple moment of flesh and blood.

Part of her wants to tell them about the horse. Part of her wants to share him, to draw them all out of their stupor, but another place, another selfish face speaks to her, saying no.

She looks out of the plastic framed window, catching the long shadows falling away towards the motorway trees, and she lets the memory of the afternoon tingle on her sunburned skin. The microwave pings and she jumps out of her skin. Adrenalin. The moment is done. The dinner cooked. She drags herself back into the flurry of dinners on trays and conversations that no one takes part in.

Nine Lives

LOOKING AT THE HOUSE from the old the old stone pillars that still held the front drive gates fast and tight, the meadow and the once gravelled drive up to the old pile looked as though they had been left untended for a century. Where he remembered a tree lined sward of thick pasture to the left of a drive penned comfortingly in by a solid wooden stock fence, and a straight run up to the house lined on the right with poplars, he now saw tangle and mess. Brambles as tall as a shire horse smothered the field, roaming at will, laying their tendrils to earth and sprouting back up in a cat's cradle of thorn and rotting berry. In those patches of ground yet to fall under the dominion of the framboise assault, there stood man-size thistles and towering clumps of nettle, as erect and hostilely on guard as the brambles were chaotic and malevolent.

The drive lay broken and twisted, with roots breaking through the once pristine canal of Cotswold stone. Here again great tufts of undergrowth were plaiting barricades against the outside world. One of the aged poplars had crashed down across the drive, acting as a second line of defence, a reserve trench, behind which he suspected there were more thorny warriors waiting for him. The gates themselves were rusted beyond hope of opening, fused together at hinge and at lock, clinging to the crumbling stone pillars for dear life. It won't be long, he thought, before they come crashing down.

As for the house not even the slowly setting August sun could bathe it in a sympathetic light. The little that he could see of the place through the shadows seemed to suggest that it was covered in Russian vine and honeysuckle and, here and there, monstrous liana fronds of brilliant white clematis. The house was collapsing under the weight of its own floral winding sheet, using vegetation as a shield against man and the elements. He could see swathes of missing roof tiles, and the ridge itself bowed at one end. The Victorian solidity of brick and stone was finally giving way to the elemental decay endemic in the twenty-first century.

"My God", he said to himself. "She's really let the place go. Still, Mary's right. We need to think about the future. She's getting on a bit, is old Aunt Billie."

Johnny Hester-Siddeley wandered back to the Range Rover parked a little down the lane and just out of sight of the house, and considered what to do next. Should he hack his way up to the house or should he perhaps try the old farm track leading up to the back yard. Judging by the state of the once publicly presentable side of the house, God alone knows what that's going to be like, he thought. He decided that rather than end up covered in scratches and have his Harris Tweed ripped and pulled to shreds, he would try the tradesman's entrance. Aunt Billie might not be up to much, but surely at her advanced age she must have some way of letting the health Johnnies and meals on wheels ladies onto the premises.

He gunned the V8 and spat stones against the crumbling dry stone wall that marked the boundary of Aunt Billie's little estate. The black four-by-four growled slowly down the lane, following a left-hand bend as the road wound down and along the far edge of what had once been North Euston Manor Farm, until he found a break in the hedgerow. There was a relatively new looking wooden five-bar gate set between the stone walls that backed the hedges, and although the track showed no signs of any other recent maintenance, it was at least clear all the way up the back of the house. In fact, as Johnny jumped out of the car and unhitched the gate, he saw that the back meadow and the old orchard didn't actually look too bad. Maybe, he thought, she just can't manage it all anymore.

Aunt Billie was an interesting old bat. She wasn't exactly a blood relative, more a giggling compadre from his mother's finishing school days, where they had become bosom chums during the social whirl of the nineteen fifties and all that debutante nonsense. Johnny's mother ended up marrying a cousin of the then youthful and engaging Billie Tuke-Hastings, but the direct line of this once numerous family of minor Gloucestershire gentry were all now long under the sod, and Johnny could lay claim to be the sole legal heir.

His mother and Aunt Billie had kept in reasonably close contact for the twenty years until Johnny's mother fell prey to an untimely maternal death, and he remembered as a young boy the occasional visit to the farm, memories filled with lemonade on the front lawn where now the brambles reigned supreme. In his memory it was always summer, always hot, and the beautifully manicured roses filled the air with perfume.

Aunt Billie, unfortunately, struggled when it came to men, and now she was eighty years old if she was a day, alone and surely decrepit, an old maid who had spent her best years looking after a sot of a brother and two inevitably ailing parents. Johnny remembered cats. He was a dog man himself.

He squeezed the Range Rover through the narrow gate, jumped out to close the gate behind him, and then drove slowly along the track and up to the house. From a distance the rear of the old farmhouse did not look too bad but now that Johnny had parked up and run his experienced eye over the place he felt more than a little dismayed. The roof would need completely replacing, the windows were rotten, the guttering was shot to hell, the pointing was in a dreadful state of repair, and all in all he wondered whether it might not be easier to clear the site and rebuild.

"God alone knows what the inside is like", he muttered. "Still, a good plot like this on the edge of a chintzy Cotswold village should fetch a whacking price whatever state it's in."

His wife, Mary, was right when she said that he couldn't leave the place to go to rack and ruin, and as Johnny was now the old girl's last kith and kin surely they deserved a little something for all their efforts. Johnny couldn't quite put his finger on what those efforts had been over the years, but nonetheless he saw no point in missing an opportunity to do both him and his aged aunt a mutual favour. It was serendipity, he thought, that no sooner had his wife mentioned the old girl, than she had telephoned asking him to attend on her at five o'clock sharp this very day.

The stable door to the kitchen was open at the top and he poked his head into the gloom within. "Hello", he shouted. "Anyone there?"

Silence.

Johnny waited for a moment or two to see if the old dear needed time to hobble from her lair deep in the bowels of the house, but not a breath of air moved. He pulled the latch on the bottom half of the door, swung the door open and was about to enter the kitchen, but before he could go any further a crisp voice rang out behind him.

"Wouldn't do that if I were you, sonny!"

Johnny froze. It was the sort of voice that aimed a double barrel shotgun at one's head. He turned slowly, feeling rather sheepish as he raised his hands only to see a short but still hearty little old lady in a bright blue-green twin-set standing next to his shiny black car with a shovel in her hand. She looked entirely capable of lifting the shovel, and Johnny knew instinctively that even were she not capable she would make the effort, just for him, just this once. He recognised Aunty Billie at once. She wore her now white hair long rather than in that typical, blue-rinsed perm, stood strongly and firmly for one of her advancing years and still had that bright green gaze that he remembered from his youth. She was a little rounder now, but she was still gracefully menacing. He switched to estate agent mode; smile, offer your hand, ooze sincerity.

"Aunty, it's me, Johnny. You remember, Christina's little boy? Christina Hester. Married your cousin, Max Siddeley. It's me, Aunty, Johnny Hester-Siddeley. You asked me to pop over."

He took a step forward, his hand outstretched and ready for a hearty welcome.

"Lemonade on the lawn", he said, schmoozing for all that he was worth. "It's been a long time, I know, but business and families.

Anyway, after your call I thought I'd do the honourable thing and come and see you, see how you are, see if you need anything."

Aunt Billie looked at him for a long moment and then snorted. She rested the shovel against the car door, the blade upright. She watched as the fattening fifty year old cove in front of her winced. Tweeds and smiles. I know your sort, she thought. She stepped forward, ignoring the proffered hand, and walked into the kitchen.

"So you're what became of Christina's boy! You're the grown-up version of the little shit who ran amok in the rose garden and puked on Daddy's Dahlias. Stands to reason. Well, you'd better come in then. I make no apologies for the place. It's how I like it. You get to my age and you find that you don't give a flying fack about what other people think."

She cleared a space amongst the old newspapers and empty tins of cat food that littered a scarred and stained antique pine kitchen table, and pointing to a rickety old carver she said, "Sit!"

This was not quite the welcome that Johnny had expected, but he'd come across all sorts in his long career as a country estate agent. Half the gentry were utterly bats, while the other half were most definitely hairy on the inside. Mind you, he thought, rough or smooth, they're all wolves, the lot of them. He ran his tongue along his teeth. He was in her kitchen and she was making him a drink, which was all that really mattered. The trick to any transaction was to overcome the initial objection. It was the start he needed. He kept smiling, and assumed the relaxed, legs crossed, hands in lap pose of one who always mixed with the finest sort of people.

"So, Aunty, how've you been keeping all these years? He asked nonchalantly.

"None of your fackin' business", was her almost joyful reply.

Enjoying the momentary discomfiture of her reluctantly invited guest, Aunt Billie busied herself filling the kettle from an ancient faucet that jutted from the wall under the kitchen window, the frame of which was as flaked and mildewed on the inside as it was rotten on the outside. The faucet juddered violently as the water gushed out. Billie sat the kettle on a black range cooker, the sort that should never be cleaned even though it relied entirely on solid fuel. Sooty dust motes took to the air as she put the kettle onto the warmer.

Aunt Billie dug around in a cupboard and found a particularly rank packet of Shrewsbury biscuits that she kept especially for visitors. After a few minutes of awkward small talk the kettle whistled, hot water was poured, one tea bag sufficing for two mugs, a scraping of milk was added so that it could float in lumps on the surface of the tea, and with a tiny, eighty year old flourish she sat down opposite her would-be relation.

She smiled sweetly as she held out the plate of rancid biscuits and asked, "Biccie, Johnny?"

He blanched visibly but took one for forms sake. "Thanks, Aunty."

Johnny took a quick, almost furtive sip of the tea and nearly spat it out all over the table, but instead he managed to swallow it manfully and smile thinly. Despite the evidence of cats, namely the empty tins of food, scratch marks on the back of the door, and a very bald and tattered grey felt mouse lying by a pot rack next to the cooker, he could see none of the awful animals anywhere. There was also a distinct lack of fur balls blowing across the stone floor and, thankfully, no smell of musk or wee.

Johnny pointed at the tins littering the table and asked, "Cats? Can't see any of the little rascals anywhere, though. Got 'em all out mousing?"

She shrugged her shoulders and replied, "Must be, I suppose. I'm sure they're around somewhere."

There was another pause during which both of them tried to smile and failed, managing only to twitch facial muscles in a distinctly inhuman and alarming way. When Aunt Billie smiled Johnny noticed some rather pronounced canines, which sent a slight shiver down his spine. Good heavens, he thought, sipping more of the dreadful liquid in his mug, when on earth did she last see a dentist?

Billie rested her arm on the table and planted her feet firmly on the stone flags of the kitchen floor. "So, Johnny, what brings you to this neck of the woods?"

Johnny swapped his legs over, feeling the first glimmer of pins and needles pricking at his left ankle. "Well, Aunty, you did. The telephone call? Just wanted to make sure you're chipper and everything's alright, really. Often thought about you, and then realised it must be years since we caught up. The wedding actually. God, twenty years goes by so quickly, doesn't it, Aunty."

Aunt Billie leaned forward slightly and almost spat at him. "Does if you're left on your own to look after half-wits and invalids." She sat back again and looked him squarely in the eye. "Anyway, it's all bollocks. You know it and I know it. Funny, recognised you as soon as I saw you peering in at the front gate.

Could always tell a Siddeley. Spivs and con-men, the lot of them. Still, nice car, so you must be good at it."

She watched him as his cheeks puffed red. "So, let's not call a shovel a mattock, eh? You've turned up because you think I called you because I want to bridge the gulf between us and leave the house to you when I die? Didn't think you'd hang about once I made the call."

She leaned forward again, this time wagging a finger under his nose. Her eyes shone a brilliant feline green, as if they reflected the fire of the waning sun behind Johnny's shoulder. "Don't deny it. Can't stand people who shilly-shally. I'm not a fool you know. I might choose to live like a recluse but I'm still in touch with the world. Keep abreast, you know, keep myself informed. Got the internet for shopping and all that sort of thing. Just because a lady doesn't want to mix with people doesn't make her mad or smell like a vat of cat's pee. You see this skirt and jacket. Marks and Spencer. Delivered to my door. Whatsername, blonde woman, looked like a pipe-cleaner, not bad in The Boyfriend as I recall, she looked very good in it on their web site. Covered up her lumps and bumps and cellulite, so it'll do for me, I thought, and I was right. And do you know what? I bought it so I could look someone like you in the eye and say fack orf. So, spit it out, Johnny, there's a good boy."

Billie slumped back in her chair and took a mouthful of the now thick and lukewarm tea. Unlike Johnny she did spit it out, all over her blue-green skirt. He flourished a handkerchief and offered to wipe. She nodded and closed her eyes for a moment, breathing hard. She seemed to have lost her sparkle all of a sudden, as though the effort of waiting for the visit and the offensive manoeuvres undertaken since his arrival had worn her out. Johnny felt just a little sorry for her.

Aunt Billie's voice was much softer now. "You're right though. No use denying it. I am getting old and this place is… a bit of a mess."

She pointed at Johnny's barely touched cup of tea. "Tell you what. Chuck that filth in the yard. In the cupboard on the wall behind you you'll find two glasses and a couple of bottles of single malt. Pick one and let's have a little drinkie and a proper chat."

Manna from heaven, thought Johnny. "Of course, Aunty, no problemo."

He threw the foul brew that had masqueraded as tea out through the open kitchen door, put both his and Billie's cups in the sink, and proceeded to open the cupboard.

"Good God, Aunty! You said a couple of bottles. There's thirty in here at least."

"I know. Every time I do a Tesco delivery I add a bottle. For the winter, mainly. Anyway, we shan't be short of a drop while we talk. The Pultenay's nice."

Johnny did as he was told, pouring out a couple of stiff whiskeys that filled the air with the smell of sweet peat and smoked wood. Billie suggested they watch the sun set across the back meadow, so they moved from the kitchen to a rickety old bench set against the back wall of the farmhouse and drank in the amber warmth of late summer and good malt. Neither of them spoke for some time, not until the sun had dipped below the tree line and then bathed the sky in reflected golds and pinks. Eventually Billie took Johnny's arm and suggested that they go inside. She was starting to feel evening's chill and her glass was empty.

They retired from the tired and shabby kitchen to the main drawing room. Unlike the tatters of the domestic area, the living room was still remarkably well fettled. A good Wilton never wears out, and the furniture, if a little on the traditionally brown side, was obviously of quality and still kept in good condition. Billie preferred table lamps to the ceiling lights, and together with the scotch and a delivery of delicious beer battered cod and chips from the village pub, which was obviously a regular arrangement, they settled down to a mellow evening of malted business.

Billie was the first to speak after Johnny had cleared away the plates and the condiments. "Now, I want you to shut up and listen, Johnny. No interruptions. Can you do that?"

He nodded vigorously, assuming that this would provide the necessary proof of his good intentions.

"Good. There are three things to discuss. One, you will phone that simpering wife of yours and tell her you're staying overnight. We have a lot of business to transact. Two, I am going to make an arrangement with you that will benefit both of us, so no chicanery on your part is needed. Three, during the night, no matter what you hear or dream, do not get out of bed. Touch nothing, do nothing, and you'll be fine. Is that understood?"

Johnny considered all three points carefully. Point two was obvious and exciting. Point three was most odd, so he ignored it. He reacted badly to point number one.

"Aunty, please don't call Mary that. She's been good to me, mostly. We have our differences but…"

Aunt Billie cut him off immediately. Now on her third glass of good malt she seemed to have regained her combative edge. "Rubbish. The moment I met her at your wedding I thought, what a silly cow. She's a snob, Johnny, but not a very good one. Knows the price of everything but never the value. You were a hound man, weren't you, Labs and the like?"

Johnny felt it best to humour the old girl. He really rather wanted to get onto point two. "Yes, Labs and a Lurcher. Still, Monty died, what, five years ago, I think."

Billie smiled. She had him. "And do you have dogs now?"

"Yes, Aunty, two of the little blighters, Bonnie and Prince."

"Don't tell me", Billie chirped, delighted that she was utterly vindicated. "Scotties! Hah! They're not dogs, Johnny, they're vermin. An abomination. Yapping shag-pile! That woman has no soul. Anyway, telephone her and then we'll get around to business. Oh, and by the way, I've put a pair of Daddy's pyjamas in the spare room along with his old dressing gown and slippers. Might smell a bit of pipe tobacco, even now, but they're not too moth eaten so you'll be nice and snug."

Once again Johnny did as he was told and if he was honest with himself the choice between spending an evening with Mary or Aunt Billie was not a hard one to make. He was more convinced than ever that the old girl was on the batty side of the equation, but he liked her balls. With his domestic arrangements made for the evening Johnny settled back onto the rather comfortable chesterfield, topped up both his and Aunt Billie's glasses, and settled back to discuss point number two.

"So, Aunty, about the house. I was thinking…"

Again she cut right through the middle of his musings like an Arabian scimitar arcing towards an exposed neck. "I don't doubt you were, Johnny, but whatever you may have been thinking simply won't do. The arrangement is as follows: You will value this property and sell it for me. I want the best possible price given the general decay and dilapidation. I will then split the proceeds with you, one half each. While I may be old and while I do find it difficult to keep this old wreck afloat, I am certainly not ready to shuffle off this mortal coil. I want half so I can travel the world. You get half as your inheritance. Oh, and once the deal is done, I never want to see or hear from you or that socially impossible wife of yours ever again."

Johnny felt that the last point was gratuitously unnecessary but was disinclined to argue the general point. As far as point number two was concerned he agreed to the terms at once, seeing something close to half a million heading his way. By a mixture of lamp and torch light Aunt Billie then conducted him around the seven-bedroom house, the collapsing outbuildings, and the cellar. Johnny made verbal notes on his mobile phone as they went around, detailing the state of disrepair in almost every room bar the well-kept drawing room, and with the preliminary inspection completed he and his aunt settled down with yet another large one. Give the old bat her dues, he thought, she can hold her liquor. For his part, Johnny was beginning to feel just a little bit tipsy.

"Look, Aunty, we'll have to do a structural and have a proper look when it's daylight. There are a number of issues, damp and the like, which will have a material effect on values. In good condition, with the land, I'd normally say about one point two mill, but as things stand we'll probably go for eight hundred thou. We could consider auction. I have a couple of friends who could help there and if we market properly we could push nine if we can convince the punters that it's mostly superficial. Caveat emptor, and all that. I can set everything in train tomorrow morning, have my people out here in a day or so, do the measurements, the photos etcetera. We might have to have a bit of a tidy up as well, for when the clients come around. What do you think?"

Aunt Billie felt suddenly very tired. She gulped down the last of her Scotch, felt her face flush with warmth, and nodded. "Sounds very like trade to me, Johnny, but then that's what you're good at, I suppose. I'll leave all that to you. I shall move out once we get to the point of visitation. I couldn't bear the thought of receiving bankers. There's a little of Daddy's cash left and I've always fancied a spell at the Ritz. Do they still do a proper afternoon tea in this Godless age?"

Aunt Billie took a lingering look around the room. There were so many memories, some of them even quite pleasant, but it was definitely time to rid herself of the past. On the mantelpiece above a red-brick crafts movement fireplace, she looked at a simple brass carriage clock, the glass of which was inevitably cracked.

"Good gracious, look at the time", she said forcefully. "Off to bed with you, my lad, it's nearly midnight. Where does the time go?"

As they were getting up to leave the room, Johnny noticed an old photograph on a solid English Victorian sideboard. "My word, is that you Aunty?"

"Yes", Aunt Billie said wistfully, "and your mother. Ravishing, wasn't she. That was our deb year."

Johnny felt a warm glow rising in his heart. "Rather a fine young filly yourself, Aunty", he said, almost, but not quite, sounding patronising.

"Yes, well, look at me. Lot of good it did me. Anyway, true beauty lies on the inside."

With that she manhandled Johnny upstairs to one of the more presentable wrecks of a bedroom. She opened the door, showed him where everything was, including the aforementioned pyjamas, an en-suite lavatory and a musty mirrored wardrobe, and then wished him bon voyage.

"And remember, Johnny, stay in your room, and ideally stay in your bed. You hear all sorts of creatures out here in the wilds of Gloucestershire, and the old house creaks and groans at night, especially after a warm day, but don't worry, everything will be tickety-boo in the morning. Remember, stay in bed."

She wished him a final farewell for the evening and closed the door. As Johnny turned to put his jacket over the back of a chair he heard a rattle and a click. How odd, he thought, it sounds as though I'm being locked in. He walked over and tried the door handle. Sure enough, the old girl had turned the key.

*

Despite the slightly odd circumstances of the evening and the fact that the mattress was far too soft and the sheets somewhat threadbare, Johnny soon dropped off, his head enveloped in a single malt haze. He usually slept in the buff but for propriety's sake he had at least slipped on the pyjama bottoms. In the brief moment before he drifted into the deep sleep of the tired and emotional after what had turned out to be quite a long evening, he listened out for the strange creatures of the night but heard nothing but the creak of his own bed springs as he made himself comfortable. The house too remained hushed and silent. Within five minutes of his head hitting the plump and downy pillow the only noise to be heard was that of a gentleman snoring.

The carriage clock in the drawing room ticked away, drawing the dull hands of time forward in their endless waltz, and Johnny drifted into the realm of the dream king, a place that he rarely visited these days. Johnny was not a man of the imagination, preferring the simple sureties of cash in his pocket and the reassurance of a drink in his hand once the sun was over the yard arm, and the sun was always over the yard arm somewhere in the world.

It took him a moment or two to realise that he was dreaming. What gave it away was the fact that he was wearing the most elegant set of dress frock and tails, and appeared to be in a large, ornately furnished ballroom. All was silent, bar the slight tinkle of crystal from above. Somewhere a window or door must be open and a gentle jasmine scented breeze made soft music amongst the brilliantly cut teardrops of the three chandeliers hanging in line from the painted ceiling.

Johnny spun round slowly on the heels of his patent leather shoes. The ceiling was divided into panels, each one depicting a famous cat. Johnny recognised but a few of the more obvious feline celebrities; Puss-in-Boots, Dick Whittington's lucky charm, Jess from Postman Pat, Arthur from the cat food commercials, Benny the Ball from Top Cat and, without doubt, the grinning beast from the Alice stories. Each panel was surrounded by fabulous plasterwork depicting alarmed birds flying between the bars of their cages and mice running in all directions amid vine leaves.

Along one wall hung pictures of the Tuke-Hastings clan and Johnny recognised Daddy from the cloud of pipe smoke hanging around his forehead. The rest of the clan, both male and female stared out of their frames with an impenetrable, almost feline grace. Opposite this imposing rogues gallery Johnny spied heavy purple velvet drapes hanging in between tall many paned windows, and in the middle of each was set a rose of stained glass. At the foot of alternate windows there was a set of glass doors.

At the far end of the room, across an acre of highly polished oak, there was a small dais set with music stands and instruments placed ready for musical hands. Johnny wandered over, clicking his heels on the floor as he walked, still spinning round and taking in the lustre and the opulence of the ballroom. The whole situation appeared quite fantastical to him, reminding him of childhood fairy tales, and, he mused, he must be in a mild state of mental discomfort made hallucinogenic by alcohol and Aunt Billie. He marvelled at his own rationalisation, and then, as he plucked a violin string, marvelled again at the resonance. In that great, empty ballroom, the sound of a single note echoed back and forth, bouncing off the walls and the chandeliers in slowly decreasing tones of pitch perfection before being absorbed by the velvet drapes.

Absolute perfection, Johnny thought, would be a glass of chilled Bollinger, and with that thought he turned and saw a table laden with sparkling crystal glasses dribbling condensation and bubbles. Johnny took a sip from one of the heavy but perfectly weighted glasses and wondered what might happen next. It was so long since he had dreamed anything that he was quite out of practice.

The dream, however, had taken control of such things. Johnny immediately heard a scattering of tiny footsteps scrabbling across the polished floor. Turning to face the little dais he was quite astonished to see four elegantly dressed rats scurrying uncertainly on their hind legs towards their instruments. Of course, he thought, the players. As he watched, the lead rat, the only one wearing a bright red sash, bowed to him before directing his colleagues to their respective seats. The lead rat then took up the violin, while the others prepared themselves to play cello, viola and bass.

"Okay", Johnny said to himself, "that just leaves the guests".

He imagined a ballroom full of empire dresses and sparkling jewels, of heaving bosoms and impossible head dresses, with gentlemen officers of the dragoons and guards in attendance, but this time the dream shifted slightly. Instead of obeying his command, there entered but the one guest. She approached Johnny from the furthest of the glass doors, walking on soft satin slippers as though she had just taken a breath of fresh air in between dances. She wore the empire line to perfection, swelling at the breast and floating across the floor. In colour the dress was the perfect shade of thick, gold-top cream, and embroidered with fine lace sporting motifs of lushly hanging cotton reels. His partner wore a sprig of vine in her long, blonde hair, and looked divine. Johnny stood and watched her drift towards him to an undercurrent of gently twisting strings. He was completely and utterly transfixed.

As Johnny's dancing partner drew nearer to him he saw a

resemblance to someone he might once have known, but he couldn't quite put his finger on who she might be. He was sure he would have remembered such an utter beauty. Her skin glowed under the lights in ambers and olives and whites, almost tabby in effect. She was slender and lean, but Johnny knew just by watching the supple way that she walked that she was attractively dangerous too.

In common with the rest of the dream, he realised that she too had a feline element to her soul. Her skin was lightly but gorgeously downed. Her eyes shone green and black, reflecting the sparkling light of the chandeliers, and if Johnny turned obliquely from her he could almost see long slender whiskers sweeping out from her perfect little button nose.

They said not a word. The rat quartet struck up in turn quadrilles, gavottes, a waltz, and finally a Queen's minuet. Johnny and his partner danced as if there could be no end to the music, no end to this perfect ball, with no words or sounds other than the perfect rodent strings passing through the air between them. Each dance merged into the next without pause, with time seeming to stand still around them. The heavy velvet drapes billowed out behind them with each sweeping pass, such was the tornadic force of their motion across the floor. Sadly for every moment of harmony, there must come a fade or a discord, and when the last bars of this perfect night were finally subsumed into the jasmine night air, Johnny felt a tear fall onto his cheek.

"Must we stop?" he asked softly. "Must this dream end, my darling, whoever you may be?"

His tabby tigress twitched her nose and almost seemed to prowl around her dancing partner, as if arching her back and swaying her rear end as cats do when ready to pounce. Her expression never changed, being that of the sublime feline smile that all cats give to the world, that knowing smile that defies your understanding. She stopped her circling and drew close to Johnny, taking both his hands in her own soft and downy paws. Johnny could smell the warm musk of fur. She purred softly, burying her head against his chest for a moment before looking up into his eyes.

She spoke in a whisper. "This is the dream, this is lap cat, my darling, but beware the beast within. This is the dream, but there is still the nightmare to come. Remember, whatever happens do not get out of bed. Please remember, my darling child."

*

Johnny's eyes snapped open. He was bathed in sweat, and the covers were twisted round him like a winding sheet. He stared into the darkness, fixing his gaze on the shape of the ceiling light in his bedroom while the vivid colours and sensations of his stunning fancy subsided into that dim realm of half-light permitted to the waking by the dream king. Johnny concentrated on breathing, slowing down his pounding heart. He ran his fingers through damp hair. He traced the contours of his corpulence, reassuring himself that the lissom man in the fantasy was gone. Mostly, though, Johnny tried to keep alive the vision of his beautiful creature, never wishing to let the last dance fade from his memory.

All that Johnny could think about at that moment was how he wanted to live in that faerie place forever. How would he ever look at Mary in the same way again? After a moment of desperate despair, he posited the alternative theory that he need not look at her in the same way. When he and Mary were together in that sort of way, things might actually be improved if he envisioned as his paramour this tigress, his tabby love. There might be something in the amorous line to be gained after all. It was while pondering on such possibilities that Johnny first noticed his erection, and then almost immediately heard a key turning in the door lock.

"Oh, bugger", he muttered, twisting round to face the door. "What the bloody hell does she want? This is so embarrassing."

The door opened slowly, swinging on silent hinges to reveal a blackness so deep that it swallowed entirely the weak shaft of moonlight that tried to sneak into the room through a gap in the drawn curtains. It was hot now, and the air smelled rank and fetid, as if Johnny were buried deep in some jungle. He smelled wet earth and dank, malodorous vegetation. From the bowels of the house Johnny thought he could hear snorts and snuffles, the sounds of night creatures in thick, matted undergrowth. He closed his eyes and stopped his ears for a moment, but nothing changed when he resurfaced. All around him he could hear the night terrors of unknown beasts, and if he stared hard he thought he could make out leaves and twisted boughs and tall grasses on the landing. And then it came to him. This was another bloody dream.

Johnny rolled over and buried his head under the pillow. If he shut his eyes and thought of sleep or sheep, then all this would go away. Sleep, however, was impossible. From out of the thick, humid air small, winged creatures continually buzzed against his exposed chest. He felt a sharp nip and realised that he was being eaten alive. Still the snorts and snuffles and squeals of life incarnate erupted all around him. He felt something bump into the bed frame and grunt like a pig. Slowly he raised the threadbare sheets up around his neck, and then sat up. In the pitch dark room he thought he could still make out the wardrobe on the far wall, and hanging over a thick rope of liana, he could see his suit and under that his shoes.

He had to make a decision. Could he simply wrap himself up in the bed clothes and wait it out? He decided that he could not. He needed the reassurance of leather on his exposed feet, of tailored cotton against his chest, and the thickness of tweed and twill against his limbs. He remembered the old girl's warning, as well as that of his tigress, but, he thought; I'm only going to put on some clothes. I can jump back into bed as soon as I've got those on, can't I?

Johnny made his decision. He leapt out of bed and landed on a thick, mucal layer of rotting leaves and vines. Twigs snapped under his heel and the black mulch of the jungle floor oozed between his toes. Something beetle-like scurried across the arch of his foot. Johnny screamed, grabbed his suit and shirt and threw them onto the bed. He panted hard, still mired in the primeval floor, but managed to steel his shaking hands so that he could make a grab for his brogues. As he picked them up a horned millipede ran out of one and up his bare arm. Johnny shrieked again, ripping his lungs in the process, but finally he managed to fall back onto the relative safety of his bed. After a few moments collecting his thoughts and parcelling them up with the abject terror coursing through his veins, he managed to shake his clothes out and dress, although he deemed it unnecessary to wear a tie under these dire circumstances.

What Johnny needed was another one of Aunt Billie's singular malts. He tried to rationalise. "This is only a dream", he told himself. "A nightmare possibly, but they're basically one and the same, old boy, so what about it? Shall we yomp down to the kitchen?"

His inner child concurred, and after a moment of deep breathing, of sucking in the hot, rancid smell of decay and death on the forest floor, he gently swung himself off the bed and placed both feet on the floor. Insects buzzed around his head, whining and whirring. Creatures unseen slithered and scuttled out of his way as he gingerly stepped out onto the landing. Everywhere, sprouting out of the walls and hanging down from the ceiling, thick fronds and razor-sharp leaves cut and smothered his crouched body. With every step a new smell of the primordial struggle erupted to fill his nostrils and his throat, making him want to wretch. He could feel the sniffling beasts of night in the jungle watching his every move. Nevertheless, Johnny pulled and pushed his way through the verdure, making for the stairs, where he used a coil of liana as a rope so that he could slither down to the ground floor.

So far, so good, he thought. Johnny waited a moment, recalling the layout of the house and getting his bearings. That was when he noticed the change. There was now an expectant air in the hallway, a brooding air, and an absence of sound. He could hear nothing buzzing, nothing rooting, nothing snuffling. It was though all fauna and insect life was holding its breath. Johnny, not being up on the jungle thing, thought no more of it. He had the taste of Scotch in his mouth and was as determined to find liquid gold in the wilderness as Cortez had been in his search for El Dorado. Except, Johnny then realised that all was not silent. At the bottom of the stairs the vegetation seemed to consist mostly of tall, thick grasses, swaying slightly in a languid breeze. He could hear the sound of tall leaves and seed ears rubbing together. He also thought that he caught the sound of something swishing rhythmically amongst the fronds.

Fear is a primal thing. From where or how this sudden realisation came, Johnny had not a clue, but he knew instantly that he was prey. The leopard was out for a late supper and Johnny Hester-Siddeley was on the menu. He tried to orient himself to the sound of the hunting cat. She helped him by emitting a low, guttural growl from somewhere near the front door.

Johnny had another choice to make. He was unarmed and an innocent when it came to big game. He stood stock still for a moment considering his options. His world constricted to a space just big enough to hold the sound of his rapidly beating heart. If he could make it to the kitchen before she pounced he might find a knife or a chair or a saucepan, something, anything with which he could defend himself.

Johnny turned slowly so that he was facing the kitchen door. He brushed a spider's web out of his hair and then crouched down in the long grass in the same way that he'd seen sprinters set themselves before a race. Unlike in his first dream, this time fat and fifty-year-old Johnny was no athlete, but he could rely on the spur of abject terror to give him speed. His mental starting gun sounded and Johnny launched himself out of the blocks, rising on the upward pump of his arms, feeling his flabby and rotund thighs curse as they tried to propel his middle-aged spread towards the safety of the kitchen.

Johnny managed three strides, perhaps half the distance that he needed, before the leopard sprang. In one savage bound she covered the gap between them, raking at Johnny's back with her powerful talons, slicing though tweed and cotton and skin as if it were thin air. Johnny fell, winded and gasping, feeling his shirt soak with blood. He turned as he fell, and a razored paw ripped across his chest, exposing bone and torn flesh to the night dark sky.

With her prey immobilised, the she-leopard lowered her head to sniff the metallic humours of fresh meat. As she lapped at the wound, she looked into Johnny's eyes and smiled her cat smile. Johnny saw there his own reflection, pale and bloodless and deathly. He also saw in those eyes the green luminescence of his once sweet and docile dancing partner. The hunting cat opened her jaws slowly, her breath hot and moist and rank with a thousand kills. Thick, warm saliva dripped off of her teeth and onto Johnny's burning face. As he started to scream, he remembered the final words of advice that his aunt and his dancing love had given him; "Don't get out of bed".

The Leopard squeezed that final shriek of horror out of Johnny's throat as her jaws closed on his windpipe to crush and splinter his neck.

When Johnny woke the next morning, he found that he could hardly move. Aunt Billie, having unlocked the door, placed a cup of freshly brewed Earl Gray on the bedside table and looked at him quizzically.

"You've had a bit of a restless night, dear. A nice cup of tea usually does the trick. There's a bathroom at the end of the landing. I've put fresh towels out for you. Give me a shout when you're ready and I'll put some bacon on for you."

Once Aunt Billie was out of the room, Johnny slowly ran his

hands over his neck and then, as best he could, down his back. He was intact and unscarred. He then gingerly moved his hand to his chest. He ached all over and in particular he felt sore and raw between the nipples. His fingers traced the ragged grooves of three long but thin scars, as if a large tom cat had raked talons across his skin. Johnny slowly pulled back the sheet. He saw there three fresh wounds, just scabbing over but still seeping little tears of blood onto the sheet.

Aunt Billie heard the screams coming from the room in which her guest had spent the night. She took a tumbler from the Scotch cupboard and filled it to the brim with a good Strathspey malt, which she then took up to her distant relative. There she sat on the bed next to him, made him drink half the glass in one go, and then gently patted his hand. She soothed him gently for a few minutes, bringing him back to the world of the living and everyday banality. As the look of dread panic slowly faded from his eyes she wiped a bead of sweat away from his forehead and spoke softly to him.

"I think it best, Johnny, if we never mention last night. I'm not sure you'll ever want to and I certainly have no intention of doing so. You should finish the Scotch and then do your ablutions. We'll say no more about it. I trust you'll get me the best price that you can for house?"

Johnny remained mute, but he found the strength to nod once. Aunt Billie raised him up on his pillow and handed him the tumbler. Johnny downed the remaining malt in one more gulp, and as the liquor warmed his veins and made his bones stiffen he started to feel a little better.

Aunt Billie patted his hand again and said, "They're just dreams, that's all."

Later that morning, with Johnny restored to some sort of order, and with firm instructions to tell his wife, Mary, that one of his batty old Aunt's cats had mauled him during the night, she bade him farewell. After he had driven his black beauty of a car out onto the lane and closed the back gate, she took a tin of something fishy out of the under sink cupboard, sat down in one of her rickety old kitchen chairs, the one next to the gently warming range, and poured herself a thick measure of her favourite Scotch. She rocked gently back and forth in her chair, spooning cat food into her mouth and smiling to herself. She whispered her secrets to the bald felt mouse over by the pot stand.

"We're looking forward to a bright future, aren't we, mousey? Little Johnny's going to get us enough money to see the world, and he'll be happy, I suppose…eventually…if he lets the scars fade. We need money, don't we, mousey, if we're going to see the world and live nine lives in the finest style."

Big Black Boots

(Loosely based on Hans Christian Andersen's The Red Shoes)

THERE WAS ONCE A little girl who ate gristle and vegetable soup just like all of the fair and dainty little girls who lived in the industrial towns of old, coke-smothered England. Her mother was very poor and in summer the little girl never had shoes to wear on her feet. In winter the girl's brooding and wretched mama made her wear clogs in the snow and, as a consequence of this, her feet were always cold and terribly sore.

The town where the little girl and her mother lived was dilapidated and failing, locked into the decline that blighted so many of the darkling centres of fading wealth that nestled amongst England's once satanic hills. Things had come to such a pass that many of the old ways and trades had all but disappeared, and the pinch-faced peoples of that scabbed landscape had to scrimp and scratch out meagre livings as best they could. Typical of this decay was an old shoemaker who sat and sewed big black boots out of scuffed scraps of worn out leather and from strips of almost threadbare felt. The boots that he made were heavy and clumsy, but they were, nonetheless, better than clogs. One Christmas the little girl's mother took all of her scratched savings to this boot maker and she bought a pair boots as a present for her darling daughter. The little girl in question was called Karen.

Both mother and daughter woke up on Christmas morning with an eager glint in their eyes. Neither of them complained about the cold, the fires were laid and lit, and the presents, such as they were, were given and received with great joy and excitement. Unfortunately, just as the Christmas goose leg was about to be served, the little girl's mother was suddenly taken very ill and she died that very festive afternoon from the combined effects of absolute poverty and the scabrous pox.

As was the custom in those days, the little girl's mother was buried that same Christmas evening to prevent any contagion spreading amongst the populace, and although big black leather boots were totally wrong for a funeral they were the only proper shoes that poor little Karen possessed. She walked bare legged behind her mother's coffin through the spare and bleak snow-dappled streets wearing her Sunday best pinafore and her new Christmas boots.

A rich old woman was driving through the town in a large, black limousine on her way home from Christmas lunch with her cousin. As her leviathan automobile wafted down the street that ran along one side of the cemetery, the old woman caught sight of little Karen through the smoked glass windows and her heart cried out for all of the lost summers that she could never regain. She felt awfully sorry for the little girl who was standing in the cold, cold cemetery on this benighted Christmas evening, so she had her chauffeur stop the car.

The wrinkled but ruthlessly rich spinster then called the parson over and said, "Look here, my good man, let me take that pretty little thing home and I promise to bring her up properly and right".

Little Karen, confused by the simple delights of the morning and the great sadness of the afternoon, was convinced that the rich old woman had noticed her because of her special Christmas boots, and she could feel the spirit of her departed mother pushing her towards the car, pushing her towards a better life of plenty and comfort.

As Karen climbed into the car the old woman tutted and said, "Well, my dear, let's see what we can do for you. A new dress and some proper little girl's shoes are in order, I think. We can't have you wandering about the house in ugly old boots like that".

When Karen and her new benefactress got home, the boots were taken away and burned, but despite these initial hardships and misgivings, little Karen was quickly won over by gifts of fine new clothes and several pairs of lovely, well-fitted shoes. Over the next few years Karen learned to cook and to sew. Her school lessons went well and she quickly grasped the rudiments of reading, writing and mathematics, and in no time at all Karen grew up to be a proper young lady. Everyone who met her told her that she was very pretty. When they heard about her lowly start in life and about how she had been saved by the rich old woman they all told her how lucky she was and how happy she must be. Karen believed every word of it except one. She knew, especially when she looked in the mirror, that she was not just pretty. Karen knew in her heart that she was beautiful.

One day, when Karen had grown into her mid teenage years, a

famous singer came to Coalminster to perform a concert in the town hall. People crowded outside the singer's hotel balcony just to try and catch a glimpse of her, and, sure enough, the singer made frequent appearances on her balcony to greet her adoring public. On one of these occasions Karen was there in the crowd. Karen loved the glitz and the glamour that seemed to shine out from the famous singer's smile. She was doubly overjoyed when she saw that the famous singer was wearing a pair of beautiful, hand-tooled Moroccan leather boots. They were, of course, much prettier than Karen's old boots, but they reminded Karen of her dearly departed mother and of the boots that she had given to Karen on that fateful morning long ago. Karen decided there and then that there could be nothing finer in the entire world than a pair of lovely, properly hand-stitched big black boots.

The rich old woman who had taken Karen in all of those years ago was a religious sort, in a Methodist way, and she wanted Karen to be confirmed. She sent Karen to Sunday school and when the day of her Confirmation approached Karen and the old woman went shopping at all of the finest stores in town, which meant in reality that they spent most of the afternoon ensconced in the rather threadbare surroundings of the Walter Henry Cheeps department store. They hummed and whispered over racks of chintz and lace, examining every dress and petticoat in close detail until, as dusk started to fall, they set out for home laden with bags and boxes full of the previous year's fashions and fads.

They had one last call to make at the biggest and most famous shoe shop for miles around. The shop was full of display stands and long, sleek, polished wooden racks full of sling backs and high heels. The assembled pantheon of footwear dazzled and gleamed, but Karen only had eyes for the finest black leather boots. Fortunately for Karen the rich old woman was by now hard of hearing and a little short sighted. She thought that Karen had chosen a lovely but demur pair of cream court shoes and she completely failed to notice Karen and the shop assistant secretly agreeing to substitute them with the most expensive pair of black lace up boots in the whole shop. The boots fitted Karen perfectly and so they were bought with a sly nod and wink towards the old lady's disabilities and her deep pockets. If the rich old woman had been able to hear, had she been able to see just how big and black these new boots were, she would never have agreed to let Karen wear them to church.

The very next day, when Karen walked up the aisle in her pretty white lace dress and her big black lace up boots, everyone stared at her. It seemed to Karen that the hand-carved figures on the tombs, that the grim portraits of old ancestral parsons and even the alabaster angels that flew above the altar were all staring at her. Her head was awash with the thrill of shocking the good citizens of the parish and when the parson laid his hand upon her head, when he spoke of rituals, meanings and covenants, all that Karen could think about was how grown up she was and how beautiful she must look in her big black leather boots.

By the time Karen and the old woman got home, everyone knew about the boots. The old woman's friends gleefully told her all about them with the politely but barely disguised relish that the socially superior members of society used to employ so well, and the old dear was furious. She and Karen had a blazing row in the sitting room because Karen, feeling her way into her adult years, answered back, but, after many tears, Karen agreed that she would only ever wear sensible shoes to church.

During the following week, the weather was absolutely stunning, and the ground became ever so dusty and dry, which gave Karen a brilliant idea. She decided to wear a long, flowing skirt to church, one that would hide all but the toe caps and the soles of her big black boots. The dust from the parched and dry earth would surely disguise how black they were, and sure enough, as they walked to church, the rich old woman completely failed to notice that Karen was wearing her black boots under her long skirt.

As Karen and her patroness approached the church they saw there, standing by the gate that opened into the churchyard, an old veteran of one too many wars selling matches at sixpence the box. Spotting a chance to do a little business he offered to clean the ladies' shoes for them before they entered the house of worship. The rich old woman sniffed a little as he doffed his cap and scraped the dry earth with a creaking bow, but his tone and manner were suitably deferential and so she put out each foot in turn so that the man could wipe the dust from her shoes. Karen, giggling, did so too.

"Good grief", whispered the old soldier as he set about wiping the dust from Karen's shoes. "What lovely fighting boots they are, little miss!" He grinned at Karen as he waved his right hand over her feet, muttering in low, wheezy tones, "Stay put in those boots when you fight".

Then he struck the sole of each boot once with the flat of his right hand before rolling away in a twenty-a-day coughing fit. The rich old woman flipped a shilling into the dirt by the old man's tray of matches and hurried Karen away and into the church, feeling as though she should wash her hands immediately.

Karen and the old woman sat in the front pew as usual. In the heat of the day the service seemed to drone on forever and when the parson started his sermon Karen could feel her eyelids drooping. She tried to stay awake but as the seconds dripped away she couldn't resist the urge to stretch her legs out in front of her and slide down a little in her seat. Everyone in the congregation stared at her as her big black boots slid out from under her skirt and the parson nearly choked on his words when he caught sight of the boots from his pulpit. When she knelt down to receive the chalice full of wine all that the congregation could see of her were rubber boot soles as thick as tyre treads. Karen, meanwhile, in her daydreaming state, forgot about everything in the world, imagining herself drinking wine from a crystal goblet fashioned in the shape of a hand tooled Moroccan leather boot.

With the service over the congregation trooped outside and said their genteel farewells. Karen and her doting foster mother, who was not as fit as she had once been, waited for their chauffeur to bring the limousine round to the gate that lead out of the church yard. She felt that in the heat of a glorious late Sunday morning it would be too much to walk home after the service. When the car arrived the old woman climbed into the rear seat with a weary sigh and waited for Karen for join her.

Just as Karen was about to climb into the car she caught sight of the old war veteran, who was leaning against an oak tree, grinning once again.

"See," he said, "what lovely fighting boots they are". He clapped his hands three times.

Karen tried to swing her right foot into the car but it refused to obey her. Her left foot also refused to move and suddenly, from nowhere, Karen felt a desperate urge to kick something. She felt an urgent and irresistible need to fight. Her feet started to lash out in every direction, left and right, catching anyone within range on their shins and on their knees. Her boots were thoroughly democratic, aiming kicks at women's ankles, children's toes and even one at the parson's nose. Protest as she might, there was nothing that Karen could do, for her boots were determined to fight.

Karen brawled up the streets and tussled down the lanes; she battered doors and kicked at cars, inflicting cuts and bruises on innocent bystanders wherever she went. In the end, and with the police in hot pursuit, all that the old woman's chauffeur could do was bundle Karen into the back of the car, with her flailing boots still sticking out of the back window. They made their escape just in the nick of time to avoid any more of a scandal than was absolutely necessary.

Once they judged themselves to be safely out of harm's way the chauffer and Karen, both of them suffering many bruises, eventually managed to untie the laces, unhook the eyes and pull the boots off of the poor girl's battered and desperately tired legs. Only then did her feet stop lashing about in the back of the car. Karen felt exhausted and not a little frightened. She was still out of breath when she got home and then, of course, she had to face the old woman's anger once again. The terrible boots were thrown out with the garbage, and with good riddance to them as far as the rich old woman was concerned. Karen was made to swear that she would never wear boots again.

Over the next few weeks the old woman grew steadily paler and more ill. She was very old, but her health was made all the worse by having to pay the doctor's bills for all of Karen's unfortunate victims, and the general medical situation was made worse by the flood of letters from solicitors demanding compensations. Then, to cap it all, the frail old dowager was summoned to have words with the local chief of police. The threat of an Antisocial Behaviour Order for Karen was probably the straw that broke the camel's back. It was all too much for the old woman and just before she fainted away at the end of that dreadful day, she insisted that Karen be grounded for at least a year.

The sad truth was that the rich old woman became steadily worse from then on, until the doctors gave up any hope of her ever recovering her old strength. Karen was really very sorry and she promised to be good and to look after the old woman, which she did with great care and love. Karen made bowls of chicken broth for her guardian, sat with her and read to her, gave her bed baths and held her hand as she drifted off to sleep in the evenings. Karen worked every hour of the day keeping the house clean and her patroness as comfortable as she could, which was hard and tiring work, but Karen was well aware that she had a great debt to pay.

One morning, some months later, a parcel arrived for Karen. It lay on the kitchen table all day while Karen cooked and mopped and scrubbed and read to the old woman, and it wasn't until late into the evening that Karen had the chance to sit down and relax. She poured herself a small sherry, which, although she was underage, she found to be of help after a long day of household duties, chores and cares. Her fringe hung limply across her forehead. As Karen brushed her hair out of her eyes she caught sight of the parcel for the first time since it had been delivered that morning.

It was addressed to her and a card said that it was from 'Dickie the Dog'. There was a message on the card saying that he had heard about the strange incident of the Sunday boots from an old soldier friend of his one evening down at his local pub, and he wondered whether Karen liked football. If she did, he said, a few of the lads would be meeting down by the gasworks on Tuesday night and she'd be welcome to tag along. According to the note the parcel contained the appropriate clothes for a night out with the gasworks boys. Somewhat disturbed but also intrigued by this strange message, Karen opened the parcel, and was amazed to see that it contained a blue and white scarf, a blue and white knitted bobble hat and those same shining black boots that had caused such mayhem after church service.

Karen immediately put the boots, the scarf and the bobble hat back into their wrappings and placed them on top of the highest cupboard in the kitchen. She dared not wear them again. She had made a promise.

But living a life made up of all work and very little play started to make Karen think. She was desperate to escape the gloom of the old house. She was a teenager, after all, and she felt as though she was missing out. She knew that she should repay her debts to the old woman for this wonderful life and all of the worry that she had caused, but that didn't mean that she was a prisoner. She could feel the weeks ageing her and she longed for just one night out, for a little bit of excitement. Every time she walked by the cupboard in the kitchen she looked up at the parcel that contained her black boots. She could feel her feet itching to wear them once again and as the days counted down towards the next Tuesday, Karen's thoughts were entirely taken up by the possibilities that beckoned to her from the top of the kitchen cupboard. She deserved a night out, she thought, and slowly she convinced herself that it would be all right. "After all," she said to herself over another glass of sherry, "what could possibly happen?"

When Tuesday finally came Karen spent the day in a high state of distracted anticipation. The chicken broth was slightly over cooked, the bed bath a little rough and the afternoon story reading just a little rushed. Eventually she managed to tuck the rich old woman up for the night, gave her a glass of warm milk and hurried downstairs. She pulled a chair up in front of the kitchen cupboard, stood on it and reached up for her boots with trembling hands. Karen put on the left boot, fully expecting havoc to break out, but everything in the kitchen was peaceful and calm. Encouraged, Karen pulled on the right boot and then she walked around the kitchen, but still everything was quiet and decidedly unwarlike. After five full minutes of walking up and down without feeling any urge to maim or disembowel, Karen decided that all of the fuss after the church service had been nothing more than a storm in a teacup.

"It was a hot day, after all", she said to herself, "and maybe I just had a conniption or something".

She pulled on her jacket, wrapped the scarf around her neck, put the bobble hat in her pocket and slipped quietly out of the back door. At first everything was just fine and dandy. The boots were lovely and snug and comfortable, obeying Karen's feet perfectly. She turned a corner and, even as she passed strangers on the night dark streets, there were still no signs of trouble. In fact, nothing untoward happened at all on any of the streets or lanes that lead towards Dickie the Dog and the gasworks boys.

As Karen turned the last corner and started to walk along a broken chain link fence beside an old disused factory next to the gasworks, she saw a group of twenty or thirty young boys in front of her. Some of them were wearing blue and white scarves, while others were wearing red and white scarves, and they were all throwing punches and aiming kicks at each other. Karen suddenly felt very, very frightened. Not only was there a fight going on, but try as she might, she couldn't stop her feet from walking straight towards the bundle of scrapping youths. She knew instinctively, deep in her bones, that she was in desperate trouble.

Karen caught sight of someone leaning against the factory wall and as she drew closer to the turmoil she recognised the grin of the old soldier who'd cleaned her shoes outside the church all those months ago. He held a long, fat cigar in one hand and as he winked at her he blew a series of perfect smoke rings into the air. Then he clapped his hands together three times.

The boots started to tingle, shake and shudder so much that Karen could feel them scratching at the loose stones and the mud beneath her feet like a bull preparing to charge a matador. Suddenly she lurched forward into the thick of the fight and started to lash out in every direction, her booted feet pummelling anything and anybody within range, and it was then that Karen realised that every single boy around her was also wearing a pair of big, black, leather, lace up boots. As she stared at the mass of bodies and faces around her she became only too aware that every one of these madly scrapping boys was screaming and shouting in pure, absolute terror. Their boots were all wildly out of control.

On and on the fighting went, with bodies lying broken on the ground and with blood splattered everywhere. Even the legs of the unconscious boys were still trying to lash out as the magic boots tried desperately to stay in the fight. Gradually the number of the fully conscious and able-bodied combatants dwindled and thinned out, until Karen was one of the last youths standing, but still her boots raged on, lusting for bursting blood and splintered bone. At that moment Karen caught sight of a small and particularly ugly looking man, more hobgoblin than human, laughing and joking with the old soldier. They were both smoking large, fat cigars and the ugly looking troll of a man flashed a gap-toothed grin at her and waved to her with long and dirty fingers.

"See you got the parcel, then", he shouted.

With one last burst of desperate energy, Karen managed to tear her boots away from the fight and she dragged them, kicking and screaming, around to the far side of the gasworks. It was like wading through thick treacle, but she hauled herself away from the fight until there was no more breath left in her lungs. She leaned against the chain link fence, breathed in deeply and looked up the street towards home and peace and safety.

To Karen's absolute horror she found herself confronted by an advancing line of black clad, helmeted and shielded riot police, who had been called out to deal with the disturbance. Karen's big black boots suddenly went into overdrive, slashing and beating at anyone in uniform who was unlucky enough to be in range. She attacked with such force that she was completely lifted off the ground. She drove into the police line like a heat seeking missile, laying into every police officer with the greatest of fury. She screamed and screamed for help, bursting her lungs with her wild pleading. Karen begged for mercy and for someone to stop this madness. She beseeched the heavens, wishing that she might wake up at home and in bed. No matter how hard she wished and begged and pleaded with her demonic boots, they simply carried on annihilating each and every member of the town's Special Patrol Group.

Helmets, truncheons and shields lay scattered across the road. Karen was in a state of total and mad despair when, all of a sudden, there was blinding flash of light. As her booted feet continued to lash out amid the bodies and the bruises, she thought that she could make out the shape of an angel or a spirit silhouetted in the brilliant white light. Slowly, and despite the gyrations of her wildly thrashing legs and the ebb and flow of charging policemen, Karen began to see that the angel's face was pure and loving. She begged for help, promising to repent her sins and to be good forever and ever and ever.

The creature of the light smiled at her, hearing her desperate plea, and started to say something but Karen didn't hear a single word. Her world went suddenly very black, indeed. With her attention fixed on the radiant smile of her saviour, and as her boots experienced a momentary sense of unease, she simply didn't notice the biggest, toughest and burliest member of the police riot squad sneaking up behind her. As she gazed into the bright white light of hope the policeman ended the fighting by crashing his baton down onto poor Karen's aching head.

*

When Karen awoke she felt uncomfortably warm. It took a second or two for her to focus properly, but when she could see straight she found herself in a red walled hall, quite alone and friendless. There were no fighting boys, no policemen and no bright lights. Karen untied the scarf that was still hanging around her neck, still feeling groggy after the blow to her head and only slowly did the events of the evening filter back into her memory. As things became clearer she started to whimper a little. Her faint sobs grew into a wholehearted wailing when she looked down at her feet and saw that her boots were gone and in their place she was wearing a pair of soft red ballet shoes. She was confused and scared and desperate for home.

Just then a door opened and Karen watched aghast as the old soldier sidled into the hall. He was still wearing that horrible grin and he was holding Karen's big black boots. He walked slowly over to where Karen was standing, and with every step his knees and hips cracked and snapped. He wheezed with every breath, and yet Karen saw within his aged frame the shape of something lithe and coiled and ravening. The old man put the boots down on the ground in front of her. Karen could hardly breathe. The adrenaline of fear raced through her veins. The air around her grew hot and fetid.

The old soldier snapped his fingers once. The boots disappeared in a puff of smoke. He snapped his fingers a second time. From somewhere above her Karen could hear the tinny sounds of Strauss waltzes being played as if through elevator speakers. The old man snapped his fingers a third time and leered at the girl. Karen suddenly felt her red ballet shoes begin to dance, and no matter how hard she tried she simply couldn't stop dancing, dancing up and down the hall. To the left, to the right and twirling round she went in some crazed sort of Irish jig.

The old soldier had swapped Karen's lovely big black boots for red ballet shoes that would dance and dance from here until the ends of days. He'd done just the same thing to other little girls and boys over the years and always enjoyed that first moment of their panic filled realisation. He watched her spin and pirouette. He watched as she screamed and yelled above the tinny sound of whirling strings and he chuckled to himself, as little devils are wont to do.

"There's beautiful", he said to himself, as he lit another cigar and started to blow perfect little smoke rings in time to the rhythm of the dance.

Civvies

AS A LABOURING PAIR of steam engines pulled in under Waterloo Station's classical girder and glass roof, and the steam from their boiler stacks joined with the vapours from all of the other troop trains hauling their heavy human cargos along these southern tracks, crowding and rowdily overlapping conversations in the packed compartment of one of the train carriages grew ever quieter. Faces appeared in the carriage windows, faces attached to bodies straining to see the welcoming fogs of the Old Smoke. Some of the 56th Londoners were coming home. Nineteen forty-five, August, and in particular, one Private Sidney Newt, a volunteer at eighteen in the summer of nineteen forty, was returning to the maternal bosom for the first time in five years. He was not entirely sure how he felt about that.

With the steely screech of wheels sliding on worn rails, and with the jolt and pull and jolt again of the slowing carriages, that brief moment of homeward bound reverie shattered. Catcalls and whistles. Windows slammed down and heads peered out into the dissipating walls of steam and coke soot. Coughs and shouts. A

Wren was in full but ordered flow along the already crowded platform that ran next to the troop transport carriage. Soldier boys tracked her in full tidal bore from train windows;

"Hello, darlin'…"

"Fancy a bit of German Sau…?"

"Oi, luv, where you going in such an 'urry?"

Countless faces. Wives and mothers and daughters. Fathers and sons and a smattering of husbands. Porters with sack-butts and trolleys laden with brown leather chattels. A party of Coldstream Guards in formation. The tin of the tannoy. The thump of brakes and buffers. The scuff of a thousand shoe leathers on hard platform stones. Shouts and screams. The sighs of true loves and families joyously reunited before hidden traumas and stresses cracked these homecoming veneers. The gentle drip of tears on shoulders and cheeks rising to form a swelling salt lake-a-lapping. The click-clack of mechanical signboards. Guards' whistles and the grind of wheels gaining traction. The inevitable tick and snick of the advancing hands on the station clocks. Sidney Newt moved through the sights and soundscapes as if drunk, oblivious to the wartime pulse and patina of the place, focused just on the step and the weight upon his shoulder. Waterloo. Another bloody war done for. The coming home of a man as unsure of his place in this grimly victorious city as that unhappy boy had been all those years ago when simply trying to get away from the Old Crow.

Banter. Six abreast across the platform. Instinctively the waiting and the watching, the working and those simply there in that moment, scuttled out of the way of Sydney's motley phalanx. Sidney's immediate host, his squad of mates, swaggered up the platform towards the open skies beyond the ticket gates, caps askew, collars undone, boots creaking with age and grime and the last of the bully days. The boys were home, all of them Brentford and Chiswick born and bred, old sands and hands of the Desert, of Italy and then the Western Approaches, and not one of them was as old as Sidney and none of them knew anything but the army slog through Africa and Italy and the rains and muds of the great northern invasion.

Sidney was a head shorter than the rest of the squad, and formed the thin, grubbily off-white, sloping, right hand flank of their meagre force as they shouldered their kit towards civilian streets. They clattered as they walked, encumbered and bagged, stock full of souvenirs and keepsakes. Sidney had a shortened German Infantry bayonet, a rusted and chipped Iron Cross and a slightly torn and grubby red Swastika flag in his kit bag, the flag being there simply because he could take it with impunity. He had a memory or two in crumpled envelope form as well. A note from a desperate Fraulein on the ration scrounge with whom he conveniently but briefly fell in love, and a snip of hair from an Italian prostitute, who had gladly let him pay for a memory that he would embellish for years to come.

There were other girls, of course. You lost a lot of inhibitions when you slogged the deserts and the mountain spines chasing one blood stained objective after another. Sidney thought about girls a lot but he had long since stopped thinking about that dose of clap and the morality of it all, about what the folks and the fragile friends back home might say. Anyway, the dose was a sort of badge of honour, a source of perverse pride.

If you knew what was good for you, you stopped thinking about a lot of things when you saw your last best mate bleed out in front of you because his feet were blown off by a mine and there was no damned medic because he too was bleeding in a ditch half a mile back and beyond. To survive you packed all of those images away safely with the other keepsakes. You left the smashed corpses, friend and foe alike, in the muds that you hoped would clog your memories forever and a day.

An assembly point. The Regimental Sergeant Major. Milling bloody chaos. Sidney reverted from the good nature of the homecoming ingénue and started to vent his more usual frustrations as a fully paid up member of the six-year time served cynic brigade. How the hell had they won the war when they could not organise the proverbial? Whistles and catcalls. The milling soldiery were all demob happy, although this particular queue was just for a three-day ticket of leave. Nevertheless, the disciplines of the war years were already fading. They were the conquering heroes. This drizzling little country owed them something. This would be their time in those sunlit uplands that Mister Churchill promised them. And Sidney, despite his reservations about what home and hearth might mean, felt once again that the West London of his timid youth was indeed the centre of a universe now expanded beyond the brittle bones and the ragged flesh of boyhood fears and the wars fought by the men that they had all become.

Sidney joined in the general barracking. "Come on, Sarge, shift your arse."

The RSM cast a baleful look over the heads of the jostling company, knowing full well that he dare not charge that annoying little runt, Private Newt, with anything worse than being homesick. He shuddered inwardly at the thought of peace. And so, with their better, homeward bound nature winning through, these soon to be former soldiers slowly adopted slightly more orderly queues, took their papers, and started to drift away into the crowded streets of Central London, becoming just one more battledress and kit bag in the random melee that was a million men slowly waking up from their shared nightmares.

*

"D'you know what I ain't never doin' again? D'you know wha'?" Sidney slumped forward in his chair, leaning on his elbows on the round, scuffed and scratched pub table at the back of the public bar in the Red Lion, just off the Great West and next to Brentford Station. The dark wood panelled walls drifted in and out of focus, hanging thick and sick with tar yellows and a tan painted ceiling. Lights burned dimly under red paper shades. The hands on the brewery clock above the bar moved to a quarter past ten. The remaining West London crew, the 56th rear-guard, was down to the last knockings. Sidney and Edwin York, Corporal Edwin York or Yorkie to his mates, were well into their backslapping cups, enjoying the fretful bonhomie's of a still vaguely grateful local clientele.

"D'you…"

"No, Sid, but I'm sure you're gonna tell us like you does", replied Yorkie, leaning back in his chair so as not to breath in the smoke from Sidney's wildly gyrating Craven 'A'.

"Sand…s'what I'm never doin' again. Fuckin' sand… Fuckin' desert shit. Sod that fuckin' Erwin fuckin' Rommel, that's what. No more fuckin' sand…"

Sydney's right elbow, the one holding the cigarette slipped off the table and the man lurched forward, slopping his pint onto the already skinned tabletop. As he slipped forward he broke the tip of the cigarette off on the table edge, dropping the lit tobacco onto the knee of his battledress trousers.

"Shit, shit, shit", he swore, brushing the embers away to reveal a neat black ringed singe mark in the coarse woollen fabric. "Oh, fuck…"

A moment or two of confused prioritisation. "…oh who gives one, anyway, s'not as though…" He waved the moment away, pulled another cigarette out of the Craven 'A' carton, flicked open his petrol lighter and lit up.

Yorkie laughed. "Always were a bleedin' liability, Sid." He paused for a moment wondering if he needed the gents. No, not urgent, not just yet. "Anyways, not even Margate, not even Brighton? No more sand never?" He took a sip of warm brown-red London Pride. He would have a Scotch with the next one.

Sidney shook his head energetically, coughed, wheezed and grinned a brown-toothed grin. "Nope, never. Nor no mud. No bloody building sites for me, mate. Strict the right side of the bookies for me from now on. That an' a bit of this, a bit of that, know what I mean?"

"Not really", replied Yorkie. He did need to pee. Definitely. "Don't s'pose it matters, though. We've done our bit. King and shit. A man's got a right to… well… something like that. We got Labour on the up now. Our time now. It's all changing. That's the thing, Sid, that's the thing to remember… talkin' of which, think on that while I go see a man about a dog." The Corporal stood up unsteadily and started to head for a door at the back of the public bar. "Oh, and I'll have a Scotch an' half. Your shout…"

Sidney nodded sagely, trying to focus on the spindles of

Yorkie's chair. He decided that some sort of definitive flanking, bar-targeted action was needed. He downed the last of his pint, pushed his chair back and started to rise in order to go the bar. As he stood up and started to turn towards the bar his previous lack of focus, that inability to form words and to count chair back spindles, manifested in a human version of the Chinese Knot puzzle. Instead of straightening up on the turn Sydney simple kept revolving, twisting so far around that he tripped himself up, shifted sideways, became tangled up with his own chair's legs and then promptly fell headfirst over the chair back and down onto the floor.

*

In the aftermath, with Sydney wrapped in a rough woollen blanket on one of the bench seats in the front bay window of the bar, the publican and Yorkie finished a late lock-in over a nip or two.

"A man can't send 'im 'ome like that, can he?" said the publican as the two late night drinkers finished their third and final dram.

"No, a man can't do that." Yorkie replied softly. He stood upright, breathed in deeply and then turned to pick up his bags. The publican followed him slowly to the front door of the pub. As the publican unlocked the door Yorkie pondered the midnight hour. He looked over at the deeply sleeping Sydney Newt and said, "Yeah, mate, all tucked up."

Turning to the publican he said, " Look after 'im. See 'im 'ome… He's a bloody hero. Wouldn't believe it, would ya? An' all this man can do in the face of that shit is stagger up South Ealing way, find a place to watch the dawn come up, an' see about 'ome tomorrow."

"Welcome to kip 'ere", said the publican, indicating a bench just like the one that Sidney Newt was currently passed out upon.

"Nah, mate. Need some fresh air." Looking directly at his brother-in-arms, Yorkie continued, "Been breathing that bastard's fogs far too long."

As Yorkie turned and started to head back up the road towards the Ealings he heard the pub door lock snick shut again. He smiled. He laughed. He wouldn't have to see that rotten bloody toe rag again for the best part of a week.

*

Gunnersbury Park at five in the morning. A body slumped against the trunk of a broad Elm under a blanket recently borrowed from a local publican. Sydney Newt was foot sore and faltering after traipsing along the Great West for a mile or maybe two if you included his odd meanderings. Sydney could still feel the dampness of sweat in his hair, a sweat broken out by the effort of heaving body, coat and kit through the still warm August night darks. All was calm now, though, as he ran his fingers through his lank brown hair. The red glow of a Craven 'A' pinpointed a sobering man's place in this sleeping city suburb.

Sidney Newt had woken up an hour or so earlier on the window seat at the Red Lion, stiff and awkward, and with a head shattered by the Fullers' barrage, knowing instinctively that he needed open spaces and clear airs. It took a lot of fumbling with locks on the tatty, boot scuffed back door of the pub, but he eventually managed to slide the bolts and turn a key that sat resolutely wedged in an old mortise lock. He had closed the door quietly, trusting to luck that leaving the door unlocked would cause no harm. He turned towards the east and then walked along Orchard and then Windmill Roads to join the main thoroughfare into the city, all the while balancing kit and swag on his left shoulder. A little way into his early morning constitutional Sydney had taken a recently liberated half-bottle of brandy out of his greatcoat pocket and nearly choked. He would, he decided, save the liquor for another day when he might once again weave fanciful stories and blind prejudices out of the hairs of the dog that bit.

As the last embers of his Elm shaded cigarette faded back into the shadows, Sydney watched the first slices of dark purple and grey slide across the horizon. He stubbed the butt of his cigarette out on the bark of the tree at his back. He dare not risk another tipple, not now that the sun was washing its face, and anyway, he preferred facing the old folks at home grubby but relatively sober. He did pour a little brandy over his fingers, though, to rub away the worst of the birdcage droppings from his gums. What he really wanted was cold water.

Sydney suddenly remembered a little local geography. Gunnersbury Park. Over by the pavilion, down along the far side of the bandstand, heading back towards Lionel Road, there used to be a drinking fountain set on a grey granite base. The thought of it brought back memories of long lost summer days. As a child he had spent hours throwing stale bread for the ducks in the circular pond by the Old Mansion house, ducks all iridescent greens and mottled browns. He immediately saw in his mind's eye Moorhens strutting along banks on impossibly thin legs. Sydney heard that distinct but delicate plop of a brown rat skimming sleekly from an exposed tree root. He remembered how his legs were always covered in grazes and cuts. He remembered the wooden slats of a swing leaving splinters in the back of his boyish thighs. Sydney could taste again the weak lemonades made up by his mother. And he felt the sting of the back of her hand, a hand wielded with a dull but penetrating weight whenever he got rowdy and over-excited under towering blue summer skies. It always came back to the back of her bloody hand. The Old Crow should have been a boxer.

Sydney stood up and stretched, hefted his bag onto his right shoulder, and set off slowly in the direction of the old painted bandstand. As he walked the shades and breaks of thinning greys in the sky above him shifted along the spectrum. Cloud edges began to take shape as the sun's rays started to bend ever so slightly through the thinning autumn atmosphere. A hint of blue. A stomach rumbling, announcing the hungers of another day. The sun stoking the old fires. Sydney felt a slight abdominal twitch.

Best get home, he thought. Might soon be time for the old back garden ritual.

He started to hurry, feeling beads of sweat break out at his temples once again. Sydney stopped walking and took off and folded his greatcoat and laid it across his shoulder before hefting the kit bag once more. He considered the greater need and decided to forget about the drinking fountain and the allure of fresh cold water. Movement eased the stomach cramps. Sydney decided to keep going. He crossed Lionel Road and cut through a break in a fence at the back of Clayponds Isolation Hospital before walking down Occupation Lane and onto the South Ealing Road.

The turn into Whitestile Road brought him to a sudden halt. The suburban, leaded bays of these late Victorian and Edwardian villas made his heart race. This was his home. Almost. The old folks lived in a small two-up-two-down on the corner of Enfield Road. Not for them and theirs the luxuries of leaded lights and tiled paths to the front door. The family home's front door opened directly onto the street. And as Sydney felt those old childhood slights of hand come to rest upon his shoulder, even as he remembered the once a week baths in front of the old iron range and the hand-me-downs and the disapproving, wrong-side-of-the-street looks, he still breathed long and hard with the anticipation of warmth and welcome.

Sydney had a plan. This was a new world. He was a soldier. The boys had a right to something better, these homeward bound lads. There would be no more back-handers, not unless they were his to dish out, although he knew in his heart that even the Old Crow deserved better than that. Wars made people change. He wondered what he might find? How were they after all of these letter free years? How would he react back in the family home? Sydney tried to remember the details of how his parents had looked all those years ago, back when he was just a boy.

As he walked slowly along the street his pulse quickened. There were gaps, plots full of rubble and weed and browning buddleia heads. These spaces were filled with burnt out brick shells and splintered window frames and scraps of charred furniture. Cow Parsley and nettles sprouted everywhere that remained broken and untended. The gaps in the fabric of Sydney's suburban streets were irregular and infrequent, but he could count by line of sight to a number high enough that it would make a man take a step backwards.

Number forty was gone. That was where Michael Bence, the kid with the polio legs, had lived with his widowed mother. Both he and Michael were single child litter-runts together, and so they had played as reluctant friends in the quiet spaces vacated by the healthy children. Michael was never destined to be a soldier. He was supposed to be one of the lucky unlucky ones, but the war got him just the same. His home was gone to bombed-out ruin. For a brief moment, and quite unexpectedly, this seemed much worse to Sydney than anything else he had ever seen.

It was still early. The Old Crow would not be stirring just yet. Sydney's Old Man worked nights on the railways… had worked nights… everything felt a little out of the usually cynical kilter. Sydney walked onto the bombsite and found a dropped but uncracked lintel to sit on. The sky was a clear, bright blue now. Early bird sounds and echoes of life were starting to brew. He lit another Craven 'A' as a tear slid down his left cheek and dropped to the dusty earth for poor little, gammy-legged Michael and his beaten down mother. The stomach cramps had eased off by now as Sydney tried to remember Mrs Bence's given name but he failed in that just as he had failed only moments previously to remember the details of his own mother's face.

 Sydney wished then that he had written home more often. Between them all they'd managed maybe one or two letters each a year through to the back end of forty-two when he had been wounded that first time. He had not written again after that. Sydney put it down to a lack of schooling, but his letter writing failures were probably a form of writer's block caused by mechanisms somewhat closer to home. In his haste to get away from the low horizons of these pre-war working class London suburbs Sydney had never felt any regrets. It was the coming home that seemed to open up sallow flaps of skin and expose those old, unstitched wounds.

Sitting on the stone lintel on the bombsite at number forty, Sydney waited out the final hour or so of his homecoming, musing as he smoked on the ways of it all, on the ways of his growing up. As a child and then a teenager he had always been afraid of both of his parents but now he realised that it was the Old Crow who iced his veins.

Soddin' Hitler was a pussycat compared to her, he thought. The Old Man was crude and bluff, but he never went for the belt or the rod. True, they could both shift a mean backhand, but she was always the heavier with the blow.

It occurred then to Sydney that the Old Man only ever went through the motions. All things seemed clear and sharply focussed to Sydney as he sat there in the rubble. She was the catalyst. She liked her gin. She liked her man hard and calloused. The Old Man played the part for her, but Sydney felt that, like most conscripts, his Old Man's heart had never really been in it. He obeyed orders with an inner resignation. Sydney changed his mind, deciding that while the Old Crow might have made a great boxer she would have been an even grander sergeant major, with Sydney and his Old Man worth nothing more than their places in the doomed front rank of the Forlorn Hope. He missed her all the same.

*

By eight o'clock the street was twitching into life. Working men and women headed out for shifts and sundry civilian duties. Sydney did not recognise them. They in their turn paid a man in battledress no more heed than another passing summer cloud. Sydney largely ignored these strangers and their occasionally mumbled 'Good morning' greetings. The first of the summer holiday, raggedy-arsed kids were on the street by now as well and Sydney had already fended off crude requests for cigarettes by the dirty little buggers too many times for his liking. He shrugged the last of the boys off, hefted his kit onto his shoulder and walked the final yards towards home.

His heart skipped a beat when he saw the four-square shapes of his childhood standing strong and firm and dusty brick red. For some years now Sydney had quite lost that sense of relief that came with small victories on the domestic front. War propelled a man outwards but turned a man inwards. The surge of adrenalin that came now with the sight of home caught him totally unawares, and the images of these familiar places blurred. Sydney paused, dropping his bag to the pavement while rubbing the heel of his hand into his watering eyes.

The dulled blue paint on the front door was peeling, revealing a combination of old black gloss and patches of wet rot. The window frames were weathered and grey and crumbling. Sydney ran a finger along the mortar line between two brick courses. He watched the mortar disintegrate under his fingertips and drop to the pavement. A succession of spindle thin dandelions and ragged worts sprouted in the dirt that sat in the cracks between wall and floor. He breathed in deeply and lifted the black wrought iron lion head door knocker. Exhaling loudly he tapped the knocker against the lion's head.

Idiot, he thought.

He raised the knocker and slammed it down. Faint heart ne'er won fair lady, and never the Old Crow. Sydney thought that he heard the sound of chair legs scraping across bare boards, but the door remained firmly shut. He felt like a prize lemon on a show stand out there on the street.

Bloody old gits, he thought, getting lazy and even more unpleasant in their old age.

Then it dawned on him. He had sat and waited out the early morning amid the rubble of number forty half expecting his Old Man to trudge home after his night shift on the tracks, but the Old Man had not made an appearance.

Must be between shifts, he thought. Definitely lazy. Try again. Harder.

This time Sydney heard more pronounced movements behind the door along with a voluble string of oaths. The Old Man was clearly in a foul temper. No change there then. The inner bolts at top and bottom slid back. Sydney heard the key turn. He waited, smiling, expecting the tidal surge of curses to break on the homecoming boy's dam of hung-over happiness. The door swung inwards.

"What the fuck d'ya want?"

Forty-something. Grubby brown trousers held up by braces atop a grey-washed vest. A rollie lodged in the corner of a downturned mouth. Stubble. Brown eyes flashing venom. Bald.

Sydney stood in the street, his kit bag leaning against his right leg, greatcoat draped over his shoulder, open mouthed.

"You fucking deaf or what, soldier-boy. Wha'd'ya fucking want?"

Sydney stammered, all the while checking the number painted on the front door. He quickly scanned the houses to left and right. No mistakes. This was the house in which he had suffered childhood.

"I… I… what the?" he muttered, feeling utterly confused and panicked. He stood there on the pavement dumb and gawping.

"Ain't got time for this shit", spat the bald man at the door. He turned inwards and reached out to slam the door closed. Sydney reacted instinctively, thrusting a boot across the threshold. He stepped forward. He was soldier, a fighting man of the 56th Londoners. His voice broke as he garbled out names and places.

"The Newts… Fred and Edie… me Old Man… lived 'ere for years. I mean… I grew up 'ere. The Newts?"

The bald man stepped back into his front parlour, giving Sydney the evils. "Don't you come any nearer, mate, You know what? Not another step, or else. Don't know nuffin' about any Newts. Been 'ere four years. No one 'ere named Newt. Nah piss off…"

Behind the staccato bravado Sydney could see blind fear in the man's eyes. He felt both strength and weakness. He could just smash the man to the floor. Easy as pie. Years of hates and frustrations. Childish rage. And that was the thing. Sydney felt as small and frail as a five-year-old boy trying to brave the schoolyard bullies while really wanting to run and hide behind his mother's skirts. Except that his mother had done a bunk. The old beaten up pieces of utility furniture were gone. The reproduction Constable above the fireplace was now just a lighter patch of white on a grubby wall. He stepped back from the gloom into the harsh bright light of morning on the street.

"Sorry…" he mumbled as the bald man rushed forward and slammed the front door in Sydney's face.

A vein-popping, bug-eyed caricature appeared at the front room window. A finger pointed threateningly. Sydney could feel curtains twitch across the street. He felt the heat of the morning on his neck. He was in shock. His mind raced. How could they do this? Not even a word? Then again he had to admit to his own faults on that score. Should he ask next door?

Sydney felt the weight of the brandy bottle in his greatcoat pocket rub along his chest as he fidgeted through his indecision. He took the coat from his shoulder, fished in one of the pockets and took the bottle out. He dropped his greatcoat onto the floor, unstopped the bottle and took a long swig for courage. He felt the bitters burn all the way down as he staggered backwards and shielded his eyes from a suddenly fearsome August sun.

Sydney stumbled in confusion and disarray back to the rubble at number forty with his worldly goods dragging behind, and resumed his seat on the lintel stone. He needed time to regroup and gather his strength for his next tactical move. In the meantime he watched crows wheel across the London rooftops. He watched dusts and airborne detritus fall onto brick and weed and stone. Insects hummed and buzzed around his head. He remained stuck in a revolving door, his thoughts and options spinning round and round but never releasing him along any one path of decisive action.

Here he was, he thought, a returning bloody hero put to flight by a fat fucker in a dirty vest.

"Fought for me fuckin' King and Country", he mumbled to the last of the pink bobbing Campion heads. He drained the last of the brandy and lit the last of his current ration of Craven 'A's. A black and white Wagtail hopped and dipped along the edge of an old flower bed now overgrown and thick with nettles.

Sydney nodded as the bird hopped right past his outstretched leg. "Free as a bird, then. S'pose that's it. Fuck 'em. Fuck the lot of 'em. Never bloody liked 'em."

The Wagtail disappeared from view behind a pile of bricks. Sydney continued his monologue regardless. "D'ya know what I ain't never doin' no more, little birdie? I'll tell ya. I ain't never doing sand no more. Never. An' I ain't never doin' fuckin' family. Never again."

Sydney's thoughts drifted to the lines and runes engraved on wood and stone that marked out the resting places of mates long gone now. Africa. Sicily. Italy. France. Sydney considered his position amid all of this carnage, past and present. He might not be a prime specimen, he mused, but he was a survivor. All those lovely boys burned and gone, and here he was, the spindly little runt finishing a ciggy in the bombed rubble of a bastard world.

Sydney stood up, hefted a now chalky white coat and kit bag onto his shoulder one more time and started the walk back towards the South Ealing Road. He felt slightly drunk and he needed to find a tobacconist. He needed a cafe with a bathroom. He headed for the posh bit of town along past the film studios and up by Haven Green. As he walked along the street towards this new and confusing post war civilisation he spoke his thoughts out loud to startled passers-by.

"Clean slate, mate, clean slate."

"Can't choose your fuckin' family, can you?"

"New world, missus, that's what we done out there."

"Got a fag, mate, for a fuckin' war hero?"

Happy Families

(Loosely based on Andersen's Hansel & Gretel)

ONCE UPON A FAIRLY recent time there dwelt in one of the gloomier districts of Leeds a family of four who knew little of the finer things in life. Their lives consisted of a daily battle with the twin demons; struggle and want. The husband and wife tried to work, but with the arrival of a son and then a daughter, they gave up what they felt to be an unequal fight. No one knew whether their situation was one that betrayed a lack of application or a dearth of opportunity. Few, it would seem, cared. The boy was called Kirk and the girl was called Ruby.

By trade the father was a labourer, although through a combination of ill luck and regular run ins with the genie of the bottle, he rarely engaged in his professional calling. His wife took her wedding vows seriously and shared the trials of their marital bed, often lying with him long after the children should have gone to school. In times of plenty the cupboard was rarely full and in times of hardship the children barely had a crust to share between them.

One night, as the husband tossed and turned in his bed with that needful worry that flows from a full stomach and fire in the veins, he turned to his wife and prodded her until she awoke. The man sighed and said to his wife, "What the bloody hell are we going to do? There's never any money left since we had those two brats. I thought we'd do well on benefits, but it barely does more than pay for you and me. With the price of fags and all, there's never enough to buy a round."

As his wife surfaced from beneath the rolling waves of slumber she groaned and mumbled, feeling for a tumbler full of bathroom tap water that should have been on her bedside table. She cursed when she remembered that she had smashed the glass earlier that night when she and her husband romped home from the pub.

"I'll tell you what we'll do", she said irritably. "We'll take them both down to the city centre tomorrow when we go to collect the unemployment. We'll park them on one of the train station benches with a bottle of fizz and then we'll tell the little monsters we'll be back later to collect them. The cops will pick them up, unless one of those perverts gets to them first. They haven't got a clue where we live, so that'll be that".

The husband looked at his wife in astonishment. He was shocked by the grim and determined tone of her voice. He considered the situation for a moment or two and shrugged his shoulders.

"Darling...I like it. Only we'd best make sure there's nothing about them that'll lead the fuzz or the social back here. And we ought to warn them about strangers".

"What?" she asked incredulously.

"Well, I don't want little Ruby being ripped apart by any of those back-street beasts".

"Sod you." said his wife. "It's that or thieving again and my money's on leaving them. I can't be doing with the hassle. It's simple. We can't afford bloody kids and it's not as though we get anything back for all our hard work. No, we'll leave them".

The argument didn't last long. The husband's heart wasn't really in it and he knew he would get no peace if he kept up his pretence of worry for the little girl's soul. They rolled over, lay their heads on their pillows and both were snoring loudly within a minute.

The sound of their parents stirring woke the two children. They had learned through hard experience to sleep lightly, for they never knew when a harsh word or the back of a hand might come their way. As quietly as mice, they sat up in their beds and listened to every word their mother and father exchanged. Ruby was dreadfully upset by the despicable fate her mother had chosen for her and she sobbed quietly into her bedclothes.

"Oh, Kirk, what are we going to do?" she whispered underneath the low rumble of nasal thunder that was brewing in the next room.

"Don't worry", said Kirk, putting a reassuring hand on hers. "I'll work something out. You're my little sister and I won't let anything happen to you, I promise".

Once the pattern of snoring and grinding teeth settled down in the next room, Kirk slipped out of the bed he shared with his little sister, pulled on a threadbare dressing gown two sizes too small for his arms, and crept downstairs. He sneaked into the living room, which was lit by brilliant white moonlight streaming in from a night bright sky through windows that had never seen any curtains. Then he went fishing through the liberally dishevelled contents of his parents' lives, contents that lived in disarray on a low coffee table propped up by three wooden legs and some house bricks. He carefully avoided the half-finished cartons of Chow Mein. He took extra care whenever his small hands brushed one of the empty cans of strong lager that his mother drank in the afternoons before going down the pub. And there, sitting under a spilled dollop of chicken jalfrezi was the object he was looking for, his parent's council rent book. He slipped it underneath his pyjama jacket and crept back up to bed.

Ruby was waiting for him when he got back upstairs, and she gave him a huge hug when he said to her, "Don't worry, sis, it's all taken care of".

Ruby really wasn't sure how he knew that everything would be all right. She thought about the two of them, small, alone and lost in the big city amongst all of those huge, hurrying adults and she felt terribly afraid. Somehow, though, Kirk's tone of voice reassured her that they would get through it all and she fell asleep in his arms with just the faintest trace of a smile on her lips.

The children's mother woke them shortly after nine the next morning, which was a surprisingly early hour for any of them to stir on a school day.

"Come on you lazy buggers", she yelled, "It's money day down at the social, so get yourselves moving. You're coming with us today".

The family made its usual peremptory visit to the world of personal hygiene, got dressed in whatever reasonably clean clothes came to hand and set out on the number seventy-eight bus that would, with a couple of changes, take them to the black heart of the city. There was little or no conversation on the bus. The two children sat remarkably quietly on the bench seat in front of their parents, holding hands as they watched the wet and glistening streets drift by outside their window. Their mother and father were equally quiet. They were suffering from the combined effects of thumping heads, dehydration and the bile churning nerves that accompany deeds such as the one they proposed to execute that morning.

On the final leg of their bus journey, the husband turned to his wife and whispered conspiratorially, "It's not natural. They're never this well behaved. It's like they know something".

"Don't be bloody pathetic", replied his sour faced wife, as she absentmindedly picked at her fingernails with a broken match head.

She hated public transport now that the buggers in the government, led by that cigar chomping public school twat, had introduced all these smoking bans. It was at least forty minutes since her last fag and she was starting to get really scratchy.

"It's a bloody good job they're behaving themselves. I'm not in the mood for any shit this morning and they'll get it if they play up. Anyway, what does it matter? It'll all be over soon enough, and we'll be off, free and easy, like magpies".

All the way to the great vaulted station that stood at the heart of the city like a huge steel-roofed cathedral, Kirk kept one hand tightly closed around little Ruby's cold and trembling fingers, while with the other hand in his coat pocket he kept a tight grip on his parent's rent book. If his parents had bothered to look into his small and grimy face they would have been chilled to the bone to see the cold and steely determination burning behind his bright blue eyes.

When they arrived at the station the family went straight through to the main concourse and found a vacant wooden bench that wasn't covered in too many pigeon droppings. The children were made to sit at one end of the bench with their father while the mother went off to buy a couple of bottles of fizzy pop and a packet of jammy biscuits.

Once she had unscrewed Ruby's bottle top and given the biscuits to Kirk, she turned to the father and said, "Okay, time to go and sign on". Then she spoke to her children in what she hoped was a reassuring and loving voice. "Oi, Kirk, look after your sister. We'll be gone for an hour, at least, so don't move off this bench. Remember, if the boys in blue start asking questions, your mums just nipped off to the loo. I don't want no trouble, so keep yourselves to yourselves 'til we get back".

With that both she and her husband hurried out of the station and headed towards the bus stop. Once they thought they were safely out of their children's line of sight, they lit much-needed cigarettes, took the smoke down into their lungs in huge gulps and started to laugh and cough all at the same time. In the station, under a huge steel sky, the two children sat quietly amid the hustle and bustle of bags and feet that rumbled by oblivious to their plight.

Kirk and Ruby remained sitting quietly on the bench for an hour. No one pestered them or asked them if they were alright. At precisely one minute past the hour, when he was sure the coast was clear, an older gentleman in a well-cut suit came and sat on the bench. He asked them if they were waiting for someone, but both of the children stuck fast to their promise not to talk to strangers. The older man asked them if they wanted something to eat and even suggested to them that he might take them to a nice little cafe just around the corner, but still they sat in mute silence. This relatively civilized introduction to importuning went on for a few minutes more until interrupted by the approach of two railway policemen. The older gent's self-preservation skills flickered into life as soon as he saw the approaching policemen, and by the time the boys in blue reached the two abandoned children the older gentleman was nowhere to be seen.

"What have we got here, then", said one of the policemen as his colleague made enquiries over his two-way radio. "Two little runaways, or are we just out for day's sightseeing?"

He tried to sound as light and as jovial as he could, but his eyes spoke a different language, revealing a mix of concern and tiredness in the face of so many disappointments. The children were taken away and given a hot drink in the office at the back of the station. There followed a succession of visitors, all of whom took the utmost trouble to check on the children's health and on their background. Kirk and Ruby refused to tell anyone anything other than that they were lost. Eventually, armed with the address printed in the rent book, the police handed the kids over to a lady from social services and filed their report, a copy of which was sent to the local police station where Kirk and Ruby lived.

There was an awful scene back at the family home when Kirk and Ruby arrived in the back of a police car. Their mother, who hadn't yet hit the cans, made a real fuss of them and told the assembled figures of authority that they were always running away and she was so relieved they had been found. She explained that her children had left for school as normal that morning and she had no idea they were playing truant in the big city.

"I mean, its fucking unbelievable, isn't it?" she said, making cow eyes at one of the police constables. "Anyway, thanks for bringing them back. I'll make sure my husband gives the two of them a right bloody bollocking when he gets back from work!"

"Back from the pub, you mean", muttered Kirk.

The lady from social services made a note to put the children on her 'At Risk' register and arranged with the mother to call back in a few days to make sure everything was alright. The policeman and policewoman who had driven the children home made a note to mark the house down as a potential source of trouble.

That evening, with a four-pack empty on the already crowded coffee table, their mother subjected both of the children to another verbal assault while their father sat slumped in an alcoholic stupor in front of the television.

"You see what you do to us, do you? Do you? Your father was so sick with worry he's gone and made himself ill. After all we've done for you. After all the love we give you is this all we're ever going to get back? We'd all be better off if they'd taken you to a home. Now, you can piss off upstairs and go to bed without any tea."

For about a week things returned to a state resembling normality. The children's parents rose late into the morning, unless it was benefits day, and hit the pubs at lunchtime. They sat watching mindless garbage on the television late into the night while they consumed more alcohol and smoked so many cigarettes that they regularly exploded in apoplectic fits of coughing. The kids did the best they could to keep themselves to themselves and to fill their half-starved bellies with scraps and leftovers from takeaways and half-finished fry-ups.

Then late into the small hours of another disturbed night Kirk woke Ruby up and told her to be very quiet. Their parents were talking about them again in the next room. The children heard their mother speaking first.

"It's all shit again. There's no money until next Wednesday unless you get off your fat arse and do some robbing or begging or something. I've got half a loaf downstairs and two fags left. We've got to get rid of those bloody millstones. You listening?"

"Yeah, yeah, listening", mumbled her husband as the wardrobe swayed gently in and out of focus.

"I read in the papers about these adoption agencies. All legal, well almost. They pay you for your kids then spirit them away to some poor sod that's got more money than sense. Two grand, it said".

"How much?" slurred her husband.

"Two bloody grand. You know a few people, you know, the ones who buy car stereos off you and that. They must be able to point you in someone's direction."

The husband felt something stir inside him, something that told him this was wrong, but he buried it again quickly. He was already complicit in the conspiracy and once committed he knew there would be no turning his wife from her course. And there was the matter of two grand to consider.

Kirk and Ruby listened in horror as they heard the conversation continue in the next room. Their father was going to start making discreet enquiries the very next day, while their mother was going to invest some of her meagre weekly allowance from the government in new second-hand clothes to make sure the kids were presentable.

"But I don't want to go and live anywhere else", whimpered Ruby. "This is our home".

"Shhh, don't cry, Ruby, don't cry. We're not leaving here. I'm going to think up a plan. Shhh, don't worry, I won't ever leave you alone". Kirk cuddled his little sister in his arms once again and rocked her gently until she drifted off into the troubled land of her dreams.

Over the next few days the children lived in a world of hushed whispers and furtive glances. While their parents made their plans for an unencumbered future and discussed the possibilities that a large amount of ready cash might bring, Kirk and Ruby spent their time in their bedroom playing with Ruby's toy kitchen set.

Their mother, having bought them some nearly new trainers and a couple of faded tee shirts each, spent the rest of her money on fags and booze. It being cold and grey outside, there was little incentive for their father to go out and find work or to relieve unsuspecting motorists of their mobile entertainment systems, and there was little food in the house and certainly no warmth. It was no surprise when the day came for the visit of the social worker that the children were left alone in the house to greet her.

When the doorbell rang Kirk answered the door and asked the lady to come in. He told the lady that his mother had just popped next door to borrow some sugar so that she could make a cup of tea and she wouldn't be long.

"So, how are you both?" asked the social worker. "No more little trips out and about, I trust".

"No, miss, we've been very good all week", Ruby called out from the kitchen.

Kirk tried to show the lady into the living room, but she said she preferred to do these things in the kitchen.

"It's usually makes people feel more relaxed if we sit around the kitchen table", she said.

Kirk followed her into the kitchen, smiling at Ruby from behind the lady's back.

The lady from social services let out a small shriek as she entered the kitchen. There, in broad daylight, Ruby was trying to light a really old and very large gas oven with a lighter so that she could boil the kettle. The lady rushed over and snatched the lighter out of Ruby's hand and turned off the gas. Then she opened the kitchen window and started to wave a dish cloth in the air saying, "Goodness me, what a terrible pong. Now, little one, you can't boil a kettle in the oven, can you".

"But I can't reach the cooker bit", said Ruby, "I'm only small".

"Here, let me", said the lady and she filled the kettle full of water, set it down on the hob and lit the burner.

"Anyway, the oven won't work. That's why it smells of gas", said Kirk.

"Really", said the lady, "let me have a look"

She opened the oven door and bent down so that she could poke her head inside. As she squatted down awkwardly with her head in the oven, Kirk and Ruby moved silently around behind her. They picked up the kitchen broom and without saying a word they hit the lady really hard on the bottom so that she rolled headfirst right into the oven. Kirk slammed the door shut, turned the gas up full and hit the button that fired up the automatic pilot light.

Having raided the lady's purse to get enough money to buy the necessary ingredients, the children spent the rest of the afternoon working out how to make pastry by reading their mother's solitary and previously pristine cookbook. By teatime every work surface, every utensil, the floor and every appliance were covered in blobs of congealed dough and snowstorms of spilled flour. The children resembled pygmy zombies from a second-rate horror flick, but there in the middle of the kitchen table was a beautiful meat pie steaming away in readiness for the return of their inebriated parents.

Sometime later mother and father rolled through the door in the middle of a heated argument about the pros and cons of holidays in the sun and gambling trips to Las Vegas. It appeared that mother was winning, and the bright lights of the Nevada desert would soon be graced by two new high rollers with money to burn. The argument ceased abruptly when the adults saw the mess covering every inch of the kitchen and every last hair on their children's' heads.

"What the bloody..." stuttered father.

"What the hell have you done now?" screamed mother.

She exploded into the kitchen in a blind rage and laid about her with extreme prejudice. Cups and plates went spinning through the air to smash on the floor and against the walls. The huge pie dish slid all the way down the table and spilled its contents all over poor little Ruby, who wailed and screeched and sobbed. Father stood in the hallway open mouthed as his wife raved and ranted at the kids and chased them up and down the stairs until she came to a sudden, spluttering, coughing halt.

While Kirk wiped the pie juices off Ruby's clothes with the bedspread, the frightened little girl called out to her mother from behind the bedroom door.

"Mummy...mummy...we only...mummy, we got some food and we wanted to make you and daddy a lovely pie for your tea. We thought..."

"You thought what exactly?" screamed their mother from the living room. "You thought you'd make my life hell is what you thought. What the blazes will the social lady think tomorrow when she comes back and finds the place looking like a bomb's hit it."

The children barricaded themselves in their bedroom, but their parents made no attempts to break in. Instead they went back to the pub, via a local car park, and didn't come home until the wee small hours.

Kirk and Ruby didn't sleep a wink that night. Instead, they talked and they talked until they made sense of the world. They carefully hid the social lady's handbag in their wardrobe, safe in the knowledge that their mother would never find it in there. It took three attempts to get the counting right, but they were now the proud owners of two credit cards, a cheque book and quite a lot of ready cash.

While their parents slept on peacefully, the children crept

downstairs and as the dawn sky uncurled from its slumbers they cleaned every last inch of the kitchen. Kirk wrapped a cloth around the broom and scrubbed the floors and the walls, while little Ruby stood on a kitchen chair and washed all of the pots. Together they scoured the cooker and when it was all done Kirk ran down to the corner shop with some of their money to buy some more ingredients and a fresh packet of cigarettes for their mother.

Towards lunchtime father emerged from his pit and stumbled down to the kitchen. He had the worst hangover in the whole wide world and he felt physically sick as he remembered the state of chaos that he and his wife had left behind them the previous evening, but when he opened the kitchen door he was blinded by the dazzle from the work tops and the gleaming surfaces of the kitchen appliances. Kirk seized the moment and gave him a nudge in the back. In his confused state the man lurched forward in surprise, still dazzled by the glittering kitchen, and tripped over the open oven door. His upper body and head fell across the hob, where Ruby was waiting with the frying pan. The rest was simple, if hard, work.

By the time that their mother surfaced to greet the day, there was a nice stew bubbling away on a slow heat in the kitchen. She couldn't remember a thing about the end of the evening and assumed that her bloke had buggered off somewhere. The kids said they had already eaten but there was plenty left if she wanted some proper food for a change. Their mother looked at them. She had no idea why they were suddenly starting to be useful, but with a fresh packet of fags laying open on the kitchen table, with the kitchen cleaned, with something smelling lovely bubbling away on the cooker and with a head that was hosting a motorway maintenance crew, she didn't feel inclined to argue. Kirk laid the table and Ruby dished up a huge plate of fresh, fatty stew. Their mother sat at the kitchen table and accepted with a shrug the food that was being served to her by her smiling offspring.

"He'll be back", she said to herself as she tucked into the first plate of proper home cooked food she'd had in a long, long while.

And for all that anyone knows this happy family still lives in one of the gloomier districts of Leeds. Social services raised the alarm when one of their staff went missing, but no one considered it possible that two small children might have something to say on the matter. With father gone, Kirk and Ruby grew up to be fit and healthy young people, living in the company of a number of long-lost uncles who visited the family home all too briefly, and never, ever seemed to be around on the day that Kirk and Ruby made stew for their mother.

Devil in the Detail

IT COULD HARDLY BE called a kick. Despite years of neglect made visible by thin, almost transparent patches of rust and jaggedly flaking automotive paint, the front wing of the little Austin Metro barely flexed under heel. It was raining fit to flood the world, a storm brewing up with the wailing mewl of legion cats being chased by battalion dogs. The driver of this last example of a long since fallen British automotive empire splashed disconsolately towards the rear of the vehicle, depressed the already sticking boot release with the heel of his right hand, and heaved at the tailgate with his left. He could barely see through the streams of water running across his horn-rimmed, circular, bottle glasses, and to look at him dripping and sodden in brown tweed and corduroy waistcoat, as thin as a rake and far too short to be a policeman, you would think him incapable of exerting the slightest force upon fresh air. He pulled at the tailgate, screwing up his scrawny, twitching features, and slowly but surely, emitting mineral groans and metallic shrieks, the metal and glass door began to inch upwards until, with the tailgate at seventy-five degrees, the little man was able to clamber onto the space made by the flattened seats, cross his legs, and utter a loud harrumph.

"Bloody car", he muttered. "Bloody sodding British Leyland. Bloody Red Robbo. Seemed like such a good idea at the time. Just goes to show you, doesn't it!"

The little man, who looked to all intents and purposes like a fifty-year old accounts clerk, the sort of man who is equally hen-pecked and ignored because his entire being is made up of nothing but disappointment, pulled a red handkerchief from his jacket pocket, wiped first his brow and then his glasses, and then finally, and with an almighty bulge, he blew his nose. It was just a question of time, he thought, just a question of waiting. He stared out of the back of the Metro, stared down the long, straight highland road, and settled himself into a damp and steamy slump. He seemed to know instinctively that eye of the storm would come from the east, from the direction that lay behind him, in his long distant past, and slumped forward as he was, he began, as he always did in such circumstances, to count the tufts in the grey and threadbare boot carpet.

*

Moving like a dense, liquid shadow across the deeps of the ocean, a black Aston Martin swept spray and stones out from under its wheels as though the driver was desperate to dam the flood before it should lift Noah's ark from dry-dock. The car bent the feeble light of afternoon, absorbing the dull residue of day under dusky thunder-heads, so that nothing definite, no edge, no gleam of paintwork could be discerned by the passer-by, and with good reason. The vehicle sported crepuscular additions and modifications such as fins and bat wings, horns, antlers, crossed bones and the flying remains of bloody pelts, and hanging from the rear-view mirror was a collection of shrunken Jivaroan heads, each one bobbling with every bump and twist as if in wild, drunken conversation. The driver of the diabolical sports coupe hammered the throttle at every turn, singing raucously and with absolute abandon every word of O Fortuna from the opening of Carmina Burana.

He wore black from head to toe, was tanned and lean under a shock of black, flowing hair, showing the aquiline profile of a true son of the Julian clan, except for the silver bar that pierced the bridge of his nose. He wore eye-liner as black as coal, and constantly flipped the sun visor up and down to check his reflection in the mirror as he spun the car through sluicing puddle and gravitational turn. To finish the demonic effect, a stuffed raven mounted on a piece of polished mahogany was nailed to the rear parcel shelf. The driver laughed out loud as he surveyed his little world of perfectly stitched cow hide, walnut veneer and deathly totem. The effect was just as he wished it to be today. In the fullest and most satisfied of baritones he let rip the lines:

"hateful life

first oppresses

and then soothes

as fancy takes it"

With the rain slanting across the road and the windshield wipers sweeping furiously across glass, the black Aston shimmied around a tight right-hand bend, sliding out at the back. Opposite lock. Ease off the power and then on again. A brief flash of red brake light in the gloom and then the snake back onto the straight and true. Revolutions. The growl of pistons exploding as they chewed up fuel. The driver beamed like a supernova going critical, lighting up the cabin with his wide, wild eyes and his deep bellow. The road stretched out before him, long and dark and shining, just as the crow flies towards a departing soul. The car kicked once and lifted at the front end as the tyres fought for grip, and then, amid a sea of spray, she bit hard into the tarmac and hauled her graceful weight forward at an ever-increasing rate of knots. The joy of it. The driver revelled in the fact that he could see virtually nothing, sure in the fact that he was master of the little that he needed to survey, certain in the knowledge that nothing in this world could alter the progress that he made towards his next destination. He knew not where that destination might be, only that he would be there when it happened, when the cataclysm erupted. He was always there. Always.

*

Out on the hard shoulder, cocooned within the thin metallic hull of his dilapidated Austin Metro, the small wee man in tweeds and corduroy had now counted for nearly an hour, but instead of marshalling his thoughts towards the infinite number of tufts woven into the boot carpets of this modern, global, automotive world, he found now that his concentration wavered. He looked up and back out along the road, and there, sure as eggs are eggs, he saw headlights piercing the dank mildews of the afternoon. Despite the driving rain and the whipping wind, he heard the growl of the monstrous motor clearly. He cocked his head, listening for the tell-tale whistle of slipstream and the dark, forbidding rumble of eighteen-inch rims, and then smiled. It was a long time, an epoch or more, since they had last met, this accountant and the onrushing demon in black, but now the time had come to ask again that one fundamental question. They were, after all, brothers of the blood, members of the same trade guild, and as such the one would surely stop for the other.

The ribbon of wet sheen running towards the horizon begged the driver of the Aston Martin to put his Cuban heeled boot through the floor, and he duly obliged. The car sat up and seemed to skim across the surface water like a steroidal jet ski, and still he pushed and pulled at the wheel, desperate for more speed. At first the driver thought that the dull, humped shape at the side of the road was just a rocky outcrop or an orphaned section of dry stone wall. The road was straight and true. He had no need to pay attention to any landscape other than that small slice of the world contained between the edges of this black speedway, and yet, as he reached terminal velocity, something made him notice the further extremes of possibility painted upon the horizon, beyond the vortex that he created.

The shape by the side of the road began to take on a disturbingly amusing familiarity. It was pig-like, a creature that grunted and snuffled through the undergrowth at the margins of every road, short and hunch-backed and wallowing. Just one second later, with another impossible distance of road covered, he saw an opened bonnet. He laughed long and hard again, booming out his mirth in the womb-like cabin of his thoroughbred steed. The thing out there was nothing more than a flea, a parasite on the arse of an Arabian stallion, and yet, like that flea, this dull object existed in imperfect partnership with the king of horsepower.

The flea could also ride the wind and run before the desert storm, just as he, the demon was doing now.

He felt compelled to look into matters more closely. He felt a sudden, urgent curiosity that brooked no flight or fancy. He simply had to prod and poke, and so, stamping on the brakes, he sent the car into a slide, spinning her round on the tarmac amid a wail of ebrased rubber and straining chassis bolts, until, with the hills and the sky melded into one grey-green-purple blur, he found himself some four hundred metres beyond the porcine wreck, facing back the way he had come. He smiled in anticipation of the stick and the squeal, and made the Aston Martin growl back along the road slowly and with extreme prejudice.

*

The diabolic driver of the Aston Martin pulled up alongside the Metro and peered through the passenger window at the wreck of a car parked on the hard shoulder. His gaze was returned from a face in obscure profile, ringed with a moist halo of condensation. A drowned rat, he thought, a drowned rodent waiting out the flood in his shabby little nest, and yet he felt a certain thrill at the sight of this weedy little specimen, as though they were joined by an invisible umbilical cord. He manoeuvred the Aston Martin onto the hard shoulder and stilled the throbbing beast. The rain seemed to be easing off, although the sky remained low and smothering. He opened his door, climbed out of the car, and stretched himself out to his full height and width.

As a physical specimen, he was entirely the opposite of the poor wretch sitting cross legged in the back of the Metro. Standing at more than six-foot-tall, with a broad expanse of muscled chest revealed beneath his snugly fitted black shirt, the creature epitomised vigour and action, an unstoppable force made flesh. As he walked he could feel his hard and defined physique ripple under tight, figure-hugging cloth. His face wore a permanent smile, a smile that started in his eyes and spread across the full depth of his features, a smile that warned, a smile that promised destruction once the fun was done with.

On reaching the broken down little heap, he wrenched the tailgate fully open with leonine ease, bent down, and peered into the darkling interior of the vehicle's boot space. "What in the name of all the fates have we got here?" he mused, grinning. "Ah, yes, the runt of the litter. Homo Patheticus. An ACCOUNTANT, if I'm damned!"

"It's all very well you saying that", squeaked the mousey little man, "standing there like Adonis, but I'll have you know I'm not afraid of you. Oh no, certainly not. I knew you'd stop…and I'm a very good accountant. The best."

The man in black paused for a second, and then stood up again, puffing out his chest, and roared, "Not afraid? NOT AFRAID! Don't you know who I am? Ha! I am Death, the destroyer of worlds, the bringer of the final pain and the ultimate darkness. I am he who sweeps away mortal dust. I am the storm, the tempest, the earthquake, the volcano, before which nothing can stand!"

Under a damp and billowing sky, he towered over the accountant, hands on hips, and waited for the whimper, but the only the sound to be heard was the scud and rasp of wind though stubby heathers and grasses, and a slight, almost effeminate cough. The little man in tweed and corduroy slid forward and sat on the lip of the boot, dangling his legs over the precipice between bodywork and muddy gravel. He looked up at the giant in black. "So am I, in a way", he said quietly, wiping condensation from his thick, bottle glasses.

"What?" roared the leviathan beast standing on the hard shoulder. He bent forward again, gripping this non-descript, runtish specimen by both shoulders. Face to face, spitting fire and brimstone and venom, he roared, "Watch!"

The world seemed to split in two, with each half spinning in a different direction, creating a whirlpool of light and matter, through which images began to appear. With each vision of destruction, the man continued to roar out his accomplishments.

"I it was who threw down Knossos and trampled the Greeks underfoot with Persian soldiers. Pompeii fell under my gaze. I was the surge that killed millions by the banks of great Huang He, and it was I who blew the winds of the Bhola Cyclone so hard that men and women crumpled."

With each item listed in his panoply of destruction, images flowed and twisted together, images of limbs and contorted faces, of blood and bone and rock, and in the midst of it all, as if conducting a violent symphony of discord, there stood the man in black, his flowing locks streaming in the winds and currents of calamitous fatality as his arms gesticulated wildly.

"See me! There! It is I who ruptures the earth to make mountains out of the sea. San Francisco was a moment of merriment, and Ashgabat and Kanto and Tangshan. The Black Death I made in your image, flea, and my coup de grace…I was the Somme and Passchendaele and Ypres, and then, when the boys came home, I was the mutant influenza. I am famine, I am a feast of mortality, and where my journeys end, wherever I choose to lay my head, there will come the end of days for millions. I was the horror propelling the imaginations at the Wannsee Conference, the obliterator of souls in their mass confusion and terror. I was Ethiopia. I am the mud slide and the flood. I am the crack and the fissure and the disintegration of Chernobyl. I am catastrophe!"

Amid the flames and falling limbs, the man in black burned and fevered, recounting every event, every malevolence, every act of desolation, and through it all he smelled again the viscera of sweet perfection, except that in the telling of these disasters, as each tale and count multiplied, so he also smelled the dust of extreme, paper-thin age. The stench of slow decay and natural putrefaction, of simple eternal failing, filled his nostrils and gagging, he broke the spell. The images vanished and the world snapped back to the dull grey of light rain falling on barren hills. He thrust the little man back into the boot of the Metro.

"You!" he shrieked, pointing at the unkempt little accountant as the man slowly emerged again from the rear of the car.

"Yes. Me." replied the accountant. "I knew you'd get there. Eventually. You've changed. When we started all this you were…smaller…less bombastic."

The accountant stood up, the crown of his head reaching only the breasts of the man dressed in black. Thrusting his hands into his jacket pockets so that he could draw it close around him to keep out the chill of the twilight breeze, the smaller of the two men stepped out into the road and looked first East and then West. There was nothing to be seen, nothing that signified light and life and hope. The monster in black took an involuntary step back towards his own car, and seemed to shrink visibly in height and width.

"And you" whispered the startled man in black, "you look so unadventurous, so benign…so invisible. How…no. I see it. Each of us becomes more and more what and how we are. For a true killer, brother, you're mean on the eye."

The accountant shrugged his shoulders, took a packet of low tar cigarettes from his jacket pocket and offered one to his companion, who shook his head. "Suit yourself", he said as he lit up and inhaled deeply. "It's not as though it makes any difference". He offered up a thin smile.

"Do you remember the bet? Of course, you do. Daft bloody question. All those ages ago, back when the apes crawled out of the trees and first began to name the rocks and the winds and the moon as gods…we agreed then that we'd each take them, in our way, and see who could claim the most souls…"

He took another long drag on the cigarette.

The lion in black tossed his mane and stood tall once again, recovering his composure. "I remember the bet", he replied, "and the optimism of our youth."

"I have to say you're impressive these days, in spite of your age, and your inventiveness is stunning. Just when I think you can't come up with anything new you give me Pol Pot…quite brilliant. You put me to shame really, with my little ways and my tidy ledgers…bar one fact. You're falling behind, brother, a long way behind in the counting. Every little death, every disappointment, every tiring of the spirit, they're all mine, remember. I am the cloud, the dullness of depressions that slip ankle and bind neck. I am all those moments when the poor creatures realise that everything is in vain. I don't do glossy, brother. I'm not the spectacular, the summer blockbuster, no, I'm the winter chill in their bones. I am the reason why they wait out the years without hope. None of its dramatic, not in your way…I mean, how do you make a public drama out of the long drawing down of a cancer, or the slow meander of a mild epidemic, or that fatal nudge into oncoming traffic? Oh, I do things with a flourish sometimes, I suppose, the knife and the psychosis, but no, my book is made up of dark matter, whereas yours lists the stars that shine for bright, sparkling mortality. Unlike you, who prefer a broad brush, I see the intricate beauty of the devil in the detail. So, brother, I've sat here in the rain with one purpose. As ever I'm here to ask…do you concede?"

With that he stubbed out his cigarette, walked away from the man in black towards the front of his battered old car, and slammed shut the bonnet. Behind him he heard a deep sigh followed by a long intake of breath. Here it comes, he thought, the pomp and splendour.

"I will never concede", roared Goliath in his mourning attire. "I have a new plan, brother, a new device, subtle and sure and global. Waters rise even as we speak. The furnace heats. A tide swells, a tide of souls that moves to my imperial call as inevitably as the seas ebb and flow to beckoning mother moon. We'll count again soon enough and see how the reckoning falls. Even then, I doubt if either one of us will give the other satisfaction."

They both stood in the middle of the road now facing one another, the giant standing with his hand on his hips, his hair thick and full on the wind, while the mouse stood hunched in his jacket, his glasses perched on the end of his thin nose. They looked each other in the eye for a moment, each of them dipping into the well of endless night, before breaking away and staring out towards the scarred hillsides leading towards Ben Mor Coigach.

"You'll be off on your way, then?" asked the smaller of the two.

"I must. Destiny calls my little fish to the net. What about you? Your transport looks a little dishevelled?"

"Yes. It is, as you put it, somewhat dishevelled. Anyway, I'm tired of it. I believe a lady of a certain age will come along the road shortly in a late model Ka. That's a safe and reliable little car, I believe, and anyway, I must have a chat with her about the disappointment she feels with her fat and flabby husband. Maybe, in her grief, I can make her an offer she won't be inclined to refuse; an autumnal, evening walk upon the mountain for her, perhaps, in return for a slow descent into diabetic coma for him?"

The brothers both smiled, being equal and opposite parts of each other, the reticent introvert and the feral extrovert, the immovable object and the unstoppable force. Before he climbed back into the cockpit of his thoroughbred machine the black clad beast stopped and turned to look once more upon the now wistful face of his twin.

"I suppose there really is no end to this, is there?" he asked.

"Not as long as there's an unclaimed soul, a red ink pen and an accounting ledger to hand", said the other, reaching for another cigarette.

Barley Sour

SHAGGY DOG. THAT'S WHAT I said to the man. A long story. It's not as though I meant any harm. You don't vandalise oak doors for no reason, not that I think it was vandalism, not in the true sense. Auden. Stopping the clocks. Just wanted to say Arrivederci Roma, thanks for all the fish, you know, so long and goodbye.

Bottom line is he was a mate. I miss the stupid bastard. We drank together. Played Aunt Sally on a Friday night. Throwing sticks at the dolly. Getting pissed, incoherent, and that's the truth. That's the bloody thing. Got pissed and got caught. Fair play.

Look, let's get a few things straight. You'll want to know what happened. Fuss over nothing in my opinion, but the law is the law. I'm not arguing, just explaining.

The way I remember, I'd had a few at The Bird, Thursday lunch time, strippers out the back, hard faced, you know the ones. The sorts that look at the walls and not the punters. Shit job, but the lads love it. It was his last hurrah, one for the boys, a touch of something noble, a dram and a vol-au-vent, sort of hushed and respectful, but that wasn't Jimmy's way.

I stayed on and had a few more bevs, catching the early shift on their way home from work. To be fair, Don, the landlord, suggested it might be a good idea if I pissed off before the eating classes parked their Mercs in the pub car park. What's a man to do? Easy. Walk round the corner and blag a pint at the Red Lion.

That's when the slate and the granite kicked me in the guts. Jimmy held, despite outward appearances, a family tradition true to his heart. Catholicism. Sunday Mass followed by dominos and a bloody good drink. I managed to keep everything straight till nine, even though the low lights were burning, but then the tears came. Already had one landlord on my case so I left the good folk of the High Street drinking club and hit the offy.

A point of honour. Kids by the door. Told them to sod off. I don't care what their parents earn, I've never taken money off a teenage alchy. Bought my own and told them where to go. Slags. No respect. Saint Paul, were he a drinking man, would have an epistling fit. Letters to Threshers.

Anyway, I bought a bottle of Grouse and headed up to where the arches are curved and keystones look anaemic.

Now, I admit the thing about the gate. It's got one of those spring loaded catches on it and I tried, but it had been a long day. No disrespect. The Good Lord, Jimmy's Good Lord, knew I didn't mean any harm. I tried a couple of times, but the flat sole of a Doc Martin boot was the only way in the end.

Rustling. The graveyard shift. Poets have words for it. Fucking creepy. Jesus. I didn't want to sleep with leathery old bats and incontinent grand-dads. The lights were on around the bell tower but there was no obvious way in. The wind was sighing in the uncut grasses around headstones. You feel like someone's breathing down your neck. At the back of the place an old bush leans white wood against a porch. The oak door.

Breaking and entering. It pays to have a long shaft screwdriver in your coat pocket. It's a village. Everything rusts. The sum total of the damage was a bust padlock.

It's dark. What do you do? Then, out of the corner of your eye you see candles in wrought iron holders in the walls. I lit a fag and set the wicks to burning. Whispers. Circles of flame. Green and gold. Mother's Union. Banners and banns. Collecting for the Sudanese. As a rule I prefer fire light in its proper place, the saloon bar grate, but I was on a mission.

By the font, to the left of the main aisle under a slatted wooden hymn board, I mounted a couple of steps. Oratory. Bloody eloquent, I was. Ten pints eloquent topped up with a quarter of Grouse. Away with the words. Dearly beloved. We come not to praise the bastard but to bury him. Jimmy Effing Caesar. Lend me your ears. Eat your heart out Christian Barnard.

Grouse is a strange blend, at least it was that Thursday. The pews were stacked with the regulation Women's Institute embroidery cushions, perfect as pillows, but the front row had old, creaking, leather medicine balls to play with. I lay down by the altar with candlelight swimming through my tears and I unscrewed the bottle top. Thin pink lips. A chill on the air. The unscrewing of absolution.

That, of course, was my mistake. Denim legs stretched out on cold flagstones. God knows I looked good. Vanity. A single voice by candlelight. My congregation was the lumps of mud on the stones that I'd scraped off the soles of my boots on the uneven edges of the slabs. I felt toppled, like a gravestone. The Word was etched on my forehead. That's what happens when you commune with phantoms and the better part of seventy hundred and fifty mil of barley sour.

Alcohol thins the blood, so they say, and a good thing too, only not when you're lying on cold stones. I started to drift, started to see things. I was sure old Jimmy was in the room. Not in person, of course, but in his box. I remember silver screw heads gleaming in the candlelight. Handles too, and soft oak veneer. I had to raise a salute, had to slur out a few odd sentimental phrases at the dry stone walls.

I toasted the box and bade Jimmy a fond farewell. Then my knees started to buckle and I bottomed out, flowing down the tube like liquid mercury on the cold night air. Last thing I remember is dragging the alter cloth down with me and wrapping it around me like a blanket. That and the laughter. Back on Church Parade after all these years. Akela would have been proud to see one of her little cherubs returning to the fold.

Missed the funeral, of course. The Old Bill took my belt and boot laces, and left me to sleep it off. Seems I made a bit of a scene. Made too much noise. As I said to the magistrate, me and God are like that over a large snifter.

I don't think he appreciated my newfound friendship with the Great Bearded One. The bugger bound me over to keep the peace, gave me eighty-hours of community service and costs. The priest was a brick, though. Waived the fine so long as I spent some of my good works time fixing up the door and fitting a new lock, which I duly did. Stupid bugger let me buy the padlock. A cheap one. You know the sort; all the keys are the same. Bought two. Now I've got my own set of keys.

These days I go round the back and cross the graveyard from the football pitch behind the church. Keeps the neighbourhood watch quiet. Just me, the Good Lord, Saint James, and a bottle of something nice to keep the chill out. I wouldn't exactly say I've been born again, but there's something comforting about the place. I miss that stupid bastard. God alone knows why, which is, I suppose, the simple way of things.

The Phantom of the Sixpenny Stalls

(Loosely based on Le Prince Desir et la Princesse Mignonne by Madame Leprince de Beaumont)

JUST BEFORE THE SECOND of the great wars, towards the middle of the last century, there was a famous movie star, whose face appeared in all of the celebrity magazines of the day. Even now, you can sometimes see him swashing his buck or romancing his true loves under a moonlit sky on a late-night re-run on one of the many satellite film channels. His hair was always immaculately black, his moustache was always pencil thin, and his eyes, even in black and white, held a sparkle and an intensity that has set female hearts racing from that day to this.

The famous movie star was no stranger to the palpitations of the heart either. Towards the twilight of his career he spent one glorious summer on location with a stunningly beautiful young lady, who was co-staring with him in a suitably melodramatic matinee feature. He fell deeply in love with her and longed for the day when he might marry her, but there was a problem. The young lady was not free to marry because she was already married to one of London's larger than life theatrical impresarios, a man famous for his quick temper. In desperation the famous movie star sought the advice of a wickedly wrinkled old socialite who'd had more than her fair share of husbands, lovers and divorces.

This aging 'It' girl lived on a diet of rouge and impossibly scarlet lipstick and when she spoke she was reputed to be able to breathe pure sulphur and brimstone. It was with some trepidation that the famous movie star called on her one afternoon to hear what she had to say about his case of unrequited love. Over tea and cucumber sandwiches the old dear fixed our movie star with a steely-grey eye and spoke imperiously.

"You know that the young lady in question is married to that hateful mogul of dodgy musical reviews. What you don't know, however, is that he was only able to persuade her to marry him because he knew about her illegitimate child. Oh yes, it's true, she had a baby when she was just seventeen. It would be an awful scandal if it ever got out. So, in return for his silence and his support in her stellar career, she has to pretend to be happily married. My advice to you is to bop him on the nose and to call him a cad and a bounder. Then you and the young lady must sell to the most lurid of our newspapers a story of tragedy and heartbreak made good by your true love".

For all of his on-screen thud and blunder, our movie star was not a brave man when it came to the realities of physical violence, but nevertheless, his love for the young lady with perfect skin was just too strong to ignore. He secretly contacted his true love and put the plan to her and without question she readily agreed that it should be done. Together they worked on their stories, on their facial expressions and on their star-crossed gaze, and influenced by the heady aphrodisiac of risks taken in extremis their mutual respect and love for each other blossomed. It wasn't long before the young lady sensed the impending patter of another pair of tiny feet.

Spurred on by the prospect of becoming a father, the famous movie actor collared the evil theatrical entrepreneur one evening as he left the first night premiere of his latest hit musical. With flash bulbs screaming in the dark night sky, he bopped the vile Svengali on the nose, cuffed him around the ears and told him what an absolute scoundrel he was. With the perfect timing borne of many years working in the mire of celebrity shame, the editor of the country's favourite celebrity magazine published a full front page spread the very next morning. Over the ensuing days the general public learned all about the young lady's heartbreak and about the sheer nastiness of the man who was soon to be consigned to marital history's list of theatrical first husbands.

It transpired that everyone who loved cinema and the fragile flowers that blossomed on the silver screen forgave the young lady and wished the happy couple a long and merry life together. All that remained was to complete the divorce proceedings, book the registry office and throw the mother and father of all show business parties.

The final petitions in the divorce case took place on a cold and foggy January afternoon. With everything done and dusted down, the famous movie star and his wife to be left the weakly glowing comfort of the lights in the court building's entrance hall and started to blend into the pale corona of mist and smog smothering London's busy streets. That dastardly old trooper of a first husband had not bothered to contest the proceedings, so neither the famous and happy movie star nor his betrothed little starlet were prepared for his sudden emergence from the gloom.

"So, you're going to marry the brazen little hussy now, I suppose", he hissed. "Well, there's nothing I can do to stop you, but I'll have my revenge. Your son, for it is a boy, will never be happy until he finds out that his nose is too long. And if you ever tell him what I've just said, he'll disappear in a puff of smoke and never be seen again".

There was an awkward moment as the theatrical impresario got his arm twisted in the folds of his cloak, but after a few seconds of muttering and cursing he managed to sweep the black cloth across his face and let out a rough edged, grating cackle.

The famous movie actor was terribly afraid, but somewhere down by his bootstraps he found the strength and the courage to turn and face the spectral figure hamming things up in front him.

"It's all rot and hot air," he stammered. "And anyway, it doesn't matter if he has a long nose. Unless he's blind or an idiot he'll know its size as plain as the…"

The actor's words shattered like glass on the empty cobblestones. The caped phantom had already disappeared into the misty night.

The actor and his bride were soon married and, despite her bump, they made a fine looking couple in all of the magazine features and on the cinema newsreels that tracked the early stages of their new life together. Their happiness was complete some five months later when a fine and healthy son was born. In true movie star style they held a huge christening bash in a big hotel, where they announced to the world their pride and joy in the fact that little Archibald had joined the family.

No more than a year after the child's birth the famous actor met a sticky end when he fell from a fly tower while filming a story about love in a lunatic asylum and his beautiful young wife was left all alone to bring the toddler up. Remaining true to her late husband's dear memory, she eschewed any further relationships and concentrated all of her time and all of her husband's vast fortune on the boy. The child grew lustily and quite dazzled everyone with his sparkling blue eyes. He gurgled delightfully through his perfectly aligned mouth and both family and friends could see that one day he would have the perfect jaw line for robust action roles. They were all, therefore, extremely upset and surprised when his nose started to grow and grow and grow.

The little boy's mother was inconsolable when she saw how long her child's nose was becoming. She remembered the parting curse uttered by her first husband and she feared greatly that she would be the cause of her son's disappearance at any moment. As luck would have it, however, all of her advisors, secretaries, nannies, friends and hangers-on said that the boy's nose was actually very fine; that it was a Roman nose and you only had to open the history books to see how important such noses were. Buoyed by these comments, she felt much better and when she looked again at her child's face his nose certainly didn't seem too long at all.

Archibald was brought up with the greatest of care. As soon as he was old enough to understand things, everyone who came into contact with him was instructed to make the best of his facial feature. Consequently, the child's favourite bedtime stories were nearly all about the terrible things that happened to people with really short noses. No one was allowed to come near him unless they too had a very long nose or was prepared to undergo an hour's worth of work with a prosthetic artist. Friends of the doting mother became so engrossed in the whole nose business that they took to pulling their own babies' noses several times a day to make them grow longer, but no matter how many times they tweaked their kiddies' snouts, not one of them ever came close to matching little Archibald's fine muzzle.

As the boy progressed through childhood and into manhood, he was provided with the finest tutors, all of whom made sure that the men of history, politics and the arts were always described as having extremely long noses. Nothing was left to chance in the boy's education. Every one of his history and picture books was doctored with sticky paper, biro and crayon to make sure that every person featured was shown with the largest of probosci. In short, Archibald grew up so convinced that a long nose was the most beautiful of facial characteristics that he would not on any account consider having his own nose an inch shorter than it was.

And so the years passed until the boy became a man of twenty summers, and his mother decided that he should have a girlfriend. Times had changed and with them had come a more relaxed attitude to courting, but Archibald's mother was determined to continue protecting her long-nosed child. She secretly advertised for a lady companion for her son, using the services of a very discreet dating agency so that she could vet each young lady for her character, for her status and for her facial features. Once she had assembled a list of potentially suitable fillies for her darling boy, she made a gift of their photographs to him and asked him to select those young ladies who might be of interest. Unfortunately, Archibald's mother did not check the photographs properly and stuck to the bottom of the pile was a picture of a most unsuitably button nosed young woman.

Archibald was completely bowled over by this femme fatale's saucy little nose. He refused to look at any of the other pictures, despite his mother's protests, and was absolutely adamant that this was the girl for him. The young lady in question was the only daughter of an oil magnate and would one day inherit a vast fortune and huge estates in several countries around the world, but Archibald couldn't care less about her wealth or her position in the social pecking order. He fell in love in an instant, which caused much consternation in the family home. Some of his mother's friends and some of his tutors had become so accustomed to laughing at small noses that they just couldn't stop themselves criticising Archibald's new-found love. Two of the tutors and a family friend of some twenty years standing were dismissed immediately and told never to darken the doorstep again.

The remainder of the staff, family and friends took the hint and learned how to deal with the situation, always thinking twice before making any further comments to the young man about the way people looked. One particularly clever acquaintance even had the foresight to tell Archibald that, although a long nose was only to be expected in any man of worth, a woman's beauty was quite another thing.

"In fact," he said to the young man, "I know a learned professor who understands Greek and Su Doku and stuff, and he said that he read this old manuscript once and even the beautiful Queen Cleopatra had a button nose".

Archibald was very impressed with this advice and he sent a

message to the young lady asking her if she wanted to meet for a drink one evening. The young lady, being a dutiful daughter, asked her father if it was permitted for her to meet this young man. When her father heard that he was the son of a famous actor, he too was impressed. He felt it would be most appropriate to marry new money to such an established and well-known scion of the arts, and so he willingly gave his consent to the meeting.

Archibald was so excited at the prospect of meeting this darling young lady that he couldn't stand waiting for her to call at the house, where his family would doubtless get in the way and be embarrassing. On the day that they were due to see each other for the first time, he called her and arranged to meet her in private at a little bar that he sometimes visited. He drove himself all the way there, never once noticing that a dilapidated and rusty old saloon car was following him at a discreet distance.

When Archibald met his paramour in the bar's secluded car park he was instantly smitten by her simple and well-proportioned beauty. He knelt down on one knee so that he could kiss her hand, just like a fairy tale prince, but as she approached him the battered old car that had been following him swept in between them. To his horror one of the rear doors swung open violently and the young lady was pulled into the car, which then roared away in a shower of stone chippings and thick black smoke from the exhaust.

The next thing that the terrified and bewildered young man heard was the ringing of the public telephone on the corner of the street. Without quite understanding why he did so, Archibald went over to the phone and lifted the receiver from its cradle.

"Listen carefully, Big Nose", said a thin, rasping voice. "You'll never see her again. She's mine now! It's payback time for your bitch mother's treachery all those years ago. And if you don't believe me ask her about her first marriage".

The line went dead and so did Archibald's heart. He was quite inconsolable and wandered London's mean streets for hours trying to work out what he could do to win his darling beloved's freedom from this evil interloper. He had no idea where he was when he finally came out of his sad reverie. All that he knew was that there was a lot of garbage in the streets, that there was steam rising from broken pipes in the alleyways and that mean looking men kept pushing past him on their way to dark deals in dimly lit bars. This was as far from home as Archibald had ever been in his life and he was very scared. He also realised that he was extremely hungry and very cold, all of which contributed to make him feel wretched and desperately alone in this harsh and threatening world.

All of a sudden, a high-pitched voice broke through the black night air and made him stop dead in his tracks. "Archie? Is that you Archie? Coo-eee…over here… in the shop doorway".

Archibald looked across the street and directly into the heavy mascara eyes of a very down at heel looking lady, who was dressed in clothes that would have embarrassed a sixteen-year-old. Her skirt was too short, and it had a slit in the side that revealed rather more cellulite than thigh. Her boots had long since lost their patent shine and her crop top revealed far too much of her very large breasts to be at all decent. Her exposed midriff appeared to be melting like an ice-cream cone on a sizzling summer afternoon at the seaside.

Shuddering internally, Archibald crossed the road and came face to face with the oldest working girl this side of the Black Death, who put on a pair of horn-rimmed spectacles so that she could see him better. The young man steeled himself and asked the old girl for help.

"Madam, I need some help finding my true love and you look like someone who knows a thing or two about the world. Can you help me?"

"Probably", the old tart replied, "But first you need some grub and a good stiff drink. You look famished and with such a silly big nose you'll appreciate a quiet spot out of eyeshot. I recognised you from the magazines and stuff, darling. Always remember big ones, me, and I certainly remember your father. Oh, yes, he had a very handsome nose if you know what I mean."

"And what exactly is lacking in my nose", replied Archibald with just a hint of a serrated edge to his voice.

"Oh, nothing's lacking", replied the senior citizen of the night. "On the contrary, in fact. There's so much of it, but never mind, deary, you can be a worthy man whatever size your nose is. Anyway, I was telling you about your father and what good friends we was. He often used to come and see me in the olden days. Course, I was a lot younger and prettier then; least he always used to tell me so over a woodbine and a nice cup of tea afterwards. We used to have such lovely chats in them days. The last time I saw him he told me all about..."

"Indeed", said Archibald, cutting across her reminiscences about his late father. "I'm really very hungry. Could we continue the conversation somewhere a little more salubrious than this doorway?"

"Posh..." said the tart. "Why don't we go over to Rick's bar? You can buy me a brandy-shandy and a bun".

She set off at a brisk pace towards a brightly lit bar at the end of the street. Archibald watched her as she walked. He could imagine that her wiggle had once been very seductive, but he couldn't quite overcome the sense of revulsion rising from the pit of his stomach as he realised he was being given the come on by someone's aged grandmother. Things just didn't seem to be sitting in the right places anymore. He followed her down the street, taking care to remain at least two steps behind her, partly out of a vague sense of social decorum and partly because of a growing and morbid fascination with the simple harmonic motion of her buttocks.

"Come in, then, deary", she said, holding the door open for him and they went and sat in a quiet booth at the back of the bar. When the waitress came over the old tart ordered two large brandy-shandies and a plate full of iced buns. A popular beat hit thumped out of the juke box speakers, repeating again and again because the bar owner only had the one unscratched record left following a minor altercation the previous week between two groups of caffeine-crazed Mods and Rockers.

"Tuck in, love, while I tell all about your dad. I'll keep it short, mind, 'cos time's money in my game and, anyway, I hate long-winded stories that go on and on forever. I mean, who needs a life story? People with long tongues is worse than people with long noses, and when I was young I never got paid for chattering with the customers. I was well known for me brevity in the gob department, I was. When I was little they used to say to me mum I weren't much of a talker. My dad..."

"Your father, I dare say, got the chance to eat when he was hungry", Archibald interrupted, somewhat rudely.

"What, oh yes, love, do tuck in, didn't I say so", said the old tart holding out the plate of iced buns towards him. Archibald was just about to take a large bite out of his bun when she put her hand on top of his and said, "I was only gonna say..."

"Look, I can't listen to anything else until I've had something to eat", cried the young man, getting quite angry now. He paused and counted to ten, remembering that he needed the old girl's help to find his beloved. "I'm sorry, do go on, while I eat. I'm ravenous to hear your story".

The old tart was very flattered by his kind words, completely missing the sarcasm that Archibald had tried to inject into that last phrase. She smiled a gap-toothed smile at him as she lit an unfiltered cigarette and blew smoke all over his iced bun.

"You're very nice for a big nose, you are".

Poxy bloody woman, why does she keep going on about my nose? thought Archibald. If it weren't for the smoked buns I'd tell the old biddy to bugger off. Why can't people recognise their shortcomings? I bet she really thinks she doesn't prattle on at all. I blame all those people who told her mother she was quiet. She really believes all that flattery and flummery. Just goes to show how sensible my mother was. She never let me be flattered or be over protected. People like that tell us what they think we want to hear and they hide our faults away. I'll never let it happen to me. I'll always pay particular attention to my faults and do something about them.

The poor boy really did believe that all of his mother's friends and servants had praised his nose because they really meant it.

He had no idea that they laughed at him behind his back.

"Look, 'mmm sorry", he said distractedly with his mouth full of slightly stale bun. He swallowed. "I'm looking for a young lady who was kidnapped this afternoon by an evil looking old man in a tatty brown car. I wondered whether you might know anything given your experience on the streets?"

"Yeah, whatever", the old tart replied. "Would you mind moving that way a little, 'cos your nose is casting such a big shadow on the table I can't see the buns..."

Archibald turned to offer her his profile while she fingered the buns to find the one with the thickest icing.

"Thanks. So, a brown car, you say. Did you get chance to speak to the old git, only if you did it might be a help, 'cos there's quite a few brown cars in London".

Archibald was about to tell the old girl about the telephone call when she interrupted, winking at him as she said, "You know, you really have got the biggest nose I've ever seen. Is everything else in proportion?"

"Really!" cried Archibald. "I wish you'd stop going on about my bloody nose. As far as I'm concerned it seems perfectly normal and I'm very happy with it. In fact, I love it just the way it is and don't want it to be any shorter, longer or fatter. It's perfect".

The old girl sat back in her seat, looking quite astonished.

"I'm sorry, Archie", she said quietly. "I really didn't mean to upset you. I want to help you find out where your little girl is. It's just that your nose is shockingly large. I'll try not to mention it again. I'll definitely try not to think about it at all, although, in truth, you could probably poke a very large rhinoceros with it".

That was the straw that broke poor Archibald's back. He was now so angry with the old woman because of her continual sniping about his nose that he stormed out of the bar and strode through the city streets in a foul temper for the rest of the night, but no matter how hard he looked or how many people he questioned, no one seemed to know anything about his stolen lover or about the evil kidnapper and his clapped-out motor. For the most part Archibald couldn't even get straight answers from the people that he stopped and questioned. All anyone in the city seemed able to do was to mock his nose and call him rude names. He thought that everyone must be quite mad, and he was in no mood to admit to himself that he was in possession of an oversized hooter. The years of conditioning and polite remarks made to him by family friends and retainers were so ingrained that he was convinced that he was the only sane person walking the city streets that night.

Meanwhile, back in Rick's bar the old tart with a heart was making a few telephone calls. The truth was that she was more than just an old professional; she was, in the vaguest sense, Archibald's Fairy Godmother, having promised his father that she would look after the boy when he most needed it. She was convinced that time had now come.

With the last call made, the old girl now knew exactly who had taken Archibald's true love and she knew where he was keeping her. She also knew that Archie would eventually end up back at the coffee bar. It was an unwritten law of street life that condemned the miserable to wander aimlessly around Soho's darker haunts for hours before inevitably ending up back where they had started out from. The old girl ordered another brandy-shandy and waited. Trade hadn't been up to much lately and she was skint, so there was no point in trying to leave until the boy returned and paid the bill.

Sure enough, at about four in the morning a weary young man stumbled back into the bar. He collapsed into the booth, ordered a double strength Americano, put his head in his hands and wept like a baby. The old girl put a comforting hand on his shoulder, slipped a grubby piece of paper under his nose and quietly made her way back out into the insomniac streets of the city.

Eventually Archibald managed to summon up the strength to drink his coffee. He looked at the piece of paper that the old lady had passed to him and saw a bill for eleven large brandy cocktails, fourteen buns and a Viennese Whirl. He was about to crumple the bill up and throw it at the waitress when he noticed that there was some writing on the other side. He turned the piece of paper over and there he saw an address and a name. He had no idea who the person named might be but the address was that of an old and disused theatre a couple of streets away. He threw some notes and some coins onto the table and ran all the way to the theatre, convinced that he would at last find a clue to the whereabouts of his one true love amongst the rotting stalls.

Breaking and entering was not something that Archibald had studied with his tutors, and so it was with some difficulty and quite a lot of noise that he eventually managed to force a window at the back of the ramshackle and degenerate building. As he made his way through the darkness he kicked various buckets, pots and pans that had been left strategically placed to deal with the many leaks that the roof had sprung during so many years of neglect. With every screech of metal on the wooden floor and with every yelp that came out of his mouth as he smashed his shins into rotting theatre seats, Archibald expected to be attacked by the hounds of hell, but nothing stirred within.

Once in the main auditorium, he saw that there was a cage on the stage lit by a single spotlight and in the cage he saw the crumpled form of a young woman, who was, he was sure, wearing the very same dress that his beloved had been wearing when she was so cruelly snatched away from him the previous evening. He ran down the aisles and up on to the stage where he tried with all of his might to break open the cage door.

Archibald's joy at finding his darling was quickly tempered by his frustration at not being able break her out of her prison. She cried and wept and begged him to set her free, but in spite of all his efforts he failed utterly. In despair Archibald thought that at least he might be able to comfort her with a kiss. She understood immediately and came towards the bars with her lips puckered. Archibald twisted and turned every which way he could, but he found it impossible to position his own lips close enough to those of his darling girl because his nose always got in the way. After twenty minutes of sheer and utter frustration, and with a nose that was black and blue from battering the cage bars, he finally sat back on the floor and, for the first time in his life, admitted to himself just how long his nose really was.

Behind the desperate couple, the house lights went up, but they were so engrossed in their respective miseries that neither of them noticed a shabby little old man shuffling down one of the aisles and taking a front row seat. Had they looked over their shoulders they would have seen a mad gleam in his eye and a bucket of popcorn on his lap, and Archibald would have heard him chuckling quietly to himself as he came face to face with the results of his curse from all those years ago.

The desperate young couple slowly became aware that they had an audience. The air around them thickened as the old man in the stalls uncoiled himself and started to slither down the aisle towards the foot of the stage. As they both turned to look at the man he doffed his shabby top hat and grinned a toothless grin.

"Got you," he snarled as his head bobbed up and down just beyond the footlights. "Been a long time in the waiting, and the curses turn you bitter inside, but it's worth it, boy, to see you here like this. Blame your bastard father."

Archibald edged closer to the cage bars, shrinking back from the papery skin and pallid, baleful glare. "What…what is this? What do you want with me…with us?" he asked timidly.

The old man chuckled. "Your mother never told you about me, did she? No, don't suppose she did. I'm the cuckold. I'm the wronged party. I'm the man with revenge in his soul."

He raised his crooked arms out wide to encompass the world. "This is it. This is my world. And you, you snivelling little shit, you are my prize. Break in you did, but you'll never break out. You're going to spend eternity here trying to kiss your little vixen, and I'm going to watch you every afternoon, watch you scab and scrape and graze that monstrous nose of yours against those bars. It's a comedy of sorts. My comedy, my last, my best, my eternal show time."

He cackled out loud and waving them away he turned to resume his seat in the stalls. "Carry on, carry on", he said with another low chuckle. "Do your worst…"

Archibald turned to his would-be lover in the cage and taking her hand in his own he sighed. "I can't believe it", he said to the girl. "After all these years and all those lies. I really have got the biggest, stupidest nose in the whole wide world!"

As soon as he said this there was a sound like thunder at the back of the stage, followed immediately by the appearance of a towering wall of smoke and dry ice. Gliding through the mist there came the figure of a tall, slinky blonde, who wiggled outrageously as she walked on air. Archibald was sure that he recognised the wiggle, but he couldn't quite put his finger on where he'd seen it before. When she reached the front of the stage the gorgeous blonde phantom took a long bow.

There was a ghostly drum roll playing from the back of the auditorium as she raised her hand and pointed it at the wretched old man, who was, by now, trying make for one of the exits. The mad gleam in his eye turned to one of sheer, utter panic, but no matter how fast he shuffled forward, the exit sign seemed to recede into the distance twice as quickly. Although he looked as if he was running forwards, in reality he was being dragged back towards the stage by an invisible will.

Archibald and his true love held hands tightly as they watched the little old man rise up into the air and pass by the cage. Underneath him a trap door opened, and he started to scream. "No, not now, you old hag, not now, damn you. Why me, why does this always happen to me? I'll get you back, you old witch. I'll get…"

The platinum blonde at centre stage winked at them both and snapped her fingers. The old man disappeared into the hole in the stage amid a shower of sparks and curses. The blonde snapped her fingers again and the cage disappeared in a puff of magician's smoke, allowing the two lovers to embrace for the very first time.

The lights snapped off and there was another crack of thunder. As the lights came up again slowly, the tart with a heart was standing where the blonde spirit had appeared, and she was smiling her soft and gentle, gap toothed smile once again.

"So, deary, won't you admit you owe me one, as it were. Not only have I saved you and your lovely little miss from that old bastard's schemes and plots, but I've also taught you a lesson. You'd never have found out how extraordinary your nose was if it hadn't stopped you doing what you most wanted to. You see, self-love is ever so destructive. It stops you dealing with your faults. No matter how hard your reason tries to tell you something's wrong, it only ever really sinks in when the problem gets in the way of something important".

The two lovers looked at her in dumbfounded amazement as she snapped her fingers one final time and made herself disappear without a trace. To Archibald's eternal gratitude the old lady's last act of kindness also reduced his nose to a more normal size, and he was finally able to kiss his darling fiancé fully on the lips to an accompanying fade out of delighted, girlish laughter.

And, of course, he learned by his past mistakes and profited greatly from his now well-proportioned good looks. With his lantern jaw, with his sparkling blue eyes and with his perfectly aquiline nose, Archibald followed in his father's footsteps and became a matinee idol on the silver screen, fulfilling his long but dearly departed father's final wish. All that remains of this story is to say that both Archibald and his darling young lady were married, that they inherited her father's vast fortune, and that, in between location shoots, premieres and promotional tours, they lived happily ever after with an enormous brood of normally featured offspring.

As for the kidnapper, that devious impresario, it is said that he appears briefly in cameo in every one of Archibald's films, his pale head floating like a spectral balloon across a corner of some vast landscape, sneering and leering and mouthing the words, "I'll get you back for this you old witch…I'll be back…"

Terry's Amazing Shin Pads

NOT LONG AGO IN Stackton-on-Seam, a town that lies in the folded valleys to the west of Manchester, a town where the chimney stacks rise up to shake hands with the sky, there was once a young boy who desperately wanted to be a famous footballer. Every day, before school, during break times and in the lowering light of the afternoons, you could find him kicking a ball against a wall or running through the streets pretending to dribble past the greatest defences the world had ever seen.

Unfortunately, the boy suffered from two serious disadvantages; he simply wasn't very good at football nor was he the most gifted substitute on the bench. His father encouraged him as much as he could but was, at heart, just grateful that his son had such a healthy hobby. No one expected young Terry to amount to very much in life.

One sunny summer day, when Terry was playing on his own at World Cup in his local park, an old man with a stoop, and who was accompanied by a sour looking fox terrier, called Terry over.

"Why are you playing all on your own, son?" asked the old man. "I thought football was a team game".

"I prefer it on my own", said Terry, jinking around the old man's legs. The sour looking fox terrier, which was called Pele, stuck out his paw and tackled the young boy with ease.

The old man looked wistfully down at the boy. "I think you're playing on your own because the other boys won't pick you for their teams".

Terry's cheeks went a very bright shade of red and he came to an abrupt and ball-less halt. Terry managed to stammer out a high-pitched "Course not", and then he just stood there frozen with embarrassment as the dog played keepie-uppie with all four paws.

"Well, I can help you", said the old man.

He reached inside his jacket and pulled out a battered old pair of faded, blue ribbed shin pads. "Do you see these, boy? These are magic shin pads and you know what that means don't you?"

Terry continued to stand there, staring at the shin pads, his face displaying the mixed pleasures of vacant distrust and horror.

"These used to belong Golden Goals Nudger", continued the old man. "Do you remember him?"

Terry searched his mind's incomplete catalogue of sporting bubble gum cards, but there didn't seem to be anything filed under the name of Nudger. He continued to stand there dumbly, his mouth flapping open and shut like a goldfish trying to remember what it had eaten for breakfast.

"Well, perhaps he was a little before your time", said the old man. "What about Chazza, do you remember him at all?"

This time Terry had no trouble locating the bubble gum card, the tee shirt and the video, and he snapped out of his vacant trance with a sense of welcome relief. The great Chazza! He had been a teenage prodigy, a master of the beautiful game, who, in the prime of his career, had spiralled out of control in a whirlwind of drink, binge eating and late-night brawls in discotheques.

"Yeah", said Terry, grinning. "Brilliant!"

"He owned these shin pads, just like Mr. Nudger before him", said the old man. "You'd never have believed that Chazza was just like you once upon a time. Aye lad, when he was twelve he was rubbish, but once he started wearing these magic shin pads, well, the world was almost his oyster".

The battered and bruised shin pads suddenly seemed to glow and to shine. Terry was convinced that he could hear the air around them crackle and fizz with electricity. Terry was mesmerised.

"I'll give these shin pads to you on one condition", said the old man. His dog was now keeping the ball in the air with his head. It sounded to Terry as though he was counting in doggy fashion and had reached nine hundred and ninety-nine.

"You can have these shin pads if you promise me you'll always love football more than anything else in the entire world".

Terry promised with every ounce of his heart and soul, for he knew that football was in his blood, that football was his reason for living. And so, with a flourish and a bow the old man gave Terry the shin pads, showed him how to tuck them into his socks and then told the dog to give the boy his ball back.

As soon as Terry started to kick his football around the park he could feel the magic in the shin pads start to course through his veins. By the time that he looked up to say thank you to the old man, both he and his dog were ambling away into the distance. They appeared to be in deep conversation and Terry was sure he heard the dog say, "It'll all end in tears, woof, it always does, woof." Terry shrugged his shoulders and got down to the serious business of dribbling successfully around all of the piles of doggy mess that littered the park's only proper football pitch.

Terry was amazed at the transformation in his skills. He seemed to possess a sublime accuracy and alacrity with a football that he had never been aware of before. By the time that he reached the far end of the football pitch both he and the ball were still perfectly clean, something hitherto entirely unheard of. Terry also noticed that his heart wasn't racing like it usually did after even a brief run. He breathed deeply, feeling his lungs fill with air. Terry felt as if he could run forever.

Terry quickly became a regular in his school team, scoring one hundred goals the very next season, which brought him to the attention of the biggest football club in the land. When he first signed junior terms with the club some of the older boys laughed at him, but Terry didn't care. With his battered old shin pads tucked safely inside his knee length socks, he ran riot through every level of schoolboy and junior football, scoring record numbers of goals at every age. By the time that he was sixteen he was ready to play his first game for his club in the country's Super League. In fact, Terry marked his debut by scoring a magnificent hat trick.

Terry was the happiest sixteen-year-old in the world and as he said in the post-match interview on television, he was over the moon. From such raw beginnings here he was doing the one thing he loved most in the whole wide world and he even got paid for it.

Of course, Terry's father handled the money side of things. He bought Terry and his mother a beautiful mock Georgian mansion in one of the better parts of Cheshire, while he devoted himself to furthering Terry's interests from a penthouse flat in the city centre.

Everything went swimmingly for Terry over the next few seasons. His goal scoring reached ever-greater levels of perfection and he was instrumental in helping his country fight their way to third place in the next World Cup. The fans, the press and all of those ex-footballer pundits on the television said that Terry was a legend in the making; that he was ten times the player Chazza had ever been. Come the time of the next World Cup every commentator expected Terry to lead his national side to the ultimate football prize. Indeed, some of the less objective newspapers even started a campaign to rename football. They wanted to call the beautiful game 'Terryball'.

One balmy spring Saturday afternoon, with his team leading by five goals to nil, Terry's manager decided to give him a well-earned rest twenty minutes before the end of the match. He had, by then, scored all five goals and it had been a long and hard season. After all, you didn't end up leading the Super League by thirty points at Christmas without some very hard graft. And so Terry was substituted, about which he was quite happy. He settled down in the dugout to watch the rest of the match next to his less illustrious teammates, just another mucker doing his duty.

During a minor off the ball fracas between two of his own team's midfield players Terry happened to glance up from the match.

His attention had been caught by a dazzling burst of light from one of the executive boxes in the opposite stand. Once Terry's momentary blindness had cleared and he had put on his airline pilot's shades, he was able to identify the source of this brilliant white light. Rays of sunlight were catching the diamond teardrop earrings of a stunningly beautiful young lady in the opposite stand and it was these bursts of pure radiance that were catching Terry's attention.

Terry nudged Crippler Cruncho, the reserve centre-half, pointed up at the executive box in the opposite stand, and asked, "Who's that?"

Crippler shrugged. "Dunno", he said, "looks some old twat an' a dog what's waving at us"

"No, up a bit, in the box, left a bit, left a bit, yeah there",

"Err...Oh, yeah, that's Bling", said Crippler, "you know, whatsername, she's a model-singer-actress, sort of".

"Bling", repeated Terry, turning the name over and over in his mind. It was the most beautiful name that he had ever heard, and Terry gazed up at her adoringly for the rest of the game. He stared so intently into her jet-black sunglasses that he completely missed the amazing comeback by his team's opponents that resulted in the match ending in a five-all draw.

Later that night in the Orgasmatron Nightclub, where the boys had gone for some shampoo and some dancing after another hard week at the tactical grindstone, Terry told his best friend, left-back and room-mate, 'Boozo' Van Honk, that he was going to marry Bling.

The world continued to turn as usual, although there were some who said that it had been turned upside down by Terry's magical footballing displays. Whether playing for his club or for his country, Terry set record after record with his amazing goal scoring exploits. No one, for example, had ever seen a player bicycle kick a ball into the roof of their opponent's net from their own goal line before. Terry and his magic shin pads were a phenomenon; they were a miracle.

The world was doubly amazed a few weeks later when Terry and Bling started to appear together at nightclubs, at film premieres and at all of the best parties. But no matter how many star-studded nights out Terry had, he never disappointed on the field of play.

Terry and Bling became what the world's press called an 'Item', appearing everywhere together. They attended every glitzy party, were invited to every celebrity bash, made frequent guest appearances on television and generally became the most famous couple on the planet.

Their world appeared to be one of endless shopping sprees, of choreographed photo opportunities, of expensive endorsements and high fashion extravaganzas. Their lives became so much a part of the general public's fascination with wealth and fame that Terry and Bling's heads filled up quite to the top with the sound of clicking and whirring cameras.

Of course, such things cannot last and eventually Terry and Bling settled into one another just as most couples do. Bling grew out of her modelling career and into the far more satisfying role of wife and mother. Terry continued to dazzle on the playing field and without quite remembering why, he stood firmly by his old and battered shin pads, even though he was offered bright shiny new ones nearly every week.

Eventually it came to the time of the next World Cup. Terry was brilliant. He led his country through all of the qualifying matches with an authority that mixed stern determination with the most sublime football skills that the world had ever seen. Everyone in the team camp, in the media and on the streets was convinced that this would be Terry's championship. This was the moment in time when he would become a true great, possibly the greatest footballer there had ever been.

Terry's brilliance new no bounds once the tournament started in earnest. He was magnificent, scoring goal after goal and inspiring his countrymen in their fight to win a place in the World Cup final. In between games, and when not training, Terry and Bling held press conferences and photo-shoots. They even had special world cup tattoos on their shoulders and they introduced fashionistas the world over to the joys of diamond encrusted toe piercings.

Journalists, players and fans alike hung on every word that Terry uttered, paying particular attention to Bling when she told them nice little stories about Terry's life of domestic bliss. The prophecies and the fates conspired, it seemed, to remove every obstacle from Terry's now undoubted ascent to the peak of footballing achievement.

On the eve of the final, in which Terry and his country would meet their greatest sporting rivals to decide who would be champion of the world, there was a knock-on Terry and Bling's hotel room door. Terry was sorting out his wardrobe for the champion's ball that would be held the following night, so Bling opened the door to find out who was disturbing their evening.

Stood there was a little old man, all stooped and grey, with a sour looking fox terrier attached to his wrist by means of a length of packaging string. In his hands he held a plush crimson velour cushion and on the cushion was a pair of brilliantly glittering shin pads. They were sewn with real silver threads and were made of the most exquisite golden cloth. On each shin pad the letter 'T' had been embroidered in genuine, full carat diamonds.

Bling's first reaction on seeing this rather grubby man and his equally grubby dog was one of mild disgust. However, when the light from the hotel room's chandelier caught the golden cloth, the silver threads and the diamonds, she completely revised her opinion to one of tolerant sniffiness.

"Tezza, babe, we've got a visitor", she called out, although she didn't invite the old man and his dog into their suite. Terry ambled out of the bedroom and joined his beloved at the front door.

"Hello", said Terry.

The old man looked at him. The boy from all those years ago was now a fine specimen of a man, a man with the world at his feet. He hoped against hope that this time things would be different.

"Do you remember me?" asked the old man.

"Erm... no, don't think so", replied Terry, after a few seconds rummaging through bubble gum cards filled with the faces of the rich and famous.

"In the park, when you were what, eleven? The dog and me? Blue shin pads?" asked the old man, hopefully.

Terry delved deeper into his collection of memory cards.

"Yeah... actually... rings a bell", he said after a moment or two. "Talking dog, right?"

"What?" the old man blurted out, before regaining some composure. "Oh, yes, well, when he's in the mood. But that's not the point. Do you remember what I told you about the shin pads?"

Again, Terry searched back through his memories. So much had happened to him, so many wonderful things, and he simply couldn't recall conversations from that long ago. He was aware that there was something he should say but couldn't quite put his finger on it. Bling looked at her nails and sighed.

"To be honest", said Terry, "I can't say I do".

The old man sucked in his cheeks and shook his head. The fox terrier looked back up at him and seemed to give a knowing wink. The old man sighed, turned back to Terry and said, "Better get this over with, then. OK, this is how it's supposed to go...I offer you these bright and shiny new shin pads in exchange for your tatty old ones. Then you the tell me to bugger off because you understand what that means..."

"Sorry?" said Terry.

The old man had a tear in his eye and a lump in his throat as he wearily muttered the words he had longed never to say again. "Just go and get those bloody shin pads".

A few seconds later, the old man exchanged the bright, sparkling, monogrammed shin pads for Terry's battered old blue ones. As the door closed on him and his dog he heard Bling say to Terry, "Nice, aren't they babe, really you."

The old man and the dog turned back towards the lifts. The little dog cocked his leg and urinated against a large potted aspidistra before turning to the old man and saying, "That's five thousand Bonios you owe me."

Of course, Terry played an absolute stinker in the final. It was as if he had two left feet and he was substituted after just twenty minutes. The rest of the team fell apart without their great talismanic leader and the country went into a deep state of mourning for a whole week after the disgrace of the final.

The next season saw Terry's fall from grace accelerate. In fact, it was apocalyptic. He scored only one goal for his great club and that was only because he tripped over his own feet and accidentally kneed the ball into his own net.

Terry retired from the beautiful game amid a welter of accusations, of public rows with Bling and general feelings of mutual betrayal. All that Terry could do, once the dust had settled and his divorce had been dragged through the mire of the gutter press, was to lend his name and his former glories to endorsements and dubious advertising campaigns. As new stars took their place in the footballing firmament, even these offers of work dried up. In the end Terry was forced to pawn his earrings and to buy a pub.

Terry pretty well disappeared from public life, earning a meagre living from his pub until that went into liquidation too. He really hit rock bottom when the invitations to play in charity golf tournaments stopped arriving on his doormat because the organisers were worried about Terry's drink problems.

However, some years later Terry did burst back into the limelight. His face, somewhat fuller and much more care worn by now, appeared on television screens and in newspapers across the world. Unfortunately, his face also appeared in Crown Court number seven, as it is likely to do if you get nicked dealing Class A narcotics.

Courtyard

BEFORE HE OPENS THE heavy wooden door that keeps the swirling winds of the courtyard beyond from raising dust spirals in the hallway, Signor Secretary Gabriele adjusts his black brocade outer vestment, straightening the hood across his shoulders and pulling down on the lapels. He twitches involuntarily at the neck and frowns at the ever-present shadows behind the door. The cuffs of his blouse are visibly fraying and it is too warm already this morning to warrant the wearing of his time served and now lovingly ink stained jerkin, but he is a man of undoubted habit. Signor Secretary Gabriele is now Second Scribe on the Listing Roster and he thinks that his stipend should at least afford him new cuffs more than once a year. It does not. He feels inevitably down at heel and frustration is a fundamental cellular component of his thin and shallow viscera.

And yet, as he pushes a wrought iron ring handle to the left to free a bolt from a splitting door frame and pushes ineffectually upon a studded door, he feels that he should not, on balance, complain too loudly or obviously. There are far too many ingrates and unfortunates beyond these courtyard boundary walls who would gladly, and most probably, he muses, violently swap his current state of boredom and his predictable sureties to assuage their own ravening hungers and hopeless disenfranchisements.

The Signor Secretary is indefatigably Second Scribe on the Listing Roster. It is not the most glamorous position, but neither is it dangerous or mutable. He is, he considers, as he lays his shoulder to the grey weathered planks of the oaken door, by and large content with his frustrations. What, after all, do frayed cuffs matter when set against the certainty of shelter and kindling and the thickly fatty roasts brewing in the hall kitchens? What are frayed cuffs in a world where he has attended the funerary rites of past secretaries and they are always laid out on their departure in new thread? Signor Secretary Gabriele is ultimately happy enough in the knowledge that with each day's walk to and fro across this courtyard he brings the sad demise of Monsignor Secretary Cannavaro, his immediate superior, a few metres nearer. The door swings slowly open onto the heat haze rising from the flagstone floor of the courtyard. Signor Secretary Gabriele squints as he wipes a speckling of woodworm dust from his shoulder.

Signor Secretary Gabriele thinks of time in terms of distance rather than the cycle of sun and moon and star. As Second Scribe he greets the days some twenty minutes before the tenth hour of the morning so that he might travel far enough to be sitting at his desk exactly on the turn of that tenth hour. His work is like his walk across the courtyard. He places one word in front of another just as he places one foot in front of another. The hand drawn lines on the ledger pages mirror the flagstone edges that mark the lane that he chooses without fail every morning and every evening.

The Signor Secretary never deviates. He opens the door that leads from his dormitory hall and heads for an identical oak door set into an identically constructed work hall directly opposite and on the square. He does not look down or to either side as he walks. There is no point. He knows from long years at the quill that the boundary walls between the halls are equal and straight and set on that same square. These days, as far as he is aware from unguarded moments of peripheral leakage, walls and bricks and mortars remain as they always have been, as they are and as they always will be.

It must be forty years, Signor Secretary suddenly thinks, since he first walked through one of those outer dormitory doors, fresh and green and scrubbed, straight from the Maimed Brothers and their administrative academy. He had not trained with distinction, preferring then the glimpse of a pretty ankle and the thrill of weed in a clay pipe behind the academy stables, but such childish things are fleeting and frivolous and gad-fly. The then merely Duster Gabriele sobered. Those first years as a glorified house maid in the ledger stores taught him, albeit not without a smart and a tear or two, the meaning and the benefit of quiet order.

Where once he may have entertained thoughts upon the nature, pointless or otherwise, of a walking, working life, he now understands that there are too many points of blinding light set into the darkening skies above a simple man's uncomprehending head. Not that he thinks himself too simple. Signor Secretary Gabriele understands the subtleties that underpin his work. The apparent tedium of transcribing ancient texts into new ledgers is actually an exercise in righteous continuity. Law is law is law. Without a safeguarding, without the constant battle cry of quill on ledger, without the endless plodding advance of the scribes in this war against time and rot and weevil, all will decay and despoil. Signor Secretary is a warrior of the word and his word is Canon Law.

His eyes adjust to the bright morning sunlight. He wipes away a little watering from behind his metal framed glasses, breathes in deeply and stares straight ahead at the door opposite his own. At this distance the walls to left and right seem to arrow in and drive his sense of perspective directly into the ledger hall. He is aware of the doors, each set into that far wall in the same proportion as they are here at the dormitory. He sets out upon his straight walk. A thought flies into his head, streaking across the empty skies of his mind like the swallows on summer wing above his head. Could he deviate his line?

Signor Secretary Gabriele is startled and he momentarily hesitates. He immediately wonders if anyone can see him. Will they sense his predicament? He pulls down again on his lapels and focuses on the straighter path. He remembers where deviations lead and such a thing, such a second thing, would surely be an undoing. He stares at his destination doorway. Those other grey and cracked oak doors are things from a forgotten past and not for him now. He will not think about the who and the why and the how. He must concentrate on that which is perfect and formed and has purpose. The Signor Secretary cricks his neck once more and takes a deep, hot breath. He steps forward again, reaching for the safety of his chosen and well-trodden path. It is then that he notices the thin stalks of dry and whitening grass poking up from an unmortared crack between these usually familiar and well-worn flagstones. Signor Secretary Gabriele is feeling quite unnerved.

His imagination is a weak and wasted thing, a gammy handed child born of incest, and he has buried it as deeply as he can under ink stains and candle soot, but still the creature fidgets. Under his wilting and grey-white collar Signor Secretary Gabriele feels the heat of the morning with manifest irritation. If he did not know better he might believe that he is again being watched this morning, as though someone has laid traps for him and expects him to falter and fail. He steps forward more briskly, feeling the first beads of perspiration form in his close cropped hair. He will be dripping by the time he reaches the far door. He feels as threadbare and darned as his clothes, and as the Signor Secretary runs a hand across his chin to feel for droplets of sweat he shudders. He has shaved unevenly. The fates are conspiring but he will not, he swears, give in. He ignores the first running droplet at his temple. Sweat or no, he will stride forward with purpose.

The Signor Secretary is long practised with the burying of speculations. He is, however, congenitally inclined towards memory. It is, after all, his daily purpose in the transcriptions. Unbidden but nonetheless clear and precisely formed, he sees again that page in the third volume of Di Matteo's case studies, On Parsimony Amongst the Woollen Brethren. Yet again this morning he shudders. He can see the curl of the downward strokes on a note in miniscule in the transcribed margin. Another clerk of the Scriptorium had penned a temptation some two hundred years previously:

He, for twill not be she,

Who leans a paw upon this page

To write a law dull with age

Would leave another versed smile

To please a clerk this long while?

That feckless reader of uninspired jottings, that bored Clerk Gabriele, was as yet determinedly of the dreaming persuasion and still resolutely impressionable. Yawning, dull-eyed Clerk Gabriele felt the tug of disorder upon the sleeve of his writing hand, and was so deftly invited into the conspiratorial heats of youthful intrigue that he too had copied out that verse in the margin of the one-hundred and twenty-first page of the third volume of the Parsimony.

At that time in his fledgling secretarial career, Clerk Gabriele worked for Signor Under-Secretary Maldini. The Signor Under-Secretary was a precise old crow, trusting of no one under the age of fifty and convinced that all young men should be birched at the beginning of every day to purge what he called 'The Twitches'. Signor Under-Secretary Maldini cawed in the treetops with the day's final reckoning. He danced the spindle legged dance of the corvid upon these very flagstones as he called a certain young clerk back to the Scriptorium door, a stripling branch swishing in the old man's right hand. Signor Secretary Gabriele can still smell the fresh sap upon his scarred shoulders.

It had taken Roberto Gabriele almost ten years to rise through the ranks of Runners and Inkers. He had trodden a sure path from humble Duster to become a man of emerging substance. He was young and fit and lithe. His nemesis was old and slow and reducing, but all it took was one look and the younger man meekly submitted to the twig and a bloody back. All it took was a signature and a moment of glee in the beady blacks of that withered crow, to see him, at twenty-five years of age, endlessly sneezing as he wiped skin flakes and rat droppings from the tops of ancient books once more in the deepest, darkest stacks.

That is why, whenever Signor Secretary Gabriele is nudged towards memory, he shudders and twitches and fidgets. He is ten years behind the curve of the moon. His celestial orbit wanes low. He too is on the cusp of mortality and yet he hungers for one more rung on the ladder. That is why he cannot falter on his path, sweat or no, grass stalk or no.

"Resolve, Roberto, resolve", he whispers to the heat haze, breaking the silence this one time. He channels his thoughts. He focusses on his world in the here and now. That is the way of it. With the sun at his back he follows the vertical tramlines, making sure that he does not step upon the horizontal rungs of mortar. It is a superstition. He feels the soft patch on his right slipper where the leather sole wears thin and is stuffed with a dried out fold of spare book binding leather.

Signor Secretary Gabriele cannot help but look away from the door in the far wall and narrow his world view to the flagstones immediately in front of him. He will concentrate on each step and only on each step. Occasionally he glances up again to assure himself that he remains on course. He finds that he is strangely drawn to the evidence of decay that he sees upon the superficially timeless floor of the courtyard. Where once upon a time all seemed perfection, he senses with the seeing that there are spaces and moments of tension in this world.

It occurs to him that things are much the same in the life of the Scriptorium. After Under-Secretary Maldini shuffled off his mortal coil he found that succeeding Under-Secretaries waxed and waned in their strict adherence to the beady-black exactitudes of the ledger. Not that the Signor Secretary ever wrote another piece of doggerel, but now that it is his turn to reckon the days, he does not begrudge an occasional ink stain or scratching out. He notes these marks and blemishes, but only as a means to know a clerk's tendencies and through that to offer guidance on the path to improvement. It is also a way of stock piling evidence to prove that some young bright-eyed thruster is not yet ready to occupy another not quite dead man's shoes.

Signor Secretary Gabriele muses on the solitary sound of his flapping slipper on the flagstones and wonders how long ice and thaw and rain and sun will take to reduce this place to the rubble of misunderstood monumentalism. He is ever alone in this walk and in these fusty musings. He is ever alone in his collared discomfiture, and yet, after all of these years of loyal and righteous service, he still fears the beady-blacks staring out from that windowless wall opposite. As he strides towards the middle of the courtyard, towards the point of no return, he believes that he can hear the faint scratching of quills on rough, hand-pressed papers. It must be that or rats at the corn stores beyond the courtyard walls. He almost smiles but stifles the urge. Nonetheless he thinks what monster rats they must be to be heard from here.

At the heart of the courtyard there is one huge single squared slab. Signor Secretary Gabriele has walked across that grey stone leviathan more times than he can recount but always with purpose and an unerring sense of direction. Today he stops. He still fears the ghosts of beady black but something stirs with his memories of long lost rebellion. He pauses and looks down at the weathered stone. As he does so the stubble at his ill-shaven neck catches on his wing collar. His lower lip pushes into his upper lip so that he pouts. His lips are a deep, ruby, heat stained red. He wonders why he's taken so long to summon this shred of nerve.

 As the Signor Secretary stares at the single slab weighing down upon the heart of the courtyard he imagines sets of calloused hands shifting flagstones into place. He sees an army of sunburned torsos and tousled, bleached heads. He marvels at the industry while sweetly aware that such a life of sinew and cracking bone would never have done for him. He wonders whether these masonic soldiers of his Lord Duke might have started their endeavours with this central installation and worked outwards or perhaps they worked in from the boundaries. His head starts to spin with the precision of such a pattern and he nearly swoons.

Signor Secretary Gabriele breaks off from his reverie and sneaks a glance at the dazzling blue sky that heaps warmth upon his black, fustian shoulders. He watches a thin wisp of white cloud drift lazily in the blue swell. Too random, he thinks. The Signor Secretary likes a puzzle based in predictable logic. During these summer evenings he often asks one or two of the more reliably intellectual junior clerks to set him anagram puzzles, which he spins round in his head as he sits on the veranda of his garden apartment in the Scriptorium hall while sipping at a small glass of pinot blushed rosé.

And there it is. Something that he has hitherto paid little attention to. A puzzle almost perfect in that it has lain here these hundreds of years and is now so worn down by flayed slippers and winter frosts that it is almost indecipherable. The puzzle is carved in full relief out of the giant slab and is made up of Signor Secretary Gabriele's favourite things; random letters of the alphabet. There are worn but fully formed letters, hints of letters and cracks and dents and rubbings, such that they form a sort of grid upon which the decaying shapes of words hang now by a thread. The Signor Secretary squats down on one threadbare knee and traces out these letters and dents, marvelling as he does at how deeply ingrained is the black ink in the whorls of his fingerprints. He forms shapes upon rough stone and stores away the pattern for his evening glass:

W—T---N

--E-M—G--S

In carrying this new and yet ancient puzzle with him as he walks briskly towards the waiting Scriptorium door, Signor Secretary Gabriele senses a subtle shift in the nature of his worldly perceptions. In the years prior to tracing the inscription he has formed a view of this courtyard as a place of quiet, solitary perfection. All is on the square and neat and maintained and smoothed. This morning, one pace beyond the mystery words, he feels as though scales are lifting from his eyes. He wonders how an eye works. Surely he is seeing the same world that he has always seen. It is, he thinks, a question of vulgar anatomy. He is out of sorts and so sees impressions of lichen and scar and scrape and moss and breaking twigs and dust and desiccated leaves and a rodent gnawed chicken bone. He does not believe in any of it.

But then it occurs to him that even this thought is a memory and unreliable. The Signor Secretary feels the heat rise once more. He wants no more of this. He has a puzzle to solve and a day to reckon. He tries to focus on each step, but as he does so he sees bare, childish feet patter across cobbles and winter muds. He is wrenched away from the skirts of a rosy-cheeked, bumptiously dimpled woman by the beady blacks and the Ducal Guard, a promising and lively child ready for the grim beaks and the cold flow of letters . He is destined the spend his years upon dusting and thin gruels and maggoty meats on Duke-Days.

 The Signor Secretary reverts to his natural antipathies and shudders in the heat broiling up from the flagstones. His regular pattern is divided and diverging. He feels thin, as though his usual deep blacks are being washed out by some other artist's watery brush. He fixes his gaze on the door and takes one last, long breath. His usually measured gait starts to twist and take on aspects of the grotesque. Roberto Gabriele breaks every rule by which he has lived these last thirty years or so. His steps quicken. He breaks into a shallow trot. Beads of sweat run down his neck and turn the discomforts in his collar to the tenfold. He cares not. All that matters is the closing of the door and the candlelight and the smell of ancient paper and the scuttle of the silverfish and the pungency of ink. The Signor Secretary is an old man accustomed to habitual slowness. To run is to debase oneself and yet here he is, hell bent on closing that far Scriptorium door with the most extreme sense of prejudice.

It is the twig and the frost scar and the chipped flagstone edges and the scattered Olive leaves that describe the world that will be. Where Signor Secretary Gabriele might think his world revolves around an appointed order, he is mistaken. This world of words, one placed after another in logical, grammatical sequence, is as much a myth as a childhood barely remembered. Signor Secretary Gabriele has lived with pipe rolls and ledgers and laws and debentures and precedent since he was five years old. As his slippered foot finally betrays him and wedges a sliver of old book binding in a crack between the flagstones not ten metres from the Scriptorium door, he falls to the floor and cracks his head on stone. With the mists closing down upon his eyes he understands that rules are worth no more than a saltshaker at the bottom of a deep blue lake.

Signor Secretary Gabriele is dazed but remains conscious. He sees his prone body from above and notices that the blood that runs from a cut on his forehead is nowhere near as black as he thought it would be. He is surprised at how thin and insubstantial he really is. He closes his eyes. He feels the tether holding his out-of-body self pull ever tighter, but then, as his head starts to clear and the nerves begin to register pain, he pulls the would-be escapee back towards his bosom. He completes the task just as he feels that iron blood run across his ruby red lips to singe his tongue with shaken sea-salts.

Signor Secretary Gabriele should get up, dust himself down, and pass quickly into the darkness of the Scriptorium. Instead he lays upon the stone flags and lets the blood slowly congeal upon his forehead and cheek. All the while he is spinning the shape of a puzzle through the empty halls of his closeted, beady black mind.

It starts with a smile. A smile becomes a smirk becomes a hissing intake of air. Signor Secretary Gabriele's cheeks burn bright red with the blood on his forehead and the heat on his lips. He snorts. He gasps. He shakes. His ribs strain cartilage. A volcano erupts in the courtyard of the Scriptorium. Roberto Gabriele laughs out loud for the first time in nearly thirty years. He guffaws. A door opens and a pale young head peers out into the bright sunlight.

"The old crow… was… wrong" splutters the Signor Secretary in between fits of violent laughter. He tries to stand. He falters and young hands help him to his feet. The tears upon his cheeks wash away the traces of blood that fell from the drying cut at his forehead. He looks at a young duster.

"Quite… quite… wrong.", Signor Secretary Gabriele says, flushing with excitement. "It's been… there all… along. Every… day…"

More heads in more doorways. A few of the black clad Dusters and Runners venture out into the courtyard, forming a semi-circle around a weirdly and obviously deranged Signor Secretary Gabriele. One or two of the Under-Secretaries dare to hope. Signor Secretary Gabriele no longer cares. He has solved the puzzle. He spells it out, tapping his foot for every crack, dent and rump of a letter:

W—T---N

--E-M—G--S

"Don't you see, boys… don't you see?" he asks. He looks at

each of them in turn and sees that they don't understand a word that he is saying. He laughs out loud again and starts slapping them all on their shoulders as he walks among them. "Don't you see, boys. It's always been there… So simple… the flagstone… so simple… it says… WRITE IN THE MARGINS…"

The Faithful Gardener

(Loosely based on Andersen's The Gardener & The Lord)

SOME MILES TO THE south of London, nestling in the gently rolling, green swathed hills of the Surrey Downs, there stands an old country manor house, which boasts the thickest of stone walls, a small but nonetheless impressive little tower and ornate white painted wooden gables. This lovely old place was once owned by a famous television personality, whose claim to good fortune and favour was based upon his inestimable knowledge of all things horticultural. He presented a weekly show about gardening and had recently been seen in the nation's living rooms helping the poor and needy to fix up their allotments and their child friendly but dishevelled herbaceous borders. The television gardener lived with his lovely wife on his modest but beautifully proportioned estate in the country, when filming and international awards ceremonies permitted.

The manor house was beautifully appointed, inside and out, sporting a novelty coat of arms above the door and a beautiful wisteria that twisted and flowered around the porch and around the front bay windows. The lawns were of the lushest, velvet green and were matched for their smoothness only by the expensive Wilton carpets that lay in the sitting room. There was not a weed in sight and the flower borders exploded with colour and vivacity throughout the spring, summer and autumn.

Given the many calls upon his time, filming new and instructive programmes, making personal appearances and in advising the great and the good about their white flies and their black spots, our good television gardener and his wife employed a rather clever man from the local village to look after their own garden when they were away. The local man was blessed with the greenest of fingers, and everyone, be they an inhabitant of the locale or a distinguished visitor, always remarked on the sheer beauty and splendour of the gardens at the manor house.

The gardens at the manor were extensive and with so many important assignments and projects to see to, neither the television personality nor his faithful gardener had ever found the time to finish remodelling every nook and cranny in the place. Adjoining the kitchen garden, to the east of the house, there was still a rough patch of ground upon which stood an ancient oak tree. This magnificent specimen stood all year round, in wind and rain and sun, standing bare and almost leafless. Instead of thick green leaves hanging from its branches, the ancient oak was covered in the large, round twig balls that made up a great city of rooks.

Ever since the tree had first raised its huge crown to the skies the rooks had made it their home, passing their history and their grandeur down through every generation until the present day, so that the bird city teemed with life and every resident rook knew that he or she was a true aristocrat. They had seen men and women come and go through the ages, but they had always been there; they were the old, the true lords of the land and the sky. It didn't matter to them one bit that men came along from time to time and raised thunder in their high-rise homes with shotguns. They cawed and wheeled, watching the fire and the thunder rise with a mixture of fear and utter disdain.

The faithful gardener often spoke with his employer about the patch of rough ground around the old oak tree. He was convinced that if the tree was chopped down he could make real use of the land and be rid of the screaming rooks to boot. Despite every good reason he could think of, however, his employer had no desire to be rid of the ancient tree. The famous television gardener always said that the great oak leant the estate an air of permanence and solidity; that it was a link with the past of this small but great house; that it was history and should stand, like himself, as a symbol of greatness and stability forever. "After all, Ted, haven't you got enough to do with the flower borders, the lawns and the vegetables?"

Ted did indeed have plenty to do in looking after the gardens, the vegetables and the orchards. He always worked with zeal, with vigour and not without considerable skill and expertise, but the truth was that the television celebrity and his wife were too busy to see the merits of his arguments about the grand old oak tree. In fact, they were often at pains to explain to old Ted that as good as he was with their little garden they had often seen flowers or eaten fruit on their travels that surpassed the specimens he grew for them at home. These conversations, these descriptions of wonderful blooms and ripe fruits, distressed old Ted, because he wanted to do the best job that he could for his employer.

One day while visiting their country home the famous television gardener and his wife called for old Ted and told him quite bluntly that the previous day they had tasted the most exquisite tomatoes. Visiting some friends in London, they had been privileged to attend a summer barbecue, where everyone, they told him, had praised these succulent and flavoursome tomatoes to the heavens. They were convinced that these luscious fruits could not be of a domestic variety and the famous television gardener asked old Ted to make enquiries, to find out where they came from and to order some seeds for the greenhouse. He was to start growing them here at the manor house immediately.

They gave old Ted the name of the fruit dealer in the city where the tomatoes had been bought and so, the very next morning, old Ted drove into town and arranged to meet the fruit dealer. Arranging all of this was no problem because Ted knew the fruit dealer very well. He was, after all, the very same fruit dealer to whom, on behalf of his employer, old Ted sold the surplus fruit that grew in the garden of the lovely country manor house. When they met, and after a few pleasantries over a cup of tea, old Ted asked the fruit dealer where these wonderful tomatoes came from.

"Why, they're from your own garden, Ted", said the fruit dealer in surprise, and he showed him the very same tresses full of beautiful ripe, red tomatoes that old Ted had sent up to town just a few days previously. This, of course, made old Ted feel very happy. He rushed back to the country manor house and told his master and mistress immediately that the tomatoes came from their very own greenhouse.

The celebrated couple could not believe their ears. "Ted, it's simply not possible. No, we won't believe a word of it unless the fruit dealer can prove it in writing".

And prove it he could. Within an hour there arrived a facsimile copy of a receipt, which clearly showed that the tomatoes had been sold to him by the gardener at Watersmeat Manor.

"Well, that's amazing", exclaimed the television gardener to his wife.

As soon as they had checked the greenhouses for themselves, they started to despatch punnets of their lush red tomatoes to all of their important friends. They were especially keen to send their tomatoes to the restaurants run by their celebrity chef chums in the bustling centres of expensive consumer consumption that shined amid the phantom lights of the capital city. They were over the moon that their modest little estate could produce such wonderful produce and did not hesitate to tell everyone and anyone about the wonders of their traditional approach to gardening. And yet, they felt compelled to tell old Ted that, after all, it was an exceptional summer and everyone's tomatoes had turned out pretty well.

A little later in the year, the famous gardener and his wife were honoured with an invitation to attend a dinner at a famous politician's house. They dined with minor royalty, with famous politicians and with an impressively ostentatious banker. They were even introduced to a famous footballer and his wife, but found the conversation wandering away from the arts of pruning rather too quickly for their taste.

The day after the grand banquet, old Ted was summoned to the hotel in the capital city where his employer and his wife were staying for a few days. They had been served with the most delicious, the tenderest and the juiciest plum pie they had ever tasted. Old Ted was told to make enquiries of the politician's kitchen staff to find out where these plums were cultivated. He was to obtain the name of the fruit, to purchase some young trees and to plant them in the orchard at the manor without delay.

It so happened that old Ted's niece was the pastry cook in the politician's kitchen. She quickly introduced him to the head chef, who was delighted to make the acquaintance of the man who had sent him such wonderful fruit and vegetables for the previous night's culinary extravaganza. At first old Ted was a little confused, but his state of mind changed to one of pure joy as his niece explained it all to him. A few months previously, when the kitchen had a very bad experience with the government catering suppliers, she had shown the head chef some her uncle's home-grown fruits that she was going to have for her lunch. Ever since then the head chef insisted on ordering fresh seasonal fruit and vegetables for banquets and special occasions through old Ted's niece, and all the while the unsuspecting Ted had been convinced that his niece was strangely obsessed by fresh fruit and vegetables.

When old Ted reported back to his employers they were quite stumped for an answer. Once again they couldn't believe what they were hearing.

"Ted, you can't pull the wool over our eyes, you know", they both said. "It's quite impossible. You can't have grown those plums",

This time old Ted was prepared. Written on official government notepaper and in the head chef's own hand, which the famous couple recognised instantly from the menus on the table the previous evening, there was a signed testament to the source of the wonderfully succulent plums.

After their initial shock subsided, the famous television gardener made sure that the whole land heard about his amazing plums. He sent fruit to every person pictured in 'Hi!' magazine that week, arranged visits to his orchards for the great and the good and started a small mail order business selling new young trees to anyone who wanted to grow their own. This particular specimen was so well appreciated that it even came to bear the famous television gardener's own name, which he thought absolutely thrilling.

And through it all, in their quiet moments, the famous television gardener and his wife made every effort to keep old Ted's feet firmly on the ground.

"It wouldn't do to let him get above himself," said the wife.

"Absolutely not", replied her husband. "We can't let him get big headed about all of this".

Old Ted, however, was not inclined to inflate his own ego. Instead, he strived harder every year to produce the most remarkable flowers, vegetables and fruits. All that he wanted was to be recognised as one of the best working gardeners in Surrey, and, with a great deal of hard work, he achieved just that, producing some of the finest specimen fruits and vegetables from the country manor garden for many years to come.

But despite his successes, his employers often reminded him that the tomatoes had been the best of all. The plums were fine indeed, but of a different nature all together and everything else since, while very good, was not a patch on those original fruits. Indeed, as good as his produce was, it was no more than a match, at best, for the produce of other gardeners. When, one year, the rhubarb wilted and turned yellow at the stem, only those poor, unfortunate rhubarb plants were ever mentioned again. It seemed to old Ted that his employers found some sort of satisfaction in being able to say, "Well, Ted, my old friend, it didn't turn out quite so well this year, did it? Better luck next year, eh?"

As well as growing the most stunning fruits and vegetables, old Ted was also something of a wizard with the flower beds. Every Saturday morning, he brought fresh flowers up to the manor house and created the most delicate or the most vibrant arrangements, depending on the patterns of the weather and the moods of his employers. One day, while reading one of his master's gardening magazines, which just happened to have an article about cottage gardens in it penned by the famous television gardener himself, old Ted read about a great national competition. Entries were invited from gardeners across the land, the prize being the chance to have your very own television programme about gardening on one of the satellite television channels. Old Ted had never considered a career in the media, having considerable first-hand experience of the pressures and the trials of it all through his employers. He was, however, intrigued by the competition's rules, which stated that to win the competition you had to produce a most unusual and new flower.

It occurred to Ted that there might be something in this, as he had spent many years experimenting with grafts, cross-pollinations and rootstocks. Hidden away, in the roughest patch of the old manor's gardens where the ancient oak tree grew, was old Ted's private nursery bed. The more he thought about it, the more certain he was that he should enter the competition.

All through the next spring, while paying attention to the manor's gardens, vegetable patches, greenhouses and orchards, old Ted carefully cultivated his special plants. It was a glorious year for growing and, amid the general praise for his floral displays and the usual comments from his employers; old Ted worked quietly and assiduously, waiting for the day of the great competition.

On the day before the competition, old Ted set off bright and early for Kew Gardens. He spent the day preparing the soil in his allocated spot, mulching, weeding and hoeing, before gently placing his prize specimen in its ornamental pot in the middle of his display. He watered his plant, brushed its stems and tenderly pricked out a few older leaves. As if responding to his loving touch, the magnificent red flower head threw up new feathers, filling out and flaming into glorious bloom at just the right moment. The next day, with the show ground full to bursting with every type of plant, with new roses, new fuscias, begonias, hostas and hebe, with the walkways full to bursting with eager competitors and excited crowds, the judging commenced.

To old Ted's delight, each judge stood for minutes on end gazing at his prize entry. Their eyes lit up when they saw the shape of the plant, its fullness and its glorious shades of green rippling in the sunlight. They seemed to melt into the dazzling display from his plant's fire-red flowers, flowers bursting with energy and vibrancy. At last, with the sun at its full height and with the crowds buzzing in anticipation, the famous television gardener and his wife arrived at old Ted's display.

They were amazed, once more, by what they saw. They walked around the plant, examined every leaf, every shoot and every stamen. They tutted and clucked, pressing their tongues against their cheeks, sucked in their breath and made notes on their judge's pads. After ten minutes they stood back and looked at each other.

"It's quite stunning", said Ted's employer. "To think that we should see an Amazonian Fritillary, and a red one to boot".

And the cries went up from the assembled crowd, "Hip, hip, hooray for the Amazonian Fritillary, three cheers for old Ted!"

All of the judges assembled next to Ted's amazing new flower, and busied themselves with their notes and their scores. The famous television gardener buttonholed each and every judge, telling them that he alone had recognised the new plant's sublime glories, that the entrant was his own gardener, who had learned his trade from a kind-hearted master, and that there could only be one winner. Despite some wrangling, and the odd fraying of nerves amongst some of the better-known judges, eventually they all agreed that old Ted was, indeed, the winner.

The next few minutes were a blur for Ted. He was given a bright purple sash to wear, a sparkling shiny trophy to hold and was made to stand just to the left of the famous television gardener when it was time for the speeches. His employer rattled through some thanks, greeted the great and the good in the audience and continued to tell everyone about the new plant. He explained that, although new to them all, it was clearly a hybrid from the equatorial regions, a masterful admixture of the new world and the old ways of the English garden. It was, he said, a stunning masterpiece of the gardener's art. The flower was the fruit of his own garden and was blossoming now because of his love for teaching and the many years of hard work that had helped old Ted to attain such levels of skill. He wanted no thanks for these services, professing only that old Ted should enjoy his moment in the limelight, safe in the knowledge that, like himself and his plums, old Ted would have a new flower named after him.

After some polite applause, and to his absolute horror, old Ted was pushed forward to make his own speech. He stood there before the assembled crowd, before the bigwigs and the celebrities, like a rabbit caught in the headlights of an onrushing juggernaut. He cleared his throat once, twice, three times and stopped. He opened his mouth to speak and then shut it again. Finally, summoning courage from the deepest wells of his soul he mumbled, "s'not a flower. It's an artichoke, a red artichoke".

To be honest, most of the assembled crowd neither understood the difference between an artichoke and an Amazonian Fritillary, nor did they care. They burst into riotous applause and cheering wildly, they carried old Ted on their shoulders all the way to a brand-new Winnebago that was parked at the far end of the show ground. As old Ted signed the contract for his new television programme, as the crowds cheered again and again, no one noticed the furious argument taking place between the judges.

"He's made a right bloody fool of you", screamed the famous television gardener's wife. "Amazonian Fritillary, my arse."

"He…he should've said something", stammered her husband, as around him one judge after another jeered and called him every sort of stupid ass that their imaginations could conjure up.

Events moved quickly after that. The famous television gardener was ridiculed for not recognising a reasonably common vegetable, albeit one of an unusual colour. The rules of the competition were checked, but it said nothing about vegetables being banned, and so old Ted's prize was safe. The world of television gardening was turned on its head overnight. Old Ted soon got over his nerves and proved to be a natural on the goggle box, with his old-world charm and his unpretentious manners.

As for the once famous television gardener, he soon found that many years of proud and boastful behaviour makes for a rapid fall from grace. With everyone's confidence in his gardening knowledge thoroughly shattered and with old scores being settled, his programme was axed from the schedules and his publishing deals quickly dried up. His newspaper column was rescinded in favour of "Old Ted's Country Ways", and before long he and his wife were forced to sell the country manor. They bought a little cottage in the village eked out a meagre living on a residue of royalties gleaned from discount store book sales and the odd spot of lawn mowing that came their way from lineage adverts in the parish newspaper.

Old Ted, on the other hand, went from strength to strength, earning a small fortune from his globally syndicated television show and from a chain of franchised garden centres bearing his name that sprang up across the whole country. Within a year he bought the old country mansion for himself and spent every spare hour he had tending the gardens, the vegetables and the fruits. At last, and with a sigh of relief from old Ted, the ancient oak tree was cut down and cleared away. In its place he carefully cultivated the most beautiful, the tastiest and the most famous patch of artichokes in the whole of the known world.

And although, as he grew older, he was tempted to get some help with the lawn mowing, old Ted could never quite bring himself to ring the telephone number of another old couple in the local village who advertised as odd job gardeners.

The Only Way to Know for Sure

(Loosely based on Andersen's The Princess & The Pea, and The Talisman)

YOU MIGHT REMEMBER A feature or two appearing in some of our glossier magazines recently about an eligible young man who wanted to get married. While this is not an uncommon thing and usually not worth too many column inches, the young man in question was no run of the mill Joe. The young man in question had, in fact, once sung a song so popular that he never found a need, financially or artistically, to bother recording any other songs. Wives, mothers and daughters throughout Britain's suburban radio land knew all of the words to the young man's song and delighted in humming along to its very catchy tune whenever it was played, all of which helped to maintain its popularity long after the song's novelty had worn off and also helped to keep the young man's income at a healthy and quietly spectacular level.

Basking in the glow cast by his brief but perfect musical

accomplishments the young man grew older living a quiet life in the countryside with his darling mother. He often thought about singing another song and had, as a result, kept himself in tip top condition, but as the years passed he found himself thinking more and more about settling down, and so it was that he decided to marry. Of course, he didn't want to marry just anybody. Whoever she might be, the young man's new bride would have to be what he called: "My Princess".

And that is why the article about the young man appeared in some of the country's glossier magazines. He was convinced that the simplest and best way to find his perfect partner in life would be to announce his desire to marry to the world by way of a celebrity photo-shoot. In fact, the article generated so much publicity that the young man found himself appearing on television and on radio shows throughout the country and his old but much cherished song was dusted off and given another airing by disk jockeys on every radio station that played popular music. For nearly a whole month the young man was the talk of the town. He was the brightest star shining above the airwaves. Once again, although in a far more mature sense, he was the dreamboat that drifted languidly through young girls' daydreams, which, given the fickle nature of the public's imagination, was a very considerable achievement.

Lured by the prospect of marriage to such a fine young man there were plenty of young ladies who made a beeline for his letter box and his lunch box. The only problem was that the young man simply couldn't tell if any of these young ladies might really be his darling princess or not. Undeterred, however, the young man travelled the length and breadth of the country, escorting each and every one these beautiful and hopeful creatures to nightclubs, to restaurants and to his hotel bedrooms. He even managed a couple of quiet evenings in with some of the not so beautiful ones. But even after all of this most diligent research the young man still couldn't find what he was looking for. No matter how hard he tried to see these young ladies in their best light, there always appeared to be something wrong with them. Eventually he returned home, being both very tired and very sad, for he did want to find his princess so very much, and it was then that the young man's dear old mother came up with a very cunning plan.

"Invite all the most famous young ladies in the land to come and stay with us", she said." Not on the same night, of course", she added just to be sure that she could manage the linen.

Accompanied by paparazzi flashbulbs and reality television cameramen, one by one the young man invited each and every one of the most beautiful and celebrated young ladies in the land to come and stay at his country pile. No matter what the weather, the season or the time of day, the house rang with the laughter of happy young people enjoying each other's company. Every morning the young man's mother delivered a lovely tray of tea and toast to his bedroom and as the exhausted but glowing couple lay in the king size love nest that had been especially arranged for them, the young man's dear old mother asked each young lady in turn if she would give her a hand with the laundry. In particular she asked each fair maid if she would wash her son's crinkly boxer shorts and diamond pattern ankle socks.

To the grave and desperate disappointment of both the young man and his mother, the young ladies behaved perfectly because they had all been brought up properly by respectably stage-struck parents, each of them agreeing immediately to the request for a bit of a scrub at the washtub. As soon as she heard the word "Yes" leave the lips of these kind and considerate young things, the young man's mother bundled the girls out of the house without a "by your leave" or any further kindness being offered.

"No, she's no good", cawed the old crow to her son as she slammed the door on yet another haplessly romantic soul. "No real princess would ever wash your smalls, boy. Ruin her nails, it would!"

This went on for weeks and weeks until, with the young man complaining about the effects of sleep deprivation, there was only one famous young lady left in the whole of Great Britain. The young man was, by now, emotionally drained, having lost count of the number of dates and encounters that he'd endured in his desperate quest to find marital happiness. The posts on the headboard in his bedroom were becoming dangerously weak as he whittled them away to nearly nothing with his little morning notches and aide memoirs. But, with time and the pool of potential brides quickly evaporating, the day came when the last of the country's suitable young women was due to arrive on his doorstep.

The young man was not hopeful. "OK", he said to his dear old mother, "we'll have some fun, but I think the socks idea stinks. Can't we just buy new ones every week?"

"You never know. A bird in the bed is worth two in the laundry, as they say"

The young man looked at his mother quizzically and let slip one of those long drawn out sighs that is the trademark of every thirty-something man who still lives at home with his dear old ma.

That evening the heavens opened upon the world and, depressed by the rain and the generally gloomy outlook, the young man all but gave up hope of ever finding true happiness. Nevertheless, and at the expected time, there was a knock on the front door. The young man opened the door with his usual flourish, a showman to the end, and was greeted by a storm of flashing electric light, and once his eyes had adjusted, to a positive vision in pink. The young lady, who was famous, as is every "glamourista", for the skimpiness of her skirts and the translucency of her pure silk blouses, stood there dripping from head to toe.

The young man smiled his sunniest smile in an attempt to alleviate her damp suffering. The young lady, known as Burberry to the common people, glowered at him for a moment before barging him aside and striding purposefully into the hallway.

"Don't just stand there", she screamed at him as the world turned a brilliant shade of gloss white in a storm of paparazzi shouts and exploding flash bulbs. The young man slammed the door shut and wrapped the young woman and her dripping designer clothes in a towelling bathrobe that his mother hurriedly threw at him. As he caught the bathrobe he thought he saw his dear old mother grinning the widest grin this side of Wonderland.

After a long hot shower, a manicure, a pedicure, two hours with her stylist and half as long again on the phone to her agent, the super-model known as Burberry was ready for the fun and games. She glided to the top of the large and ornate staircase in a positively charged shimmer of discotheque fashions and demanded champagne. Then, as she descended the stairs in large, but strangely and compellingly graceful platform boots, she explained to everyone that she had sold the picture rights for the evening to Howdy! - the celebrity lifestyle magazine beloved of the little people.

The young man's dear old mother was a true brick that night. She soaked the labels off of every bottle of Cava before it was served, and she handled with absolute tact and aplomb every request for pizza, for nail varnish and for some decent bloody music. The young couple got on famously all through the evening, cuddling up on the sofa, talking, eating Marmite on toast in the small wee hours and generally adopting every pose and every smile called for by the photographer. The evening was, despite the early rain affected shenanigans, a resounding success.

Eventually, with the photographers long gone and with the young couple safely tucked up in bed, the young man's dear old mother sat quietly in the kitchen with her gnarled old hands wrapped tightly around a steaming mug of cocoa. The grin on her face was as wide as the Grand Canyon as she flicked her top dentures forward absentmindedly to relieve the irritation to her palate caused by some very annoying biscuit crumbs. Her body swayed gently in time with the sound of creaking mattress springs coming from her son's bedroom.

Bright and early the next morning the young man's mother tapped on her son's bedroom door and walked into the room carrying the usual tray of tea and biscuits. She threw open the curtains, letting the room flood with glorious summer sunshine, and as she stood there, silhouetted in her curlers and her power-shouldered dressing gown, she started to sing. The old lady's gravel laden voice was perfectly suited to the tune: "Oh, what a beautiful morning".

"Aaaarrrggghhh!" screamed Burberry, as the dulcet tones of cock-crow dipped in beneath the duvet cover and dragged her into the world of sunlight. "What the bloody hell is that?"

She yanked the duvet cover back up over head and started to swear loudly. The young man rolled over slowly, opened one bleary eye and made a slow-motion lunge for one of the mugs of tea. From under the duvet cover the disembodied stream of oaths and imprecations continued unabated, and as the young man tried to sip from the life-giving tannin elixir, his latest paramour started to thrash her legs around wildly.

Finally, and in a real one hundred and ten percent hissy fit, she surfaced from under the duvet and screamed, "Shut the friggin' curtains. It ain't nat'ral bein' awake before bloody lunch time".

It took all of the young man's guile and persuasion to coax and persuade his new paramour to keep her head above the duvet cover and to accept that it was, indeed, a very beautiful morning. It was only with the greatest reluctance that Burberry allowed herself to become accustomed to the brightness of this early hour.

Once her eyes started to focus properly, she let out another, huge, lung-bursting scream. Stood there right in front of her was the young man's wrinkled old mother and in her arms she was holding a plastic laundry basket full of crinkly, used boxer shorts and stiffly soiled socks.

"What the…" stuttered the young lady. "If you think I'm going anywhere near those things then you're bloody barking. Haven't you got a maid?"

The young man leaped out of bed and spun his mother round by her waist as they waltzed around the bedroom in a dance of pure joy. Teacups shattered and biscuits crumbled underfoot as they danced and sang. It was all over. At last they had found the perfect match; at last the young man had discovered a real princess. And so, with the pre-nuptials agreed and with the photographic rights sold to the highest bidder, the young man finally got his heart's desire and married his darling princess.

The young man and his bride jetted off to their honeymoon paradise sponsored by a company that made coconut filled chocolate bars, and in return for a few more photographs, a short video and some encouraging words, they were given a wonderful time on golden beaches lapped by azure seas. Their evenings were a riot of dancing, laughing and the after-hours bliss of the marital bed, and after all of this the happy couple even found time to sit quietly as the dawn rose and talk of life, love and their plans for the future. They were so very happy, and everything seemed to be working out perfectly for them, but as the honeymoon neared its end, they couldn't help noticing that all was not well between them. There were no fights, no disagreements, nor was there any petulant posturing, but nonetheless, during their long dawn conversations they became aware of a doubt nagging away at them beneath their true, true love.

The doubt that each of them felt was this: will I always be as happy as I am now?

They checked their legal agreements through, clause by clause and swore to each other in front of various newspaper and television reporters that they would always be true, but no matter how vehemently they protested their love for one another the doubt always remained. Finally, with that hook of uncertainty still snagging and scratching at their hides, they decided to seek out a talisman, a lucky charm that would protect their love for each other forever and ever more.

In their professional capacities they had both heard about a foxy old publicist who spent his summers on this very same Caribbean paradise isle, a wily old dog of a man who was held in the highest esteem by stars and celebrities the world over. He was wise and powerful, and it was said that he always knew how to give the best advice, even in the middle of the greatest of hardships and miseries, and so, over a mint julep or two by the side of the old man's pool, the young man and his princess told him about their problem.

When the wise old publicist heard their story and thought about everything they had told him, he turned to them both and said, "Journey to the four corners of the world. Ask every famous married couple if they're truly content. If they really are, then ask them for a couple of signed photographs that each of you can keep with you wherever you go to remind you of your love for each other. That's the surest remedy for your problem. And if you want, I can arrange for a documentary crew to accompany you every step of the way".

The documentary idea was tempting, but the young couple resisted the old man's inducements. They wanted this journey to be a pure expression of their love, unsullied by grubby fingered commercialism.

The very next day Burberry read about a famous film star and his wife in one of her favourite glossy magazines, a couple who had been happily married for over forty years and even had a barbecue sauce named after them. What could be better? The young man and his adoring wife immediately flew to Hollywood and as soon as they arrived they telephoned the film star's agent, who happily arranged dinner for the four of them at a swanky restaurant on the strip. During dinner the young man asked his guest if his marriage was truly as happy as it was rumoured to be.

"Of course," was the reply. "Except for one thing. We have no children, unfortunately, at least not from our marriage".

The talisman was not to be found here then.

On their way back home, the young couple stopped off in New York, where a wealthy business tycoon lived, who was rumoured to have found true happiness in a long and successful marriage. The tycoon was only too happy to entertain such well known newlyweds and he invited them to a party with all of his friends, acquaintances and prospective business colleagues.

When asked the same question he replied, "Why yes, indeed, we really are very content. My wife and I lead the best of lives. Our only regret is that we have so many children. They cause us so many headaches and heartaches".

The talisman was evidently not to be found here either.

The young couple continued to seek out every happily married celebrity couple in every city and in every country where really famous people lived, but nowhere could they find anyone who could say a "yes" without adding a "but". Eventually, and with heavy hearts, they gave up their quest and headed for home.

When the happy couple disembarked from their Jumbo Jet and left their first-class seats in the usual state of long distance disarray, they found themselves in the middle of another media scrummage. Hundreds of reporters and photographers vied with each other to get the best quotes and the best pictures, and in the middle of this ruck and maul the young prince and his lady wife spotted a tired looking man and woman sitting in the middle of the airport concourse. These two frayed individuals were playing lovingly with their twin sons. They seemed oblivious to anything going on around them. The husband, his smiling wife and his happy sons seemed to exude a sense of calm that was quite unique and perfect in this rushed and bustling world. Breaking free of the media circus, the young man and his new wife rushed over to the happy family group and asked them the same question that they had asked all around the world.

"Yes, we are very happy", said the man. "With my wife to comfort me and my children to keep me young I'm extremely happy and content".

The young man grinned at his new bride. Remembering the words of the wily old publicist, the young man said, "If we make you famous, you know, fifteen minutes and all that, could we have a signed photograph of you? You can even kiss Burberry on the cheek if you like".

The older man looked at his wife in horror and his cheeks burned red with indignation. He managed, however, to summon up his reserves of inner calm before turning towards the young man and saying, "Bugger off! Don't you know who we are? Don't you recognise us? How dare you be so patronising, you little shit, you one hit bloody wonder".

The young man looked blank. His beautiful new bride looked blank. Around them pandemonium broke out. The gentlemen of the press surrounded the family and completely ignored the young man and his beautiful new wife. As the young starlets started to slink away, confused and not a little annoyed, they heard the familiar shouts and barks of the hounding press pack:

"Over here, Prime Minister…"

"Give us a smile, Brenda, love…"

"Any comment on the single currency, Sir?"

And so the young man and his wife returned to their new home, which they had recently bought in a prime location just to the northeast of London's orbital motorway. They were tired, disappointed and frustrated. The very next morning they telephoned the wily old publicist and gave him a piece of their combined minds, but having listened to their ranting and raving for nearly a whole minute, the old dog smiled to himself and asked the young couple, "Has your journey really been such a waste of time? Haven't you learned a great many new and wonderful things?"

The young man thought about this for a few minutes. His new wife also stopped short of her final insult and gave these wise words some serious consideration. The young man took his bride's hand in his and spoke gently to the old man on the other end of the telephone line.

"Well, I suppose we've both learned that to be content you need nothing more than just that - to be content".

He looked into his wife's hazel eyes and smiled. She looked back at him for a second, grinned and then taking the handset from him she said, "Or maybe we've learned that that there's more than one way to skin a cat...we're too young to settle down. I've been offered a part in an 'Adult' movie by Jean Paul Robespierre, you know, one of them blokes we met in Hollywood and I've always wanted to do some serious acting, so thanks for the advice but..."

With their respective lawyers flexing their considerable egos and with the press pack baying like wolves, Burberry hopped onto the next transatlantic red-eye. Despite his grief, and with his deeply tanned six-pack still in fine shape, the young man overcame his tragic flirtation with married life, secured a new recording contract and within a month he released a new disk full of sad little love songs, which sold millions of copies.

Burberry's film, while not a critical success, was watched by millions the world over and as the young man set off on a world concert tour, Burberry found herself on set playing the lead in a new film, this time with complete sentences for her to speak.

In their respective hotel suites on opposite sides of the world, the young man and his soon to be divorced wife considered the lessons they had learned from married life. True love might be a holy grail worth chasing, but in its absence a good marriage with plenty of publicity did wonders for the old bank balance.

In hotel rooms on opposite sides of the world the young man and the young woman looked at their reflections in the bedroom mirror and smiled to themselves.

"What a perfect marriage..." they both thought and as one being they picked up their bedside telephones and rang down to order more champagne.

The Television Bride

(Loosely based on Andersen's The Most Incredible Thing)

THE WORLD HAS SEEN many marvels during recent years, and one of the many things that helps to illustrate the fusion of technical modernism with the established status quo is the way in which England's ancient feudal institutions have embraced the social and political structures of modern times. Nowhere is this more obvious than in the mutual fascination that the high and the low of the land have for the world of television. In fact, television is so popular in Great Britain that even the royal family, when not entertaining foreign presidents or giving the halls of Buck House a fresh coat of magnolia emulsion, spend their evenings with their eyes glued to the box.

In this febrile atmosphere of ratings wars and popular novelty, an executive producer at a small independent production company came up with a marvellous new idea. Rather than employing actors to tell classic tales, to make people laugh, or to inform and to educate, he hit upon the novel idea of making ordinary people the stars of television shows. He called the idea by the following name, 'Dropped on your Head Television'.

This was because he wanted people to understand that it was real, and like being dropped on your head, it sometimes hurt those who participated in it. Most of all, however, it was called by this name because it was funny watching other people making complete fools of themselves, and pretty soon nearly every television programme featured ordinary people trying to win small fortunes, to become movie stars and generally being the nastiest of nasties in the woodpile.

'Dropped on your Head Television' became so popular and so addictive that Betsy Windsor, our wise old Queen, called all of her courtiers and all of her political advisors before her and made an astonishing announcement.

"Whoever can do the most amazing thing on our royal television, whoever can show the most ingenuity and talent, will win the hand of our grand-daughter in marriage together with half of our personal estates and investments as a dowry."

The whole country went wild with excitement. All across the land hopeful suitors practiced their funniest party turns and their most amazing performance art works in the hope of winning the princess' hand in marriage. A sizable number of women entered the competition too, for the country has, in recent times, embraced social inclusiveness and is open to a wide variety of ideas.

True to the generally accepted format of such television shows, there were weeks of auditions held before an expert panel of judges, all of which were televised. The ratings were measured and found to be off of any known scale and every night, come the appointed hour, the whole country stopped dead in its tracks to watch one poor unfortunate after another being ridiculed by the judges.

The airwaves were filled by singers who couldn't sing, by jugglers who dropped their balls and by contortionists whose bodies were as stiff as boards and refused to do what they might once have been capable of. The viewers laughed at inventors who made thingamabobs that didn't work and at flu-riddled scientists who claimed to have a cure for the common cold. Every sphere of human endeavour at every level of competence was represented in the auditions, night after night after night.

The experts sat and watched each contestant, and as all such experts are trained to do, they sat there in po-faced silence until, with a flourish and a wicked gleam in their eyes, it came to the time for judgement. Each desperate contestant was made to stand in front of the panel of judges on a spot marked with a silver star, and almost without fail the judges poured torrents of scorn and condescension down upon their heads. These ordinary people cringed and winced as the experts subjected them to crushing and horribly patronising witticisms, The ultimate aim of this personal degradation was focussed on one thing; to single out only the most exceptional talents, while ensuring that the audience at home was vicariously thrilled and titillated by the humiliation of those who failed.

And this was, as our dear and wise old Queen knew very well, the whole point. Only the strongest and the most robust contestant would be a suitable match for her grand-daughter's spirited nature. Only the most inventive and talented of her subjects would be able to engage with her grand-daughter on a mutually fulfilling and intellectual level. The weeks passed, and the judges ripped contestants to shreds until at last there were only twelve of them left in the competition.

The whole of the country was ablaze with talk of the Grand Final. At every crossroads, in every bar and in every factory canteen, there was only one topic of conversation. For a whole week the twelve finalists were made to live in one of Betsy's smaller palaces, where their every waking and sleeping hour was broadcast to a mesmerised and adoring public. The Queen even forgot to attend a diplomatic dinner because she was so engrossed in the goings on in the 'Big Suitor House'.

With audience figures going through the roof and with advertising revenues hitting all-time highs, the executive producer was, of course, paid a big fat bonus. He was also offered a promotion to the position of Head of Light Entertainment with the BBC, which would have been fabulous had someone on the board of governors not insisted on inserting a clause in his contract forcing him to keep a whole twenty percent of the schedule for factual content.

On the given day and at the given hour each of the remaining contestants revealed their final masterpiece. The first contestant performed a stunning new aria. The second conducted the London Symphony Orchestra in a stirring rendition of his brand-new symphony. The remaining contestants performed popular songs of wit and charm, painted pictures in sublime colours, formed living sculptures, delivered the world's first coherent theory of everything and even wrote a best-selling novel live on television. Everyone, however, agreed that the most amazing thing of all was the human television.

The judges used every hyperbole in the thesaurus to describe their joy and amazement. The studio crowds went wild. The human television was astounding. It was incredible.

One of the contestants made a suit out of the finest electronic wizardry, which turned his body into the most beautiful, the most versatile and brilliantly clear television screen ever invented. He even made a special series of videos to show on his body and as he slowly revolved under the hot studio lights, as he turned from judge to judge, each programme was revealed in all of its glory. The Queen and her family, who were sitting on the judging panel for the final, could do nothing but gasp in sheer ecstasy.

On the contestant's back there was an image of Moses on the mount, typing the first of the Ten Commandments into a laptop computer; "Thou shallt have no other Gods before me".

On his right arm there appeared a video of an exhausted messenger falling to his knees in a crowded Athenian marketplace. Although in the throes of death he reported to his people that the Persians were defeated at the battle of Marathon.

On the contestant's left arm Adam and Eve danced around an apple tree in full bloom, bothered neither by their nakedness nor by the tambourine-playing snake that accompanied their wild gyrations.

On his bottom you could see depictions of the four seasons, each appearing in sequence, in full bloom and in sweet surround sounds that made the world appear so delicate and fragile.

Along the length of his left leg the great artists wove images and colours in a collage, in a riot of tone and line, just as if the contestant were a kaleidoscope.

His right leg showed the Muses, one for each of the arts, leading the great poets, writers, painters, sculptors and thinkers by the nose.

On his head played theorems and equations, numbers and symbols, representing the sciences. These images culminated in a sequence of grainy pictures depicting John Logie Baird, the inventor of television, as recorded at the dawn of the broadcast age.

Finally, displayed across the man's broad chest, there were images of riot and unrest, of the dispossessed and the establishment locked in mortal combat. As the image zoomed in, as a police baton was raised in anger, the images metamorphosed into flowers blooming around the heads of cherubs born aloft on rainbow wings. This, of course, was the triumph of hope.

Everyone in the television studio was absolutely mesmerised by the melange of imagery and by the cacophony that rose up from the merged soundtracks. It was, they all said afterwards, quite the most amazing thing. It was a work of art without compare.

All that remained was to crown the only possible winner of the competition, and after the ceremony to place a laurel wreath on his head was complete, the contestant removed his fabulous suit and revealed himself to be a fine looking young man. He was handsome, strong and tender. In short, he was everything that the princess could have hoped for and the Queen and her consort were overjoyed that their plan had worked out so well.

All in all, and after a few questions about prospects and family lineage, they were so pleased that they had found such a suitable young man for their grand-daughter that it was agreed the marriage should take place there and then with the cameras still rolling. Cheers and hurrahs went up in every living room in the kingdom. Bottles of fizz were popped and toasts were drunk.

The director of the broadcast panned his cameras around the studio and zoomed in on every smile and every grin as the audience pulsated in time with the continual explosion of flash bulbs and the shouts and screams of the wildly happy crew.

All of a sudden, the screams of joy turned into screams of dreadful fear and panic. In the middle of the studio set there was a huge puff of black smoke followed by the loudest thunderclap imaginable. As the smoke began to clear, the shape of a large, muscular man could just be made out.

"STOP!" yelled the man. "That suit isn't the most incredible thing on television. This is!"

And with an enormous sledgehammer the giant proceeded to smash every transistor, every microchip, every filament and every capacitor in the wonderful television suit. In a furious, seething storm of blows the stranger destroyed the suit right in front of Good Queen Betsy, her family and every member of the watching audience, both at home and in the studio. The royal family, the judges, the technicians and the watching public looked on in amazement as the stranger stood firm and roared, "I did that. I have power in these hands greater than life and death. I'm the victor!"

After much consultation and some legal wrangling, the judges reached an agreement. "It's true." they said. "In destroying this work of art, this marriage of the Muses with technology, this stranger has, indeed, shown himself to be the most astounding of all things."

Of course, there were rumours. It was said in some quarters that the drama of the finale had been arranged as the final coup de grace in the search for the ultimate televisual experience. But, even if it were true, most of the general population agreed with the judges and so within the hour the stranger came to stand beside the princess in London's great abbey at Westminster.

The princess was, understandably, not at all pleased with this turn of events. She tried to argue with her grand-mother, but mindful of the rules and of the power of the moving image, she could not change her grand-mother's mind. The ratings and the weight of public opinion were too great. Any change of heart now would drive their poll ratings into the floor.

All around the princess the ladies of the court sang and celebrated the occasion as the great and the good of the England's green and pleasant land, the celebrities and the superstars, assembled to celebrate the marriage. The streets thronged with revellers and the abbey was illuminated in the glorious ambers and reds of candles and torchlight. Beside her the stranger, her husband to be, swaggered and gloated over the princess, with his head held high, sure and certain in the winning of his prize.

At a signal from the Archbishop of Canterbury silence fell upon the assembled crowds. The ceremony was about to start. Priests, pastors and holy ones of all religions stood and opened their mouths to begin the first incantation. As they uttered the very first word of the ceremony the most horrendous wailing drowned out their massed voices and the air was filled with the thud and boom of bass notes and percussion. All eyes turned towards the huge oak doors at the far end of the abbey and there, advancing down the aisle in the once famous television suit, was the beaten finalist.

Ladies swooned and fainted. Men gaped and started to sweat as the apparition walked. It was like seeing a ghost for the very first time, for there in the middle of the church was an ogre, a hobgoblin, a wraith, which moved, in vengeful fits and starts on two stiff legs. Every cobbled together panel on the suit showed disfigured and disembodied images. The patched together speakers broadcast sounds of groaning torment, growling like rabid dogs. No one but the man in the suit could move a muscle. Slowly, in an agony of horrific imagery, in a barrage of deafening vibrations, he staggered up to the altar and came to a halt directly in front of the princess and the lofty stranger.

The man in the suit raised his right arm. In his hand he held a television remote control, which he showed to the assembled crowd. He pressed a button. One by one the images that played upon his broken body writhed and bit at the air, spinning and rising up from their broken screens to take shape and solid form in the real world.

First Moses, then Adam and Eve, the marathon runner and all of the other famous and virtuous people in the videos appeared in physical form. Moses pinned the stranger's feet to the cold flagstones by dropping his laptop computer onto them, while Adam and Eve chastised him for his pride and for his covetousness. Each character appeared in turn, making the stranger quake with terror until, finally, a horribly disfigured cherub flew up above the stranger's head and laid him low with a police baton.

In every home in the land, on every sofa, the entire population of the country sat transfixed by this gruesome and entirely unexpected scene. This vengeful, this fascinating series of events held them in total thrall. It was, without a doubt and despite all that had gone before, the most incredible thing ever seen.

The princess was the first to come to her senses. She stood before the man in the ruined and spectral television suit and called out to the assembled dignitaries, "He will be the one. He will be my husband."

The young man pressed another button on the remote control and all of the phantom images faded into the shadows cast by the candles that illuminated the great abbey. The terrible discord that had filled the evening air wound down to nothing more than a faint hiss before falling into the deepest, darkest silence. The young man peeled the suit slowly from his weary body, walked up to the princess, took her hand in his and turned to face the awe struck line of ministers, priests and holy souls. As the young man leaned forward and kissed his bride to be softly on her ruby red lips, Betsy Windsor, the congregation and the viewing public all stated to sob tears of pure joy. Throughout the land men, women and children reached for boxes and packets of tissues.

Outside of the abbey, in a pantechnicon in a fenced off area, the director of the television broadcast cut to close ups of the young couple. The young man smiled to camera and there was a diamond flash of light around his head. Speaking softly and warmly, like a close and beloved friend, the television show's anchor-man informed the viewers that they would be right back in the thick of the action after a short message from the programme's sponsors...

Upwardly Mobile

(Loosely based on the Grimm brother's The Fisherman & His Wife)

ALTHOUGH LIFE BY THE sea might appear to be idyllic, it is not without its problems of season and poverty, and there was once a poor fisherman who lived with his long-suffering wife in a caravan on the cliff tops that rise up from Cornwall's craggy southern coastline. Apart from a few casual jobs that he managed to get during the summer season, when Britain's residential masses poured out of their suburban homes to spend two weeks basking in the melange of weather systems that blow in across the great western seas, he spent most of the year fishing from beaches and rocky breakwaters, eking out a meagre living by selling sea bass to local restaurants and pubs.

Towards the end of another summer of variable weather, with the seasonal work drying up, the fisherman went down to his favourite spot on the beach and cast out his lines, settling down in a rocky hollow to wait for the bounty of the oceans to come his way. He spent a happy hour musing on the vagaries of fortune and on his wife's incessant drive to better her lot by putting up new net curtains and buying things in the end of season sales, before, all of a sudden, the line went taught and his float was dragged under the waves and out of sight.

The fisherman played out the reel, letting the fish take enough line so that it wouldn't break and then he hauled and spun for all he was worth. It was, quite possibly, the biggest fish he had ever landed and was sure to be worth a pretty penny. He worked as diligently and as carefully as he could so as not to lose his prize. Eventually, after much travail and having expended a great deal of energy and sweat, the fisherman finally caught sight of the great fish he hoped to land. He was stunned to see that holding on to his line for dear life was a soaked, bedraggled and half drowned man in sailing gear. The fisherman planted his rod into the sand, wedged it fast with some rocks and waded out into the surf to rescue the poor unfortunate from the heavy swell and from a wind that whipped the spray up and around his ears.

"Please…help…me", gurgled the waterlogged tourist as he finally managed to grab hold of the fisherman's coat sleeves, and without a moment's hesitation the fisherman dragged the man to safety on the beach. Having checked that there were no broken bones, the fisherman dashed up to an ice cream kiosk at the head of the beach, borrowed a mobile phone and called for an ambulance. Then he went back to the stricken man and tended to him with great care until the rescue services arrived.

As the half-drowned man was placed onto a stretcher he placed a soggy but readable card into the fisherman's trembling hand and whispered, "My name is on the card. I'm in catering and if ever you should need anything at all just call me. I'll do whatever I can to help you. You've saved my life".

The local paper took pictures of their resident hero and by the time that the fisherman got home to his caravan, his wife had heard all about her brave husband's stirring deeds that afternoon on the radio. She pressed him to tell her everything, which he did, including the part where the poor unfortunate man had promised to remember them if they ever needed help.

"Did you ask him for anything?" said the fisherman's wife.

"No, not at the time, I didn't think it was right", replied her husband, "and anyway, I wouldn't know what to ask for".

"Typical bloody man", said his wife, as she looked the now dry business card over for the umpteenth time. "You can start by calling this number and asking him if he could help us to get a proper little cottage in the village. This caravan stinks and it leaks and winter's coming on".

The fisherman walked the half-mile to the nearest telephone box and called the number on the card. The phone rang a few times and was answered by the businessman's wife, who, on hearing that it was the fisherman who was calling, immediately promised him that she and her husband would sort this small thing out.

"After all", she said, "everyone should have somewhere warm and dry to live and it's such a small thing to do to repay your bravery and your kindness".

Within a month the paperwork was done, the local council searches were completed, and contracts were signed. Well before the final onset of winter's driving rains and howling gales, the fisherman and his wife were snugly settled into their new cottage home, complete with brand new furniture, a proper telephone line and a lovely new kitchen. The cottage even had a pretty little courtyard garden with a greenhouse in one corner so that the fisherman could supplement the family diet by growing a few vegetables and fruits in the spring.

The fisherman remarked to his wife as he carried her over the threshold of their first real house, "Well, love, this is where true happiness begins".

She looked at him quizzically for a moment before replying, "We'll see".

That winter was full of beating winds and horizontal rain. The seas towered above the bunkered land in their grey majesty, and the couple, blessed for the first time with central heating, lived as well as they had ever done.

The fisherman thought the world was a beautiful, a perfect place, until early on a bright spring morning his wife turned to him and said, "You can't swing a cat in this place. It's really getting me down, and as for the garden, well, it's no more than a yard. It reminds me of the sort of place my grandmother used to live in. What we need, especially if we're going to have a family, is a nice three-bedroom semi-detached house with a proper garden. Call your mate and tell him I'm in the family way and we need something bigger".

"Darling, darling", exclaimed the fisherman, "that's wonderful news, I had no idea. But do you really think I should ask our friend again. I mean, he was very kind, but we can't keep asking for more. The cottage is snug and warm, and we've got two bedrooms, couldn't we make do here?"

"Rubbish!", said his wife. "You saved his life and he can't put a price on that. Pick up the phone and ask him".

Reluctantly the fisherman telephoned the businessman again and this time he got straight through. He explained that his wife was expecting and that, although they appreciated his kind gesture, the cottage was really a bit small for a growing family. He apologised but asked nonetheless for a three-bedroom semi-detached house with a garden and a swing.

"Of course," said the businessman. "I understand. I've got a couple of kids myself and I know how it is, never enough space for the nappies and the toys, and your wife will be getting anxious about her little nestlings. Leave it with me. After all you did, how could I possibly refuse?"

To make things run as smoothly as he could, the businessman bought the cottage from the couple, which, given that they never had a mortgage in the first place, meant that they pocketed a tidy little sum. Then he made them a gift of a beautifully decorated, modern semi-detached house on a quiet new estate in a local seaside town. The house had the latest in modern kitchen appliances, a brand-new corner bathroom suite, fitted wardrobes in all three bedrooms, and a lovely garden in which the businessman had a swing, a climbing frame and a sand pit installed. Within a month, and with late spring in full bud, the couple took possession of their brand-new home, invested some of their newly acquired cash in a sporty little hatchback car, and paid for a family membership at a local country club and gymnasium.

Strangely, the fisherman's wife did not suffer from morning sickness, nor did she eat for two, gain weight or find cute little knitted bootees of any interest whatsoever. It turned out that she had misread the results of the pregnancy testing kit, and although disappointed, she told her husband that they should keep practising in the bedroom of a Sunday morning. In the meantime, she spent a great deal of her time at the country club and gymnasium, toning her muscles, keeping her figure in trim and joining a number of other upwardly mobile wives for coffee mornings, hair appointments and tennis lessons.

Towards the end of summer, on a balmy Sunday afternoon with the barbecue embers glowing in a corner of the garden, the fisherman raised a glass of sparkling Chablis to his wife and said, "Darling, what a life. There's money in the bank, we've got a lovely house, and I've finally been able to afford the best fishing rods that money can buy. We couldn't be happier, could we?"

His wife lay back on her sun lounger, shut her eyes and murmured, "No dear, probably not".

The next morning the fisherman's wife woke up early. She had not slept very well, her head being full of ideas and schemes, and so, as the sunlight streamed in through the bedroom window, she nudged her husband awake with her elbow. "Come on, wake up, I've got something to say".

He turned over slowly and opened one eye, feeling that slight dullness around the edge of his thought processes that suggested that maybe he had supped one glass too many the night before. Once he was able to focus he realised that his wife had that look on her face that signified trouble, not of the 'You Bastard' variety, but of the 'I think we should' variety. He sat bolt upright in bed and waited.

"Now that I've finally got your attention", she said, "I want to discuss our present living arrangements. Ever since we joined the country club, I've had to put up with the airs and bloody graces of all those other women. I don't mind that you don't go to work, in fact I like it, but how will we ever afford one of those big, new, detached five-bedroom houses with automatic gates like the ones at Seaview Park? How will we ever be able to afford brand new cabriolets and a swimming pool?"

"Are you saying you want me to get a job?" asked her husband after a moment or two casting his line out amongst his early morning thoughts.

"No, dear, I'm not. I think it would be much better if we asked our mutual friend for bit more help. I mean, if he buys this house from us and gives us a lovely new executive home, we'll be able to put one over on those bitches at the club, won't we. We'll be the only ones out of all of them who have independent means".

"You've got to be joking", replied her appalled husband. "I can't ask him for another house. It's just wrong. No, I won't do it".

Breakfast was a frosty affair and the fisherman decided that this was one of those times when absence would definitely make the heart grow fonder. He packed up his rods and his brand new multi-compartment bait box, loaded them into the back of the car and spent the rest of the day sitting on the beach waiting for the fish to start biting and for his wife to stop snapping. He didn't get home until dusk had fallen and was very surprised to find a beautiful candlelit dinner waiting for him, a dinner that was suffused with the sound of romantic strings and a look in his wife's eyes that meant that he would be getting very little sleep that night.

Unfortunately, the mood was broken when, over a large cognac, his wife revealed that she had phoned their mutual friend, had told him about her husband's terminal illness and had persuaded him to make her poor spouse's final year or two truly comfortable. The fisherman was disgusted with his wife's behaviour, until, with the screaming and shouting turning into the inevitable sobbing and sniffing that always closed down their arguments, she explained just how much their current house was worth and what that meant in terms of their future lifestyle.

Before the autumn leaves started to fall, the happy couple had moved once again, this time to the gated residential community called Seaview Park, which stood in beautifully landscaped surroundings on the fringe of the lovely, picturesque Cornish village of Fowey. They also spent just enough of their newly banked cash to park two matching cabriolets on their substantial, shingled driveway.

The only dark cloud on their horizon was a note from their benefactor that had been pinned to a bottle of champagne that awaited them on the day of their arrival in their new home, offering his sincerest condolences on the sad news about the fisherman's health and saying that he would consider it an honour if they would invite him to the funeral, long may that day be postponed.

Apart from the discomfort caused by the occasional call from their friend to enquire on the fisherman's health, the couple thoroughly enjoyed their new life embedded in one of the higher strata of the aspirational middle-class cliff face. Without a mortgage to worry about, the funds that they had received from the sale of their previous, modest abode provided them with a solid foundation on which to base their daily activities. The fisherman still caught sea bass when time permitted, and he still sold them on, although usually to a higher class of establishment nowadays. His wife embellished her life considerably with good quality clothes and jewellery, buffing up her ego and fluffing her aura so much that she became a leading light in the social whirl at the country club. She even took up golf to while away the hours when her husband was otherwise engaged with lines, reels and lures.

The fisherman's was a happy soul and he thanked his lucky stars for the gift that they had made to him of a strong and purposeful wife. Even in those far off days in the caravan, she had known how to manage their affairs, limited though they may have been back then, and he was quite content to leave the day to day nitty-gritty of bills and services in her capable hands. As long as he had enough cash in his pocket to put petrol in his rather sparkly cabriolet and to fund his passion for angling, he simply didn't have a care in the world, and so things progressed for nearly two years until his wife made an announcement over breakfast one morning.

"Have you seen the local paper this week?" she asked.

"No, not yet", replied her husband.

"There's an interesting feature on the front page. Our mutual friend is opening a fish processing factory just down the road in St Austell, which might come in handy now that we've run out of cash".

"I beg your pardon", said the fisherman. "What do you mean, we've run out of cash?"

"All gone", said his wife. "I don't know how you expect us to manage with all of that expensive fishing gear you keep buying. Anyway, I was thinking, maybe we should ask him to give you a job. Factory Manager would do nicely".

"But I don't know anything about fish factories. Catching the odd bass is one thing, but I've never managed anything other than my own time, and besides, he's hardly going to take me on in my current state of health, is he!"

"Oh, don't worry about that. Tell him a faith healer or something has cured you. It's a miracle, heavens be praised!"

"I really don't want a job…"

His wife looked at him sternly, crossing her arms and assuming a position where her body language needed no translations. "Ask him…"

Reluctantly and with a heavy heart, the fisherman telephoned the businessman and they arranged to meet to discuss the possibility of the fisherman joining this new business venture. The truth of the matter, however, was that the businessman wanted to see for himself just how marvellous his saviour's recovery had been. According to the man's wife he had been knocking on death's door for months now and it was quite amazing to think that he was fit and well once again.

During the telephone call the businessman decided not to remark on the fact that he had seen the fisherman sitting on the beach with his rods and his lines on more than one occasion during his recent trips down to the south coast to seal the deal on his new factory with the local council planning authorities. He also decided that it would be better to deal with the matter of his friend's phantom offspring face to face.

On the businessman's next trip down to review progress on the building of his new factory, the two men met for a pie and a pint in the local village pub. After exchanging some pleasantries and reliving that fateful afternoon once again, entertaining all of the drinkers in the place for a good half hour, the two men got down to business.

"So", said the businessman, "you're interested in working for me at the factory?"

"Oh, absolutely", replied the fisherman. "My wife thought that with my extensive experience around fish you should make me your factory manager. She wants…I want fifty-thousand a year and six weeks holiday, plus healthcare and gym membership for me and my family".

"Very reasonable for someone qualified to take on that sort of responsibility. When can you start?"

"A month or two, after the summer, probably", replied the fisherman nervously.

It all seemed to be going too easily and although they appeared to be getting on famously, there was something in the businessman's eyes that seemed to take all of the warmth and cheer out of the day. At the end of the meal the two men said their goodbyes to the landlord and headed for the car park, the businessman promising to drop his friend a line shortly to confirm the details discussed.

As his friend and benefactor walked over to a luxuriously large red saloon, the fisherman stood quite still in the middle of the car park and stared open mouthed at the space where he had parked his car. It was gone. He rushed over to his friend's car and tapped on the smoked glass windows, gesticulating wildly at the vacant spot where his lovely sparkling convertible had been standing.

"Gone…stolen…car", he stammered.

"Oh, don't worry about that", said the businessman. "Hop in and

I'll run you home. We can sort everything out there. It's always happening these days, especially with popular models like yours".

The fisherman sat in stunned silence as they drove towards his fine executive home at Seaview Park. He was shocked and hurt, feeling decidedly violated and dirty and angry. He was also deeply impressed by the sheer opulence on display inside his friend's sumptuous motor car and in between fits of pique about the riff-raff who walked today's streets, he wondered whether he could get a car like this as a perk of his new job.

They drove up the hill that led to the big electric gates at the entrance to Seaview Park just in time to see a large removals lorry pulling out of the estate followed by a ranting, screaming harridan dragging behind her a couple of suitcases and an old and battered fishing rod. In the background two large looking gentlemen in suits checked a clipboard list, closed the front door to one of the houses and put the keys into a black leather briefcase.

The businessman stopped his car, told the fisherman to wait and with the help of the two suited gentlemen, he put the screaming woman's suitcases in the boot and opened one of the rear passenger doors for her so that she could get in.

"You bast...", was all that she managed to yell at him before one of the suited gentlemen clamped his hand firmly over her mouth and bundled her onto the back seat. The two minders then climbed in and sat on top of her, remaining seated upon the squirming woman all the way to their final destination. The fisherman stared alternately at the businessman, at his very big and burly associates and then down at his prostrate but still struggling wife.

After twenty minutes of driving, during which the fisherman's wife gradually lost the will to fight and bawl, the car pulled up at the head of the cliffs that rose up above the beach where the fisherman, his wife and their mutual friend had first bumped into one another. The newly homeless couple were manhandled out of the car without a further word being said by anyone and left standing on the loose stones and thinly grassed topsoil at the top of the cliff where they had once lived a spare and shabby life in a caravan. The businessman put a sealed envelope into the fisherman's hands, climbed into his car and drove out of their lives forever more.

The envelope contained a short note, which the fisherman gave to his wife to read.

Dear…

You and your wife are thieving bastards. You lied about everything. When you've saved enough of your unemployment benefit, sue me. Now you've got what you really deserved all along.

Your one-time drowning friend.

In the bottom of the envelope was a set of keys to a brand-new second-hand caravan that was parked on top of the cliffs in exactly the same spot where the fisherman and his wife had lived before they had met their no longer mutual friend.

About the Author

Clive Gilson was born in 1962 into a household steeped in sport and rhythm. His father was a senior amateur and lower-league professional footballer, while his mother, equally formidable, was an award-winning ballroom dancer. Their spirited household didn't just hum with ambition, it danced to it.

After earning a degree in History from Leeds University, Clive took an unexpected turn into the then-nascent world of information technology in the late 1980s. Yet, the call of story and stage never left him. Alongside a thriving tech career, he freelanced as a journalist and book reviewer, earning one small by-line in the national press, and also spent over a decade performing in village halls and professional theatres across the south of England.

A true inheritor of his family's sporting zeal, Clive later pivoted into live sports broadcasting. In the 1990s, he became a trusted rugby 'stato' for the BBC, ITV, EuroSport, and TVNZ, bringing insight and analysis to major tournaments including the Heineken Cup, Six Nations, World Sevens, and Rugby World Cups.

As a writer, Clive has made his mark across genres. His debut novel, *Songs of Bliss*, was published in 2017, followed by *A Solitude of Stars* in 2019. Since then, he has released three acclaimed short story collections, *The Mechanic's Curse*, *The Insomniac Booth*, and, in 2025, *Melodies in Black Ink*.

He is also an award-winning poet and the author of a biography detailing the life of a former professional footballer, namely his father. Since 2018, Clive has served as Managing Editor of the Firesides Tales Project, a global storytelling initiative that has published over 30 collections of folktales, fairy tales, myths, and legends from around the world.

Today, Clive continues to write fiction rich in folklore, memory, and quiet transformation, combining his deep love of narrative with a lifelong fascination with the human spirit.

For more about his work, visit clivegilson.com, where stories are always waiting to be found.

ORIGINAL FICTION BY CLIVE L GILSON

- *Songs of Bliss*
- *Out of the Walled Garden*
- *The Mechanic's Curse*
- *The Insomniac Booth*
- *A Solitude of Stars (Cry Havoc, part 1)*
- *A Symphony Of Sorrows (Cry Havoc, part 2)*
- *Melodies In Black Ink*
- *Acts Of Faith*

AS EDITOR – TALES FROM THE WORLD'S FIRESIDES

- Tales From The World's Firesides is a book-led storytelling project shaped by Clive L Gilson's long interest in folktales, fairy tales, myths, and legends from many parts of the world. Its purpose is to gather old stories into clear, readable UK English while keeping faith with their origins wherever those origins can be traced.

- At the heart of the project is the belief that traditional stories are more than curiosities from the past. They carry traces of people, time and place. They show how people made sense of the world.

- Tales From The World's Firesides seeks to present those tales in a form that modern readers can enter with ease, while still feeling that they have come from somewhere particular.

Reviews

I have edited Clive Gilson's books for over a decade now – he's prolific and can turn his hand to many genres. poetry, short fiction, contemporary novels, folklore, and science fiction – and the common theme is that none of them ever fails to take my breath away. There's something in each story that is either memorably poignant, hauntingly unnerving, or sidesplittingly funny - *Lorna Howarth, The Write Factor*

*Ragged A**** Ruffian* reviewed on Amazon in the United Kingdom on 27 January 2021 - A truly heartwarming, interesting, story with a wonderful narrative. Unquestionably a splendid read

A Solitude of Stars: With deft turns of phrase and an imagination that would make Philip K. Dick jealous, Gilson foresees a dystopian future, the seeds of which are definitely being sown right now. The story is a chilling glimpse of what may come to pass, warmed by a thread of love that raises the narrative beyond despair. I found the stories disturbing and breath-taking in equal measure. The Apparat and Dirigiste tribes are ranging across our solar system seeking peace by waging war, raising the question; is humanity actually capable of peace? A riveting read. - *Rob Swan, The Write Factor*

Songs of Bliss gripped me from the start - I had to read right to the end. Loved the humour. Impressed by the surprising empathy that I felt for rather - on the face of it - unlikeable characters. Look forward to seeing it in print. - *Maighdean-Mhara, commenting on Authonomy*

I just wanted to thank you once more for your help acquiring this beautiful collection. It's found a new home at the top of my library. I've already stumbled onto some wonderful stories in a couple of the collections, and I can't wait to get more. Have a wonderful holiday and a great new year... - *Richer Daniel Laporte, California, December 2021*

Melodies In Black Ink: A collection of darkly captivating short tales, each inspired by the melodies that move us, the lyrics that linger, and the stories hidden between the notes.

Gilson (editor of the international Fireside Stories series) offers a dark, poignant collection of genre-crossing stories, all inspired by songs, that explore the fragile intersections of love, loss, resilience, and the shadows we carry. Ranging from children with superpowers to accounts of blossoming love, abusive relationships, unexpected pregnancies, and the isolating rhythm of a machine-driven society, Gilson's stories capture raw textures of the human experience in a key suggested by their musical inspirations, which include lushly brooding tracks from Kate Bush, This Mortal Coil, Angel Olsen, The Cure, and Youssou N'Dour (the sublime "7 Seconds," a duet with Neneh Cherry.) Gilson has a gift for moment-to-moment storytelling that grips and then lingers, like Gorilla Glue stuck to one's fingertips, resisting even the harshest solvents of reason.

Life goes wrong in unpredictable yet resonant ways throughout these 26 compact tales, and Gilson's vivid portrayals of scenery and emotion make it easy to lose oneself in these narratives, drowning in a wave of feeling that refuses to let go. From the Scottish Highlands to space travel to the blood-soaked earth of Danish-Viking battlefields—told from the perspective of Ulfhednar and his sacred wolf, Ulric—these stories span wide imaginative terrain. Despite some big ideas and SF elements, characterization is compelling. "The Jakey and the Nae Chancer" introduces Elliot and Fiona, who have perfected the art of detachment, the latter of whom "was almost certain that her heart was too delicate to risk breaking again." One of the most heart-wrenching stories, "Be Well," is inspired by a devastating loss. It's a piece that does more than tug at the heart, it reaches in and seizes hold with unrelenting intensity.

Adding a unique dimension, each story concludes with a toast to the song and artist that inspired it, an invitation to experience these briskly potent stories on another sensory level, with a soundtrack tying words to melody, emotion to rhythm. Melodies in Black Ink is not light reading—but it is deeply moving, with haunting emotional rewards.

Searing, surprising stories of urgent feeling, inspired by beloved songs.

The US Review of Books
Professional Reviews for the People

Melodies in Black Ink: This work is not just another set of tales linked together by a myriad of characters who sometimes appear in more than one narrative. In fact, this is much more than just another short story collection. It is also a reflective, musical journey. Accompanying each story is an explanation of the song that inspired the writing. Most impressive is the wide expanse of musical genres, artists, and songs included in this book. From Wardruna to Metric to Blue Oyster Cult to Dot Allison, the book's audience will experience a musical journey unlike any other. The incorporation of the notes discussing each inspirational song provides an informative background. It also provides historical context, along with the author's personal anecdotes, about each song.

What makes this book even more realistic is its honest, vulnerable, and sometimes gritty portrayal of the characters and their existences. One story in which all of these themes and characteristics culminate is "Going Underground." It is a story in which even the main character's name, Daniel Grimes, reflects the character's harsh, gritty environment and existence, as well as the difficult decisions Daniel must make. Daniel embodies rebellion against the status quo after having lived a life in which he originally "played by the rules. All it got him were ration credits and a little coin, enough to rent a bedsit and eat slop." "Going Underground" is a daring story with a dystopian tone. Deepening that dystopian tone is the fact that the author cleverly disguises the story's time period, and the tale can be read as either occurring in the past, the present, or the very near future.

Music lovers will appreciate this book because of the role music plays in each and every story. The stories, too, are a testament to not only the power of music but also of the necessity of interdisciplinary studies and the humanities. The stories are a novel type of ekphrastic writing in that, rather than responding to visual art, the stories are responses to music. The fluid, poetic writing in each story mirrors the magic and lyricism inherent in the songs the author utilizes. These stories are powerful, emotional, and moving. Most of all, they are beautifully and unquestionably human.

RECOMMENDED by the US Review

Book review by Nicole Yurcaba